D0336371

THE DOOM LIST

THE DOOM LIST

Gerard O'Donovan

This first world edition published 2020
in Great Britain and the USA by
SEVERN HOUSE PUBLISHERS LTD of
Eardley House, 4 Uxbridge Street, London W8 7SY.
Trade paperback edition first published
in Great Britain and the USA 2020 by
SEVERN HOUSE PUBLISHERS LTD.

British Library Cataloguing in Publication Data
A CIP catalogue record for this title is available from the British Library.

ISBN-13: 978-0-7278-8903-4 (cased)
ISBN-13: 978-1-78029-690-6 (trade paper)
ISBN-13: 978-1-4483-0415-8 (e-book)

All Severn House titles are printed on acid-free paper.

Severn House Publishers support the Forest Stewardship Council™ [FSC™],
the leading international forest certification organisation.
All our titles that are printed on FSC certified paper carry the FSC logo.

Typeset by Palimpsest Book Production Ltd.,
Falkirk, Stirlingshire, Scotland.
Printed and bound in Great Britain by
TJ International, Padstow, Cornwall.

FOR ANGELA

ONE

'Hey, Johnny, com'n ha'e a look o'er here.'

The light had drained from the cloudless sky when tuft-haired Homer Junger crested the dusty, scrub-covered incline and stared into the yawning abyss below. He and his best pal Johnny Rosten had been waiting hours for this, ever since Homer discovered his oil-engineer pop had left for work without his treasured Eveready flashlight, a forbidden magic wand that conferred the power of lighting up the dark even unto the hands of a twelve year old. Now, out here in the arid wilderness, half a mile from his parents' cozy frame house on one of the newest subdivisions in the county, there was nothing but dark to explore beyond the twinkling city's edge far off in the distance.

It was time.

Neither of them knew what they were hoping for, or how far they had strayed from home. Such thoughts hadn't shadowed their minds. Their sole aim was a night adventure of untold possibility, of sneaking out and braving the dark alone like their movie-cowboy heroes, Tom Mix and Hoot Gibson. Astride imaginary palominos, they had been hoo-hawing and slapping their galloping hips since they made it out of earshot, competing to lasso rocks and shrubs with their twist-cord lariats – rustled from Johnny's pop's 'useful' store of tools and cable – for as long as the light had lasted.

'What'cha got, Hoot?'

Johnny scrambled up the rise and flattened himself on the ground beside Homer on the lip of the drop to the gully below. In the dusky gloom Homer caught the sheen of the nickel-plated flashlight in his hands – he had let him carry it awhile as a gesture of just how much their friendship meant to him, but

Johnny didn't seem so keen on handing it back now the moment had come. Over a foot long, the torch was heavy and Homer feared he might drop it, so intently was Johnny pushing the little switch on the tubular body back and forth with no result.

'Here, gi' it here, you're doin' it wrong,' Homer scolded, reaching over to take it back. But Johnny wasn't giving.

'Y'have to twist the cap off, c'mon.' There was a squeal of frustration in Homer's voice now. He grabbed at the top of the flashlight just as Johnny laughed and pulled it away and the thin metal cap turned and came off on the tips of his fingers and fell, shimmering and glinting with barely a skitter, into the murk below.

'No!' Homer's only thought now was of the walloping his pop would give him. Getting to his knees, he wrestled the flashlight back from Johnny's grip and directed the beam downwards. Freed of the bonds of his imagination, all he could see now in the sharp yellow light was a dense tangle of vegetation in the gully below, a thorn thicket with fat fleshy cactus heads bulging up through the gaps, spikes white and painful-looking in the harsh light. Ranging the beam right and left he saw nothing else on the gully floor below but dirt and stones, until a glint of something caught his eye ten or twelve feet down and he became aware of Johnny's hand on his arm, tightening.

'Look, look – there, d'ya see it, it's there.'

Before Homer could stop him, Johnny twisted himself over the edge, forearms propped on the rim as his shoes scrambled against the dirt wall beneath to give him purchase.

'It's OK, c'mon,' Johnny said, rolling on to his behind now and inching his way down the earthen slope, looking heroic picked out in the yellow spotlight. 'It's easy. Han' me down the lamp and you come too. You gotta come down, too.'

Homer really wasn't sure but did as he was bid, rolling the heavy flashlight down to Johnny and following, scrambling down the dusty slope on his rear end as the yellow beam turned up on him. Now he was at the foot of it, he felt a kind of nauseous euphoria seize him as the adventure became suddenly real and, framed by steep earthen banks, the night closed in fully on them.

Johnny was already ranging the torchlight against the towers of thorn and cactus arching over them, branches and suckers thrown out like ghostly arms. All they needed was the glint they'd caught before. But everything looked so different down here, it was impossible to tell where it was, where exactly they had seen it before. Hearing a sudden scuffle to their left, both boys jumped and turned and shrieked, grabbing at one another in the dark even as the beam in Johnny's hand caught the white underbelly and pink ears of a jackrabbit scuttling into the brush. They giggled wildly in relief, the flashlight twisting in Johnny's hands so wildly it caught, off further to their left, the sought-after glint of metal.

Or was it?

Something felt plain wrong to Homer, the glimmer too far beyond the edge of the thicket, too high somehow, for a nickel cap he'd been sure had fallen to the ground. But Johnny was gone again, skipping and scuffling across the loose stony ground towards his bewitching goal. In the dark Homer had no choice but to follow, his heart already in his mouth for what they might find. Johnny was three maybe four yards ahead now, when suddenly he stopped still as if he'd turned to salt, the flashlight beam pointing up into the tangle of thorns in which a darker night seemed to have gathered just above. In the wavering light Homer saw the darkness too, a shape of something big suspended in the dense overgrowth, hanging there as if dropped by God himself, one arm loosely dangling, dry rivers of blood crusted on the fingertips below the grey parched hand and wrist on which a cheap metal watch glittered in the flashlight's glare. The trembling yellow beam shifted, revealing a pale parched moon above that slowly resolved into a face drawn in horror, fly-blown sockets of eyes pecked out by birds, dry thorn-torn cheeks scabbed and flaking and, from between a halo of bared, gall-yellow teeth, a bloated tongue hung obscenely.

Nothing but the sound of his own screaming breached Homer's ears as he tore up the slope and raced blindly for home.

TWO

I t was a little after midnight and the party was beginning to wind down in the sophisticated, rather muted way that was characteristic of the Oasis. The band had gone home, and Tom Collins was leaning against a baby grand on the small stage, chatting with an elegantly dressed woman who was sitting at the piano and caressing the keys absently, eliciting a gently entrancing melody. Mary O'Hara was around the same age as Tom, which is to say some years older than most of the bright young movie folk who populated the room. Like him, too, while she was certainly possessed of good looks, the finer points had perhaps begun to unravel a little thanks to the lateness of the hour and the temptations of the club's well-stocked, and better-hidden, cellar.

'Rex is just so—' O'Hara broke off her playing to look Tom intently in the eyes. They had been idly trading the latest movie-colony gossip and complaining about the endlessly oppressive heat, but now it seemed she was taking a turn for the maudlin. 'He's just so mysterious, you know. Like every true artist.'

Tom couldn't tell whether O'Hara was being ironic or simply drunker than she looked. Her party had come in after a long day's shooting on their current movie over at Metro, then attending a screening of their last – which had just emerged from the cutting room for the first time. The picture had obviously gone down well, even if the screening room was like an oven. All were in high spirits.

'Yeah, I'm sure it's all that artistry and mystery of his that gets you girls a-flutter whenever he comes in the room,' Tom said, grinning.

He looked across the dance floor to where Rex Ingram was sitting at the center of an adoring entourage of twenty or more. The man had the looks of a god. Tall, lean, loose-limbed and with jet-black hair slicked back over a noble brow, he was as strikingly handsome as any of the actors surrounding him.

And at barely thirty years old he was, by any measure, the most wildly feted of all the younger movie directors in the colony.

'You're just jealous.' O'Hara flapped a hand at Tom. 'Though how he could have settled for that talentless little slip of a thing, I will never know.'

Now he knew O'Hara was drunk. It was not like her to be ungenerous. Especially not towards Ingram's wife and leading lady, Alice Terry. Sitting alongside Ingram, Terry was, from the little Tom knew of her, an exceptional young woman in her early twenties, possessed of a serene, ethereal beauty and eyes that seemed to, as the fan magazines might put it, pierce the very soul. She talked a lot of sense, too. Together they looked like the perfect couple.

'I think maybe the hooch has gone to your head, Mary. Can I call you a cab?'

But O'Hara acted like she hadn't heard, instead reaching out and stroking Tom's chin with a maternal fondness. 'Not like you, clever man. You got the best catch in the whole of this rotten town, didn't you?'

He could not disagree with that. Glancing around the room he sought out Fay Parker, actress, singer, owner of the Oasis and, to his mind, too, unquestionably the best catch on the West Coast – and the whole of the rest of anywhere, for that matter. As so often, Fay now seemed to materialize from nowhere, leaning across the back of the chair in which Ingram was sitting, talking confidentially with the director, who in turn whispered in her ear. As if she could feel his eyes on her, Fay looked up and smiled across the room at Tom, and with an elegant twist of her hand got Ingram to look across at him, too. A moment later, the director was on his feet, and the two were striding across the room towards him.

Fay extended a hand again in a faintly courtly gesture. 'Tom, I don't believe you've met Mr Rex Ingram?'

Tom held his hand out to the beaming young man. 'Mr Ingram. It's a real pleasure. I'm Collins. Tom Collins. I really loved *Four Horsemen of the Apocalypse*.'

'No, no,' Ingram said, batting away the compliment. He grabbed Tom's hand and shook it enthusiastically. He had a surprisingly firm grip for an artist. 'Call me, Rex, please. One harp to another, like.'

Tom must have raised an eyebrow.

'Mrs Parker tells me you're a Dubliner, like myself.' Ingram's accent – a touch exaggerated now for effect – put it beyond doubt.

'Born and bred, yes,' Tom said. 'And I couldn't get out of there fast enough.'

He didn't anticipate the guffaw of agreement this elicited from Ingram and the renewed pumping of his hand that it produced.

'I'm with you there. Best appreciated from a distance.' Ingram laughed again and nodded amiably towards O'Hara. 'But as Mary here will tell you, I always say the only fellow you can truly depend on when you're in trouble is a fellow Irishman, don't I, Mary?'

O'Hara grinned and flicked her eyes heavenwards. 'And I always say "Just 'cos my name's O'Hara, that don't make me Irish".'

While they laughed at that, Tom noticed Fay signaling to him, as if he should ask Ingram something, which could only mean one thing.

'Well, as Fay might have told you, Rex, trouble is the business I'm in. So, if there's ever something I can help you out with—'

Ingram put a hand up sharply, smiling still. 'Mrs Parker says you're the best private enquiries man in the business. If you're that good, it's certainly good enough for me. Maybe you could find the time to come and see me at the studio sometime?' He looked away distractedly a moment, and his eyes were even more intense when he looked back. 'Tomorrow morning, ideally, if you're not committed elsewhere. I have a small problem on which I'd appreciate your advice. But if you don't mind, I'd rather not spoil my night out by discussing it now. I just love this place. I was telling Mary the other evening how much I adore the idea of North Africa. It was she suggested we should come here.'

Ingram turned to Fay again and gave an airy wave towards the shimmering rose-pink and celadon silks that were draped, tent-like, from the ceiling and down the walls, the hanging pierced-metal lanterns casting a low light that barely penetrated the club's dimmer recesses – and combined to give the Oasis its distinctive mood of a dark desert encampment.

'You know, Mrs Parker, you have created a place of fantasy suited to my soul here. In this heat, one could almost believe it real. Ever since I was a youth at home in Ireland, I have wanted to visit the deserts of North Africa, wash myself in the spirit of the Mohammedan, so to speak. I was fourteen years old and with my parents visiting friends who have a castle in the county of Offaly, when a young lady of the house handed me a beautiful, Morocco-bound copy of *The Garden of Allah* by Mr Robert Hichens. Have you ever had the pleasure of reading that wondrous adventure yourself, Mrs Parker? I would make a movie of it tomorrow, if only Selig didn't hold the rights . . .'

An hour later, a dozen or so of the party were still firmly encamped, the only ones left in the club, seated in a wide semi-circle – the focal point of which, inevitably, was Ingram. What had been a quiet murmur of conversation had become louder and more heated once the subject turned to the topic on everyone's lips that week: the imminent arrival in the colony of the industry's newly appointed 'movie czar', Will H. Hays. For five months he had been gas-bagging from a plush office in New York about how he was single-handedly going to clean up the Sodom that was Hollywood. Now he was heading West on his first 'fact-finding mission' to the creative epicenter of the movie industry – and nerves were on edge.

'It's the beginning of the end, I tell you.' Ingram, in full rhetorical flight, held the small group in thrall, his handsome face a touch more florid, his hair in minor disarray. 'The nerve of the man, thinking he can tell us – *us*, the community of artists who have been making movies and fortunes for the studios for years – to bow our heads to *him*, who knows nothing of us and what we achieve.' Ingram jabbed a forefinger in the air. 'Well, not me. I see no cause for all this hoopla. Hays is nothing but a shifty wheel-greaser of the lowest kind, who cares as much about the movie business as I care about politics – and that's precisely nothing. All *he* seeks to enhance is his own reputation. All *he* can do is point the accusing finger and get in the way of people making the only thing worth making, and that is *art*. God damn all politicians, I say; may we rid the world entirely of their parasitic, self-serving kind.'

The faithful hung on his every word, a babble of approving voices egging him on, keen to hear more. But O'Hara, also more florid now, shushed them down, wanting to be heard. 'It's all well and good your saying that, Rex – and, I agree, the man's self-regard is outrageous. Take this mass rally he's invited everyone to attend. Thirty thousand people expected? It is ludicrous. But I was surprised to see your name so heavily associated with it.'

'My name?' Ingram sat up in his seat, puzzled and affronted.

'Certainly – and Miss Terry's.'

Ingram's face darkened and he shifted again to share a glance with Alice Terry. 'Did you know anything about this?'

Terry shook her head, equally bemused.

O'Hara looked around, focusing on no one in particular. 'Does anybody have a copy of tonight's *Herald*?'

On Fay's instruction, a copy of the newspaper was brought from behind the bar, and O'Hara opened it eagerly to an inside page, handing it to Ingram folded open on a quarter-page advertisement for the event, encouraging the people of Los Angeles, and particularly those associated with the movie industry, to attend upon Hays's speech at the Hollywood Bowl the following weekend. Over an outline drawing of the venue, the banner '*Every star will be there*' was flying atop three columns of names, prominent among them the director's and his leading lady's.

Terry leant in to peruse the page more closely but said nothing. Whatever her thoughts were, Tom reckoned, she wasn't as keen to advertise them as Ingram.

'It's a goddam outrage,' Ingram grunted. 'Publicity probably wrote down the first names of any consequence that came in their heads. There is no way on earth I would lend my support to the vile little booster, especially at a public rally. Who in hell's name does he think he is, calling half the city to worship at his rotten feet? Is he Will H. Hays or Jesus H. Christ? He's doing nothing in my name, that's for sure. I'll instruct them to remove it tomorrow.'

Again, the coterie murmured their approval; one or two even cheered. But O'Hara had the bit between her teeth and was determined not to let the subject drop. 'You mean you're going to snub him, Rex? For the whole week?'

Ingram sighed and pushed back a hank of hair that had flopped over his face. 'I wish I could. But no, I'm under orders to attend the private luncheon that the studio heads are hosting for him at the Arts Club on Tuesday. It's been made abundantly clear to me that my future with Metro is dependent on my attendance. Which, ordinarily, would be enough to guarantee my absence, but, with so much in the balance just at the moment, I rather think I'll have to go along with it. If only to sit at the back and scowl. And I must admit, I am curious to see the rat-faced little succubus in the flesh. Perhaps I'll be invited to stand up and voice my opinion of him to his face.'

Before his acolytes could encourage him more, Terry put the brake on. 'No, you mustn't do that, Rex. There's no point getting a black mark against your name just for the sake of it. Not before we know if all they say of him is correct. You won't want Hays singling you out for his first Hollywood grudge. And, surely, it is only fair to allow the man an opportunity to make his case?'

'Not if all he utters are weasel words, it isn't,' Ingram said, though now his heart didn't seem quite so in it. 'And what else would a politician have to say about our business?'

Ignoring him, Terry laughed to herself and turned to O'Hara. 'What dear Rex has omitted to say is that we are unable to be in Los Angeles for the rally in any case. Due to that other, more pressing event requiring our presence in New York.' She pointed a finger teasingly at Ingram. 'Someone seems to forget that *The Prisoner of Zenda* has its gala premiere at the Astor Theatre, Times Square, in less than two weeks and, you know, I suspect we will find ourselves on a sleeper heading East at more or less exactly the time Mr Hays will be stirring up the Bowl.'

Ingram gave Terry a look of such admiration, Tom had to wonder if she'd made up that travel plan on the spot to dig him out of a hole. Either way, Ingram broke into a broad grin and sat back again, relaxed. 'And what a relief it will be to breathe in again the reviving air of civilization for a few days.'

That might have been the end of it had not the prim, gray-haired, elegantly mustachioed figure of Edward Connelly, one of Ingram's older regulars, leaned in just then, enunciating in gossipy undertones: 'Speaking of black marks, I can't help wondering if we wouldn't *all* be well advised to rein in our revelries for a time. I keep hearing this scoundrel Hays is compiling a list of people to be barred from screen work because he considers them unsuitable or undesirable. *Unclean*, if you will.'

'I can't think why you would worry about that, Ed.' Ingram said. 'You're so widely known as a man of impeccable habits. It's too preposterous to believe.'

'Not if you talk to Mary, it isn't,' Connelly said. 'And she should know, she's the one with friends in high places.'

All heads turned towards O'Hara, who sat forward eagerly again. 'Sure, I do, and I'd say Ed has it about right. It's not just the movies we make. Hays says he intends to root out anyone he considers to be, in his words, a "liability to the decency, moral standing and public perception of the movie industry." Lots of good people who came out here to Hollywood precisely to get away from sermonizing crazies back home will find themselves having to get habituated to looking over their shoulders again.'

Someone in the company, Tom didn't see who, quipped: 'We won't be able to get so much as a shirt when the costume departments are cleared out.' But it fell on deaf ears. A gloom had fallen over the group, and only Fay seemed willing to ask the inevitable question. 'You are being serious, Mary? Do you really have the dope on this?'

O'Hara nodded gravely. 'I'm afraid I do, and the signs are not good. I know I probably shouldn't say this here, but I had it on good authority only yesterday that Roscoe Arbuckle is at the top of that list.'

'But poor Roscoe was innocent,' Fay said, glancing over at Tom quickly, shocked. 'Everyone must know that now, surely.'

'Innocent or not, he's finished. And not just finished, but set to be made an example of, for all of us.' O'Hara was talking in an undertone now, and soberly. 'Zukor's done a deal with Hays and agreed to shelve the two films Roscoe finished before his trial. And to rip up what's left on his contract. If what I'm told is true, the same fate awaits anyone who steps out of line in the next few months. Zukor, Laemmle, Lowe, Fox, the lot of 'em – they all lay down like lambs and agreed to give Hays a free hand to take whatever action he wants – *carte blanche*.'

'*Carte noire*, more like,' Connelly sniped. 'I heard someone call it "The Doom List".'

'That's exactly what it is,' O'Hara agreed. 'A list of the doomed. And whatever you might say now, Rex – or any of us – you know you won't want to find yourself on it. Look around. All this wealth, this fame, this fine living and freedom. They can take it away from any of us in the blink of an eye. Sure, Hays will come among us all smiles and handshakes and bonhomie – but beneath that cloak of conviviality he will be hiding a sword of fire.'

'Oh, Mary, you go too far, surely?' Fay reached out and took Tom's hand. 'You're making Hays sound like one of the horsemen of the apocalypse.'

There was a ripple of laughter, the gloom broken, as all eyes turned to Ingram to see what he would say. 'Rex,' the cry went up, excitedly, like it was some new parlor game. 'Which one of the four would Hays be?'

Ingram had been uncharacteristically quiet, a look of inwardness broken only by a quick glance at Tom, and then away again. But the enthusiastic mention of his greatest success to date seemed to pull him back to reality.

'What do I care?' he muttered impatiently, beneath his breath, until he realized how many eyes were on him. Then the smile returned and he gave them what they wanted, a quick laugh and a sharp retort. 'Hays? There's only one of 'em the conniving little sleeveen could possibly be. Pestilence, God damn and blast him. Pestilence!'

Later, when the party was gone and the clear-up completed, after the house lights were doused and the doors locked and the last goodnights wished to the waiting staff, when they were alone again together in the apartment above the Oasis, Fay said to Tom: 'Mary was in high spirits tonight.'

'Spirits being the word.' Tom whistled silently. 'She was determined to get a scare into everyone about Hays.'

'As was Ed Connelly, too.' Fay put her brush down on the dresser and swiveled from the mirror to look at him. 'Such a charming man, usually. There were quite a few concerned faces in the room, I thought. Did you notice?'

Tom nodded. 'I noticed Ingram giving me a queer look when Mary was talking about having to be more watchful. I wonder what he's got to hide?'

'I imagine you'll find out when you go meet him tomorrow.'

'I hope so.' He smiled wolfishly at her. 'I could do with the business. Did he give any hint of it to you?'

'None whatsoever. We were chatting and he asked me about you, how long we've been together. He was so delighted to hear you were Irish. Then, when I told him what you do . . . well, you saw for yourself, he jumped right up and made a beeline for you.'

'Must've been quite a recommendation you gave.'

Fay raised an eyebrow teasingly, then turned back to the mirror and resumed her combing. 'That dear young man, Samaniegos, was looking pretty downcast, too, I thought.'

'Which one was he?'

'The young Mexican, of course – Ramon Samaniegos.' She turned again in disbelief. 'You must have noticed him.'

Tom had a vague recollection of a glowingly good-looking but sullen-seeming youth in a well-cut suit.

'Such a handsome boy,' Fay continued. 'They were saying he outshines everyone in this new *Zenda* film of theirs. And that Ingram is determined to make him an even bigger star than he made Valentino.'

'Can't say I see it. He looked like a kid to me. Barely whelped.'

'Oh, Tom, really. Be serious. You said you didn't see it with Valentino either, remember, even with women fainting all round you in the movie theater.'

'What can I say?' Tom put his hands up, surrendering. 'All I know is, if the press boys can call Valentino a pink powder puff, heaven knows what they'll come up with for that kid when the time comes.'

'You might not be far wrong there.'

'Meaning?'

'Oh nothing, forget I said it. Call it a woman's instinct, if you like.'

Tom twisted the pin out of his collar, removed it and put it with the others for laundering, along with his cuffs. He took a hanger from the wardrobe and stood a moment, shirt in one hand, hanger in the other, distracted.

'Is Mary really so well connected?' Tom asked. 'I mean, enough to know all that about Hays?'

Fay turned from the mirror again. 'So I'm told, but I'm not at all sure how. Something to do with her ex, I expect. But as she refuses ever to talk about him, he is a mystery she keeps firmly to herself. Not that it matters, Hays can't hurt her. I know she comes from money because she mentioned it once to me before. Somewhere in the Mid-West, I think.'

'There's not a drop of Irish in her, anyway,' Tom said, emphatically. 'Despite that *nom de plume* she adopts.'

Fay stood up, a playful light in her eyes as she approached him. 'You know, I sometimes think I'm the only girl in the colony who goes under her own name.'

He couldn't help but laugh at that. 'And there was me thinking that's the only part of you that is still your husband's.'

Fay beamed at him, delighted, as if she had actually forgotten for once. 'Guilty as charged, darling.' She put out a hand and drew him towards her. 'Maybe *you* are the only truth-teller around here, Mr Collins . . . At least, I assume you are Tom Col—'

He kissed her before she could go any further with that.

THREE

I t was four months since he had taken the lease on the two-room office on Gower and had it stenciled on the ground-glass door panel: *Tom Collins, private enquiries.* It still gave him a kick to see it, first thing every morning. But today he was more surprised to find the door already unlocked and, inside, Mae sitting at her desk, post sorted, poring over the morning newspapers.

'Hey,' she said with her usual big grin. Twenty years old and she'd lived more than most. Harder than most, too. Yet the grin was always ready to hand. A mask like any other, just nicer. 'Hey, yourself. What're you doing in so early?'

'Couldn't sleep with the heat,' she said. 'Had a yen for some nice iced juice, so hopped a trolley and came on over here. You know as well as I do, Sammy's is best.'

'Did you get one for me?' His eyes snagged on the empty glass on her desk, his mouth watering at the tantalizing dregs of sun-bright orange at the bottom. He could all but taste the tang.

'Sure, but then I drank yours, too, it was so good.' She laughed. So typical.

'Well, thanks for the thought, anyway, I guess. Is there any coffee, at least?'

'Sure.' She signaled vaguely towards the minuscule kitchen. 'I'll make some in a minute.'

Shaking his head, he moved on through the open door into his own office and thought he heard her laugh. Then, hanging his hat on the rack he saw it: a half-pint bottle glowing orange and frosted with cool runnels of condensation in a dish of ice just out of reach of the sunlight shooting in the window.

'Got ya,' she said, never taking her eyes off the paper.

Forty minutes later he was still struggling to put the final touches to a report on a rising young movie star's brush with the law at Long Beach, for Pete Smith over at the

Pickford-Fairbanks Studio, when the phone rang in the outer office. He glanced at his watch absently and decided he should be going. Mae came around the door.

'That was Mr Sennett. Wondering again why you haven't got back to him.'

'You tell him yet?'

'Not until he's polite to me.'

'That's the spirit.' He got up and grabbed his hat. Nothing was more than an arm's length away in his office. 'I'm going over to Metro now, but I'll be back by lunchtime.'

'Who you seeing over there?'

'Rex Ingram.'

'Oh, my, seriously?'

'Sure. He was out at the Oasis last night, asked me to drop by.'

'Can I come?' Her face was lit with something not far short of adoration. 'Who wouldn't want to be Alice Terry, right?'

'They looked pretty tight last night, all right.' Tom gave her his best grin. 'Can't say he looks any great shakes to me, but Fay's in your camp. Says it's a shame to keep him behind the camera. I say, always play to your strengths.' He laughed. 'And, sorry, but I need you here, to take all those big-time calls while I'm gone.'

She gave him a skeptical look. 'All I know is I should never have given up my job at the Oasis. At least I got to meet some interesting people out there, instead of being chained to a telephone all day.'

'Your gratitude knows no bounds.'

He knew she was only kidding but he felt for her. It had been slow this past week. And so hot. She was a bright girl; too bright for taking phone messages, typing and filing.

'Give it time, Mae. They'll be queuing up here, too, any day now. It'll happen.'

He only wished he could be as confident about that as he sounded.

A block south of Santa Monica Boulevard on the intersection of Romaine and Cahuenga, the Metro studio was a sprawling concatenation of the industrial and the artistic. It was as ramshackle behind the scenes as any studio in Hollywood yet distinguished by a fine, white post-Colonial frontage erected to mask the expanding clutter of offices behind. Stepping in under the grand colonnade, Tom approached the gleaming white reception desk, expecting to be kept waiting – given the late hour the Ingrams had departed the Oasis – while a pass was arranged. But to his surprise, the smartly dressed, briskly efficient desk clerk said he'd been informed that Tom was expected. Handed a pass card with his name already printed on it, Tom was directed across the street to the Lot 2 stage where Mr Ingram was at work, and had been for hours.

'Look for the *Black Orchids* chalks,' the clerk said, with a twist of his fingers suggestive of writing on a blackboard.

Tom loped out into the sunshine, weaving through the unbroken ranks of automobiles parked on Romaine – an increasingly common sight around the studios now and a sure sign of the shared prosperity of studio employees. Across the street, the gate guard tipped his cap and directed him towards an enormous glass-walled stage, a building that seemed to get bigger with every step Tom took. The air was filled with the constant cacophony of industry – set-building and breaking, a wash of competing mood music and the non-stop chatter and bark of busy human voices. Players in costume stood about in what shade they could find, feasting on that staple of all studios, gossip, while awaiting new scenes and set-ups. Even the path to the stage entrance was clogged with vividly painted stacks of flats and overflowing prop trollies, most with tarps pulled back for ease of access. Safe enough from rain for now, Tom thought, glancing at the achingly blue sky above. Only the most precious or delicate items were protected from sun and dust.

He excused his way past the huddle of gabbling actors round the doorway and pushed in through it. Inside, the heat was intense in the vast, glare-bright space. Every window on the lower walls was open to the maximum, in hope of catching a fugitive breeze, but there was none. Deep-looping folds of muslin hanging from the rigging above diffused the direct light as much as possible, but nothing could be done to ameliorate the stifling heat of a July day under glass in Hollywood. It simply had to be borne. Shading his eyes with a hand he peered into the dazzle and, amid the din of hammering and shouting, heard Ingram's distinctive Irish tones above the others, barking orders at the far end of the building. He had hardly got halfway along when he was intercepted by none other than Alice Terry.

'Thank you so much for coming, Mr Collins.' Despite the heat she looked, in a long, white, delicately embroidered linen dress, as fresh and cool as a spring morning. 'Unfortunately, we are in the middle of re-shooting a key scene.'

He was flattered she remembered him. They chatted idly a moment or two before he recalled something from the evening before. 'I thought I heard last night that you weren't working on this movie, Miss Terry.'

'No, I'm sitting this one out. But Rex likes me to be on set regardless. He believes I have an ability to see through the tangles he gets himself into sometimes. I'm not altogether sure he's right, but perhaps I am a mite less excitable than he can sometimes be.'

She gave him a slyly amused glance and Tom reckoned he saw why Ingram had fallen for her. That mix of serenity and mischievousness, so unlike the regulation *hauteur* of the standard movie diva.

'We're due a break for luncheon when this scene is concluded,' she went on. 'Although if you were familiar with Rex's working practices, you'd know I can't promise that will be any time soon.'

'I don't mind. So long as I can stand here and watch.'

Though he had no desire to be involved in the process himself, Tom had long had a fascination for the mechanics of movie-making. Ever since he was first sent out West in 1917, to ride shotgun for Doug Fairbanks on *A Modern Musketeer*, he'd been entranced by it. And even now that he'd been out on his own for the best part of a year, he still missed the feeling of shared endeavor he had enjoyed every day for five years working at the Lasky studio, of being involved in something bigger and more important. Of striding through the lot every day and being a part of all that bustle, business and barely contained madness. Every chance he got now, he loved to stop and watch a scene or two being shot.

Miss Terry directed him to a chair facing on to the set, but he preferred to remain on his feet, propping himself against one of the huge steel uprights that supported the arching glass roof. The scene was of an interior space arrayed in decadently luxurious fashion. Great swathes of heavy damask silks and satins, densely embroidered with glittering beads and miles of metallic thread, formed a proscenium arch of sorts, through which the cameras ranged upon a circular room of both antique mystique and disconcerting modernity. The walls were formed by long, shimmering columns of silver silk and pale grey chiffon, the floor was a sunburst of monochrome rays exploding from a central gilded yellow circle in which stood a gold table bearing a glittering glass orb. Richly decorated ancient urns sat around the floor edge, statuettes of bronze and gold on thin marbled surfaces, and a vast Biedermeier sedan supported still more silks and gem-encrusted cushions. The effect was quite disorientating, an opulence rooted more in the mind than any particular place or time.

'It's a remake of *Black Orchids*,' Miss Terry explained. 'One of Rex's own scenarios. I wonder, did you see the original? It made his name out here.'

'Sure,' Tom said. 'A few years back, I remember it. The one with the ape, no?'

'Whatever you do, don't say that to Rex!' Her laugh took the sting from the admonishment in her voice. 'He'd much rather you saw it as a towering work of gothic genius – which happens to feature an orangutan in a minor kind of way.'

Tom laughed too. 'I only mentioned it because I worked with that ape Joe Martin once, on a monkey flick at Lasky's. He was a nice old fellow. Was pretty smart for a creature kept in a cage. Him and me, we got along.'

'How wonderful!' Her delight was almost physical. 'You'll enjoy this scene then. He features in it.'

'Joe Martin? You're kidding me? Joe's still alive?' Tom wasn't sure whether to be delighted or appalled by this news. He had heard somewhere that apes could live to a great age, but what kind of life could it be for the poor creature, kept behind bars and only brought out once in a while to caper about in front of a camera.

'You might find him changed. It seems his advancing age is

betrayed in his temperament. Apparently, he's very jealous of Miss La Marr's affections.' Again, she gave Tom that mischievous grin. 'Not the first hairy ape to go that way, I'm told.'

'I can believe it!' Tom laughed.

He had heard that Barbara La Marr, sultry screen vamp, was playing a major role in the movie, and had noted she hadn't been among the Ingram entourage at the Oasis the night before. She hardly needed to be there in person as her name was never far from other people's lips; one of those rare screen goddesses with such a natural gift for publicity that her reputation blazed out in advance of her screen performances rather than after them.

'If you saw the movie before, the story hasn't changed much,' Terry continued. 'Miss La Marr plays Zareda, a vampire countess who sets a rich old count and his artist son against each other in a fatal battle for her affections. It's all shadow, seduction, dungeons and excess – and not much story. But dear Rex is determined to have another stab at it, convinced it will be his greatest ever, and I do not doubt the box office will agree. Especially since I convinced him that Miss La Marr, far better than I, would suit the vampire role.'

Tom glanced at Terry while she was looking away, unsure whether she was joking or not. However talented she might be, he couldn't see vamping coming very naturally to her. Just then a shout went up and Ingram emerged from the wings and walked across to the largest of the three tripod cameras aimed at the scene, speaking with a spare, whey-faced individual in an outsize flat cap who was standing by, ready to crank, looking like he conspired to spend all his time working in California's golden light without ever stepping directly into it.

Ingram called across the floor to an assistant and immediately, from behind, actors began drifting towards the set. First out was the instantly recognizable figure of La Marr, a tall, startling blend of willow and curve, dressed head to toe in a high-necked gown of flowing black silk. With her hair covered in what appeared to be a turban, a veil of black gauze hanging before her eyes, all that was visible of her face was an exquisite curve of jaw and her mouth, china-doll lips painted a deep, glossy black. The effect might have been humorous if she hadn't radiated such an extraordinary air of sensuality, so strong and dense and enveloping it took Tom by surprise when every muscle in his body tensed in instinctive physical response. He had seen La Marr on screen with Doug Fairbanks once before, and heard colleagues talk of her in crudely salacious terms. But here in close proximity he felt a potent carnality as she sauntered sinuously across the stage and perched at one end of the richly gilded Biedermeier sofa that dominated the set.

'Is this where you want me?' La Marr asked, her voice gentler, richer than expected, as she lifted her chin to the light in a melodramatic pose. Ingram said nothing, deferring for now to his cameraman, who asked her to adjust her position minimally. Meanwhile, Edward Connelly had also walked out, entirely eclipsed, and was arranging himself beside her, expertly flipping back the wide coattails of his morning suit to take his place on the sofa. Dressed as an aristocratic old roué, his mustache accentuated by black greasepaint upturned at the sides in the manner of a vaudeville villain, the effect was jarringly comical set against La Marr's sultry exoticism. But Ingram seemed more than happy with that, laughing out loud and encouraging him to be sure to repeat the tailcoat gesture once the cameras were rolling.

'Ed's playing the baron,' Terry whispered. Tom had almost forgotten she was there. He could tell she knew it, her amused eyes holding his now, a smile playing on her lips. 'The priapic old goat is obsessed with winning Zareda's favors.'

Before she could say anything more, they were silenced by another shout, this time of 'On your marks, folks.' It sent the two actors scurrying apart as on to the set loped the shambling orangutan Joe Martin, alongside his old keeper – Schott, Tom recalled his name was – whose hand he held in his like a corpulent toddler in a burnt-orange horsehair suit.

Tom's heart sank at how unhappy the creature appeared, but lifted again when he saw the look of delight fire up in its eyes when it caught sight of Miss La Marr. Joe instantly released Schott's hand and scampered across the set, embracing her round the waist and legs with clearly reciprocated affection.

'Oh, look who it is. It's my fat little monkey pal,' La Marr simpered at him, appending a chatter of mewing and clucking noises.

As the keeper ducked out of sight behind the drapes, Ingram's shout of, 'OK, roll 'em' went up, and the cameramen started cranking steadily. Responding to coaxing from Ingram beside the camera, Connelly entered, bowed gallantly, and proffered a gift of an extravagant rope of outsize pearls to La Marr's temptress. She responded by hanging them round Joe Martin's neck and uttering a teasing, melodramatic laugh. As Connelly oozingly encouraged her to sit beside him on the davenport, Joe Martin followed, settling on the floor against La Marr's legs and toying with his new necklace while fixing her admirer with a curious stare.

Now, at Ingram's urging from offstage, the baron went up a gear in his schtick, taking Zareda's hand and drawing it towards him in a pantomime seduction, while she pretended to resist. All went well until she pulled back playfully, and the baron leant in to plant a kiss on the back of her hand. Whereupon the staring ape went ape. Letting loose a baleful snarl, it hurled itself across La Marr, clamped its enormous jaws round Connelly's offending hand and wrapped its long right arm around his neck, wrestling him away from his paramour, and off the sofa, crashing in a terrifying death roll on to the floor.

A momentary paralysis of panic seized the room before complete pandemonium broke out. Schott threw himself at Joe Martin, attempting to drag him off Connelly, but to no avail. Two cameramen joined the fray, hauling at and thumping the creature, desperately attempting to separate its jaws from the screaming actor's hand to no avail, with Ingram close by in the background shouting instructions uselessly and La Marr backing away, mouth open in horror, a hand pressed to her belly. Tom could see the ape was determined not to give up. Back hunched, Connelly's bucking head tucked in under one long arm, warding off blows with the other, Joe Martin was hunkered down for the long game.

Only a tug at his sleeve brought Tom out of it. Terry, her features drawn in shock. 'Oh, my lord. Can't you do something? It'll be the death of them both if you don't.'

She was right. Ingram, somehow, had gotten hold of a rifle and, roaring at everyone to stand clear, was raising it to his shoulder to take a shot.

'No!' Tom hollered at him and jumped between gun barrel and beast, blocking Ingram's sightline. From the Biedermeier he grabbed a cushion that shimmered beneath the studio lights with iridescent silk and glittering gold brocade, and waved it, hunkering down and urging the others back, moving slowly, sideways-on towards the animal, holding it out for him to see.

'Joe, Joe look, for you,' he said as calmly as he could above Connelly's muffled moans, waving the cushion again. The ape glanced once, the sparkling fabric catching his attention. He looked away again to check the room. His attackers had receded, a hush had fallen all around. The creature's jaw slackened on Connolly's wrist, but his headlock on the actor did not. The cushion was just beyond his reach.

'Come on Joe, it's me, Tom. Remember me, buddy?'

Joe Martin's glittering black eyes looked up past the cushion and locked on Tom. Dimly at first, then in an instant, the creature's eyes seemed to widen in recognition. He withdrew his long arm from round Connolly's neck, and hurled himself at Tom, grabbing the cushion and clambering awkwardly but enthusiastically into his arms as Ingram and others rushed in to drag Connelly away.

Tom embraced the animal's weight as well as he could, fending off the enormous leathery hands and lips exploring his face, the tugging on his hair, the intense aroma of overheated, overexcited primate, until Connolly and the others were out of sight and the set was cleared of all but Tom and the keeper, Schott. Only then did he untangle Joe Martin's limbs and set him down, the incident apparently forgotten, the intelligent eyes seeking out La Marr, perhaps, but in her absence settling on his shell-shocked keeper, towards whom now, all friendships reaffirmed, Joe Martin waddled contentedly.

FOUR

'They sure knew what they was doing, dumping him in that spot.'

He could have said it a million other ways, and Detective Thad Sullivan would have been no less offended by the manner in which Gil Reynolds, constable of Inglewood County Sheriff's Office, was speaking to him.

'Could'a been there months. Nobody would a'knowed it.'

Reynolds was a short, squat, round-bellied officer with a sun-flushed, flap-jowled face and a bristling salt-and-pepper mustache that made him look permanently irritated. He had been sitting downstairs in the lobby of Los Angeles' Central Police Station when Sullivan walked in through the arched doorway and had pounced on him unannounced, demanding an immediate interview.

As soon as Sullivan spotted the 'Inglewood' stitched on his shoulder badge, he knew what Reynolds had come about. He had already absorbed the shock of the headline on the front page of the *Los Angeles Times* over a long and fretful luncheon in a quiet cafeteria two blocks down on Spring. Now he feared his worst suspicions would be confirmed. But, shaken as he was, Sullivan didn't betray it. He told Reynolds brusquely to hold his horses a minute, as he had to go upstairs and see his captain on urgent business.

Sullivan didn't have anyone to see. But it gave him time to give his face a splash of cold, reviving water, get some air on the sweat-drenched armpits of his shirt and gather his thoughts, before going back out and calling Reynolds upstairs to his desk in the detective bureau. By a stroke of good fortune, the usually bustling office was largely empty, so there was no chance their conversation would be overheard by one of the many busybody snoops round about whose curiosity would be pricked by the sight of a County uniform. A good opportunity to brush Reynolds off, hopefully. Maybe get rid of him for good.

But it didn't work out like that. Even before he settled in the chair, Reynolds asked Sullivan straight out if he'd seen the story. Sullivan said he had, like any professional would, then waited while Reynolds told it over again his way, anyway. How the two boys had been brought in by Bud Eckland, screaming and jabbering about finding a dead man, and dragged him out to a gully in the hills, full of sagebrush, cactus and a mess of prickly pear, and there was this body stuck high in a clump of thorns, obviously thrown down there from above, all black and grey and twisted and stinking like a ripe ol' cheese.

'Couldn't even get close to him 'fore sunrise.' Reynolds had a wheezing way of talking on the inbreath, like he'd run half a mile for every step he'd taken up the stairs.

'Had to leave him till the boys from Matson's funeral parlor was free to get him late afternoon. Figured it wouldn'a matter none to him. An' it took hours. Couldn' get the truck up the hill. Had to carry ladders in and cutters for the cactus. Hours. In all this here heat, too. Matson's boys said we was lucky he dried out so much in sun already. Face all leathered up an' black as a Santa Clara prune.'

'So you've got no idea who he is?' Sullivan asked, thinking he should demonstrate a flicker of interest at least.

'Own mother wouldn't know him. Jeeze, I don't never wanna see nothing like that again.'

'Or how long he'd been there?'

All Reynolds did was shrug vacantly, wrinkling his nose and mustache like he was breathing in the stench of death again. 'Could'a be weeks, could'a be months, doc says.'

Sullivan saw enough in that to want rid of it, quick. 'Well, sounds like a tough call, Reynolds. But what I don't see is what's it got to do with us here in Central?' He swung one of his massive arms out and around to indicate the office in general. 'I appreciate we might not look too hectic today, but we are a very busy squad and this looks to me to be Inglewood County Sheriff all the way. So, unless you can tell me different, I'll need to be getting on.'

Reynold's eyebrows arched up and a harder, more skeptical look fell across his face. 'I would'a thought it was obvious, detective. I don' care one whit about Central. I wan'a know wha' can *you*, Detective Sullivan, tell me about this fella.'

Sullivan didn't have to fake his astonishment. 'Me, for Christ's sake?' he spluttered, the shrillness of his native Limerick coming to the fore. 'You told me already you don't know him from Adam himself. Or how long he's been there. How in hell's name would I know any more than you do about him?'

'Well, we jus' felt you got to.' Again, Reynolds gave him the hard eyeball. 'The crows an' other critters gnawed 'way mos' of what he got on him. Mortuary boys found a wallet in his pants pocket. Nothin'. Whoever killed him must'a cleaned it out and put it back 'fore they dumped him. When doc put him on slab, he peeled what was left 'a the suit away from his skin – an' found a slip of paper in the inside pocket. Only thing left on him.'

Reynolds smirked knowingly and, as if prolonging the pleasure, tapped each of his chest pockets in turn, then unbuttoned and pulled a billfold from the left. Slowly, delicately, he drew out an embalmed-looking piece of paper, horribly stained a marbled yellow and deep brownish red. Unfolding it carefully, he handed it over to Sullivan, never once taking his eyes off the big man now, gauging his reaction.

'Ain' easy to make out, all the stains an' so on. But seem' mighty like a name and badge number to me, so I looked it up. And guess what?'

Sullivan's eyes bugged as they adjusted to the faded scrawl on the paper and deciphered what was scrawled beneath the stains.

'Where the hell did he get this?'

Glancing up, Sullivan caught the remains of the smirk fading from behind the officer's ridiculous mustache, and his dislike of the County cop dropped a level deeper.

'That's my badge number.'

'So it is,' said Reynolds. 'You' name, too, if we readin' it right. An' tha's what we'd like to know, too. Where *did* he get them? Tha' ain't by any chance *your* handwritin' on there, detective, is it?'

FIVE

Having endured a final malodorous hug before helping Schott load him into a stifling hot crate on the back of a flatbed truck, Tom waved goodbye to his pal Joe Martin and made his way round to the dressing rooms. The studio doc was there by now, pushing a concerned throng out of Connelly's room and assuring everyone he would be OK, that he was in no immediate danger of losing a hand, though his patient had had a serious shock and desperately needed to rest. Ingram was among the first to leave, apparently both relieved and entertained. As soon as he set eyes on Tom he rushed over, gratitude pouring freely from him along with laughter.

'Would you credit it? I said it last night, didn't I? Tight spot – fellow Irishman! Well, you've put that beyond any doubt now, old man. Beyond any doubt.'

He repeated this again, and more, with no less enthusiasm when Terry came over to say she was going home for an hour. Ingram, deciding the day was lost in any case, dismissed the crew for an early lunch and invited Tom to his office for a drink.

'We should probably talk about what you asked me over for this morning,' Tom said.

Ingram's shoulders sagged as if he had forgotten about that and his expression darkened.

'Yes, yes, OK, the marvelous Miss La Marr,' he said, as if that explained everything.

Tom's interest was instantly piqued. Aside from arousing acts of erotic jealousy in apes, La Marr had a unique gift for drawing attention to herself. And not always to her benefit. Despite her undeniable beauty, her taste for on-screen vamping had always kept her firmly excluded from the top roles. Was there, maybe, more to it than that?

Ingram crooked a finger and set off, inviting Tom to follow as he entered the maze of connected wooden cabins that made up the stars' dressing area. La Marr's room was not big, but it was as opulently fitted out as an empress's boudoir. Ingram barged in without knocking and Tom followed, his impression akin to that of entering a perfumed grotto, with bouquets of fresh-cut flowers crammed into jugs and vases on every available surface. All such thoughts were dispelled as soon as he caught a sight of the actress, hunched over her dressing table, one hand to her forehead, the other cradling her stomach, her face pale to the point of illness and apparently struggling for breath.

Ingram rushed over, showering her with concern. La Marr responded with thanks, but once she caught sight of Tom lumbering in behind, a veil went down behind her eyes and another, more public self, appeared to take hold. She pushed Ingram away, chiding him gently for fussing so much, and forced a smile to her lips which she directed at Tom, turning in her chair and struggling to her feet.

'This is Collins, the private man I was telling you about,' Ingram said, sitting down heavily on a satin-draped trunk.

'Oh, my. And our hero of the hour, too, apparently. Well, you certainly know how to inspire confidence in a girl, Mr Collins.'

La Marr extended a hand horizontally towards Tom. Uncertain whether he was expected to kiss it or shake it, he opted for the latter and was entirely unnerved when a jolt of something animal coursed from his fingertips to his loins, bypassing his brain entirely. He checked her face to see if she had felt it, too, but if she had she was hiding it well.

'Rex told me he asked you over. Just as well, I say.' She laughed lightly and held Tom's eyes. 'If it hadn't been for you, I might've had to worry about my hairy little friend. Is Joe OK?'

Tom smiled and nodded. 'Joe's fine.'

'And Ed?' This directed to Ingram. 'How is the darling man?'

It was only then that Tom noticed it. The high-necked black dress she wore was now unbuttoned at the front, revealing a sliver of glossy black silk chemise beneath. Something in the way it parted as she turned to listen to Ingram's reassurances, in how the fabric clung to her belly as she twisted round from the waist, revealed a very considerable bump. He remembered then how she had cradled herself protectively before, and he tried to conceal his realization. But La Marr was too quick, catching his gaze fastened on her a moment too long, the question forming in his mind. She stepped back weakly, a kind of defeat coming over her as she slumped into her chair and raised a hand to her forehead again.

'Oh, what's the goddamn use, Rex?' she said, with a resigned sigh.

Ingram had seen his reaction too and, putting a consoling hand on her arm, he turned to Tom. 'Well, there's no point trying to hide it, is there? It's one of the reasons we asked you here, Collins. Miss La Marr is going to have a baby and we can't afford for anyone to find out about it. As you may or may not know, she's between husbands at the moment.'

La Marr gave a little snort of scornful amusement, but Ingram ignored it.

'A scandal would not be good at any time, but more so just now. What with all the publicity around our new movie coming out and, especially, with Mr Hays in town over the next few days.'

Tom recalled Ingram's wary glance the night before and wondered if this could really be the source of it. If so, he wondered why. Unless he was the father, of course. But for all Ingram's concern, he wasn't giving that impression.

'Well, I'll help in any way I can,' Tom said. 'But I'm honestly not sure what I could do. Seems to me you're handling it pretty well yourselves. If it hadn't been for that business with Joe, I'd never have noticed anything.'

'Goddam ape,' Ingram said. 'I'll have the wretched creature put down.'

'No, Rex, you will not. It was trying to protect me.'

'Don't be crazy.'

'It probably was,' Tom said, ignoring him and addressing La Marr. 'Your condition might have contributed, ma'am. They say some creatures sense these things better than we do. But I still don't see how I can help. That costume does a better job of covering it up than I ever could.'

'We spent enough getting the damn dresses right.' There was little hint in Ingram's tone of the bitterness you usually got from directors on the subject of money. If anything, he sounded proud of it. 'I employ only the best, Collins. And Seitz, my cameraman, reckons he can hide anything if he positions the camera right. That's why we brought all of Miss La Marr's scenes forward, to try and wrap before she becomes too . . . well, too obvious, I guess. Today was supposed to be her last day on set. That damn monkey's put the hex on that now.'

'Oh Rex, you'll find a way around it. You always do.' La Marr was looking a little more composed now, the color coming back in her cheeks, and she sat up straighter in the chair as if readying herself for business. 'And anyway, this is none of Mr Collins's concern. It's not even what you asked him here to talk about, now is it?'

'There's something else?'

'Sure. Can you believe it?' Ingram said, laughing ruefully and shaking his head again. 'When I said Miss La Marr is currently without a husband, I was being a mite inaccurate. In fact, she appears to have an excess of them. Because one of her supposed former husbands has come back on the scene, claiming not to be former at all, and threatening to kick up a stink about it.'

'Oh, Rex, you know it's not as complicated as all that,' La Marr complained.

'Isn't it? I'd like to see you explain it any better.'

'I'm sorry, I'm not entirely following you,' Tom said. 'Former husband? Not former at all?'

La Marr leaned forward a little in her seat, then thought better of it. She fixed him with her gaze. It was as if her tiredness, despair, even her condition, were all forgotten now as her eyes lit up again and enveloped him.

'Mr Collins, I wonder . . . did you see a feature about me in *Photoplay* last month, written by Mrs Rogers St Johns?'

Tom smiled. 'I think everyone in Hollywood saw that one, Miss La Marr. Made quite a splash.'

'And tell me, what did you think of it?'

'Honestly, I thought it was puff for the fans. I mean, most of these articles are, aren't they? Apart from anything else, I remember she spent a lot of words talking about your beauty, and how it's fading. I'm not seeing that.'

He wasn't sure why he said that, or why he felt the need to grin at her when he did. La Marr simply seemed to invite it, and she as good as purred with pleasure when he did.

Ingram laughed drily. 'Well, that's all fine, but there was more truth in it than you might imagine, Collins, especially relating to Barbara's marital entanglements.'

Tom raised an eyebrow. 'If I remember right, she said one of your husbands was a brain-sick married man who duped you into marriage before dying in the operating theater. And your first husband died falling off a horse, am I right? So, I'm thinking the problem can't be with either of them. And given that you're what, twenty-five, twenty-six at most, ma'am?' – she nodded at the latter – 'I'm guessing there can't be too many other husbands around.'

'That's very amusing of you Mr Collins. But the fact is, this man was never my husband. Only someone I spent time with once and who is now claiming we were man and wife.'

'And were you?'

'He says he has a marriage license,' Ingram broke in impatiently. 'And that he'll file the petition on grounds of infidelity.'

'OK.' Tom was beginning to see the problem now. 'So, does he have the license? That's all the proof he'd need.'

'I don't see how,' La Marr said, though she didn't sound entirely convinced.

'The problem is he *says* he has it,' Ingram broke in again. 'And whatever about going to the police, his lawyer says he'll take it to the newspapers first. Infidelity? A baby? It amounts to the same thing. Even without Hays in town we couldn't afford for this – any of it – to get out.'

'You say he has a lawyer involved?'

'Yes,' La Marr said. 'A ball of slime by the name of Roth. You know him?'

Tom shook his head. He knew plenty of lawyers. Some were square but for most, as far as he could see, it was hard to tell which side of the law they worked on. 'Could be dangerous, though. And you, Miss La Marr? What does your lawyer say? I imagine you must have one.'

She gave him a funny look. 'Well, yes. Frank Drew. Do you know *him*?'

That was the first good news he'd heard. 'I do, as it happens. I worked with Frank a couple times over the years, when I was with Lasky. He's a good man. Straight up, and smart with it.'

'Well, what we'd like is for you to work with him,' Ingram said. 'Maybe the two of you could put your heads together and come up with a plan to get rid of this Deeley and his slanders – any way you can.'

Tom didn't like the sound of that. 'Deeley, that's his name?'

'Yes, Ben Deeley,' La Marr answered. 'He's an actor, but I doubt the no-good bum has worked in months.'

He nodded, the name sounding vaguely familiar. He turned to Ingram. 'Look, if you're looking for someone to rough this guy up, you've come to the wrong man.'

'Naturally we wouldn't want that, Mr Collins,' La Marr said quickly. 'All we want is for him to go away, as quietly as possible. *The Prisoner of Zenda* comes out in two weeks. It is my biggest role to date, and everyone says it will propel me to the first rank. I can't afford for that opportunity to be thrown away.'

'That's another thing I don't get,' Tom said. 'Metro must have a lot of money tied up in that movie. Not to mention this other one you're shooting now?'

Ingram shrugged like he didn't care. 'Approaching a couple of million, yes.'

'So why haven't you taken this to the studio and let them take care of it? You must know as well as I do, a studio – even a medium-size one like Metro – has the resources, the lawyers and fixers and publicity men to deal with this so much better than one private guy ever could. Especially when there's so much at stake.'

Ingram looked more than a little irked by that and his reply was emphatic. 'No, Metro can't be involved.'

'But they're the people with the biggest interest here. You must've made a stack for them with *The Four Horsemen*. Not to mention what they've got wrapped up in these next two. I mean, no one could have a greater interest in promoting and protecting your reputation. And Miss La Marr's too, now, what with her predicted to break so big. I'm guessing they would be a whole lot keener than you imagine to help you protect their investment.'

Ingram's face reddened and the determination in his voice deepened. 'Absolutely not. No one at Metro must get wind of this, under any circumstances. This is a private, personal matter. And must be dealt with as such.'

Le Marr reached out a calming hand on Ingram's arm. 'What Rex is not telling you, Mr Collins, is that he put his reputation on the line to cast me in *The Prisoner of Zenda*, in the face of very considerable opposition from the studio. They did not regard my "reputation" as an asset. And they desired me even less for *Black Orchids*. Rex only got his way by threatening to quit Metro if they didn't grant him autonomy. The flip side of the deal was they said he was on his own if any problems arose, that they would wash their hands if he got into trouble. And with Mr Hays coming to town, who knows how they would react?'

'Sure, but when it comes to the bottom line, they might think different. We're talking money here. Lots of it. With so much at stake they're bound to recons—'

'Look,' Ingram cut him off angrily. 'I care nothing for their money. Or this goddamn studio. And as for Hays, the man can rot in hell. All I want is for *Zenda* to come out and to be seen by the whole world. And for *Black Orchids* to be the triumph it undoubtedly will deserve to be – once we get it finished. We have put our hearts and souls into these projects, Collins. And I will not have some little glad-handing shyster politician come and take all that away from me. So, please, when I say this is the way I want it done, this *really is* how I want it done. We will pay you whatever you like, but Metro must know nothing of it. Do you understand me? Absolutely. Nothing.'

Tom was beginning to see how Ingram acquired his reputation for getting his own way on things. There wasn't much room for maneuver, or misunderstanding, there. But before he could say anything further there was a knock on the door.

'Christ, what is it now?' Ingram said, jumping up and stomping towards the door. From the hurried exchange when he opened it, his presence was clearly required urgently. Somebody wanted him out on the set.

Before exiting he looked back. 'Will you take the job, Collins?'

Tom put his hands up, a small surrender. No point trying to

do himself out of paid work. 'Sure, I'll see what Drew has to say.'

Ingram was visibly relieved. 'Good, we'll talk in a couple of days, then.'

With that he left the room and Tom turned to Miss La Marr, about to go the same way himself. 'I'd better get down to Drew's office, see what he's got.'

'Thank you, Mr Collins. But I already know Mr Drew is in court all day today. The earliest he could see *me* was tomorrow, at three. You're welcome to join us then.'

It sounded like a good enough way of getting everything he needed to know, as there would probably be matters she needed to discuss with Drew that she wouldn't want to share with Ingram.

'In that case, I'll see you there tomorrow, Miss La Marr.'

He reached for his hat but, to his surprise, she put out a hand and folded it small and soft round his outstretched fingers, gently staying him. 'No, wait a moment, Mr Collins, if you would.'

Again, he felt the visceral charge of her touch shoot into him, stirring something ancient and involuntary. He was pretty certain too, now, that she was entirely unaware of the effect. If anything, the seriousness of her tone suggested her thoughts couldn't be further elsewhere. He was relieved when she released his hand to pat the seat beside her, the one Ingram had vacated.

'Please, sit down,' she said. 'There is something else we need to discuss.'

SIX

Tom declined La Marr's invitation to sit beside her. Whether she was aware of its effect, or not, her physical proximity was the last thing on earth he needed to be thinking about.

'Are we still talking about your troubles with Mr Deeley?' he ventured.

'No, this has nothing to do with that, thankfully,' La Marr said. 'But it does involve Mr Ingram. And he mustn't know anything about it. At least not for now.'

Tom put a hand up, as politely as he could. 'I'm sorry, Miss La Marr, I'd better stop you there. Mr Ingram's the one who's taken me on. I can't go behind his back.'

He said he should go but she wouldn't hear of it. 'No, no, please, it is nothing to do with Rex, I promise. It's something that only came up this morning. Please, hear me out and if you cannot help, then perhaps you could recommend someone who can.'

He didn't have much choice but to agree to that.

'Tell me, Mr Collins, did you happen to meet dear Ramon, last night?' La Marr asked. 'My colleague, Mr Samaniegos, that is? Rex said he was with the party at the Oasis last night. I was too tired to attend. But I'm not sure Rex would have let me anyway.'

Tom nodded. 'I saw him there. He was in the company, that is. But I didn't actually speak to him.'

'Did nothing strike you about him?'

Tom made a face that vaguely suggested nothing at all.

'He's a shy boy, at the best of times. So very beautiful – and possessed of a beautiful soul too. But he's not at all worldly.'

'I'll take your word for it.'

She looked at him quite sharply then. 'I haven't known Ramon for very long, Mr Collins, but already I count him among the loveliest and most sensitive men of my acquaintance.'

Even as what Fay had hinted the night before about Samaniegos rose in his mind, it was turned on its head completely when he saw her stroke her belly again while she was mentioning the boy's name. Again, she caught his gaze, though this time she responded by laughing out loud.

'No, no, Mr Collins. He is not the father. I see that even you find that a little hard to believe.'

He felt the color rise in his cheeks and grew impatient. 'Maybe we should just get to the point, Miss La Marr. Is he in some kind of trouble?'

'Yes, that's exactly it,' she said, relieved by his bluntness. 'He telephoned me in a state of considerable distress this morning. Said he'd got himself into a "situation" and life wasn't worth living anymore.' She paused, savoring the drama of it. 'I was shocked, he sounded so low. But he calmed down when I told him I'd see what I could do to help, though I didn't know what precisely. And then, there you were, appearing out of nowhere just now. And I thought, well, maybe you could pay Ramon a visit for me. And see if anything can be done to get him out of this fix he's in.'

Tom waved that away. 'And what, exactly, is this fix?'

'Well, that's something I think only he can tell you. I'm sure all you'd have to do is call in for a half-hour and give him some advice and reassurance. You do have that worldly look and dependable way about you Mr Collins, if I may say so.'

She all but purred at him as she said it, and he found himself nodding despite himself.

'Well, I suppose if I can't see Drew until tomorrow, I could see him instead.'

'Oh, how simply marvelous of you! I'll call ahead and tell him you'll be right over. I will pay you for your time, obviously. And if it's something you decide you cannot help him any further with, because of Rex, then maybe you can point him in the right direction.'

Tom felt as if he'd been railroaded, but there was something in those eyes, the purse of those lips that rendered him powerless to resist. He shook his head, more to clear it than to offer a negative, and a modicum of sense finally returned. 'OK, I'll try, Miss La Marr. But Mr Ingram has got to be my priority.'

'Oh, worry not. So long as you have some advice to offer Ramon. I am so concerned for him.'

'I'm on my way.' He thought this would settle it, but she only become more effusive.

'Oh, thank you so, so much.' She rose from her chair and, extending her long, elegant arms, she grasped his two hands at once, her extraordinary eyes half-hooded, her lips beaming with gratitude. He hardly knew whether to be mortified or aroused but, fortuitously, there was a knock at the door and a young woman entered, her eyes widening a little as she took in the two tall figures standing just inches from one another.

'Oh, I'm sorry—'

'No, no – come in, darling,' La Marr said, wafting over and drawing her into the room. 'Mr Collins was just leaving. What is it?'

'There's this reporter guy out on the lot,' she said, flicking another curious glance at Tom. 'He was looking for Mr Connelly first, but now all he's interested in is you. He's been over by the other dressing rooms asking everybody where you are.'

La Marr visibly blanched and both Tom and the girl had to help her sit down. 'Oh lord,' she sobbed. 'I can't be seen by anyone in this state.'

'Can't you ask security to get rid of him?' Tom asked the girl.

She shook her head. 'He has a pass and says he has permission to be here. We got someone over to see him off anyway, but he disappeared. And no one saw him leave the lot.'

'Did you get a name?' Tom asked.

'Yeah, Olsen, they said at the gate. From the *Herald*.'

Tom cursed under his breath. 'I know Olsen. We can't risk him seeing you, Miss La Marr. There's not a hack in Los Angeles with a better nose for a story than Olsen. Believe me, I have good reason for knowing that.'

La Marr looked as interested as she was troubled by that, as if – even in the midst of panic – she was filing the name away for future reference.

He turned to the girl. 'Is there another way out? I can try to distract him while you get Miss La Marr off the lot.'

SEVEN

Tom didn't have to go looking for Olsen. He had barely stepped out of the block into the dazzling daylight before he heard his name called. There was only one person that nasal bug-whine of a voice could belong to, and the thought of him pinged the hairs up on the back of his neck.

'Hey, Collins? Tom Collins, wait up there, brother.'

He looked back over his shoulder, feigning surprise. Sure enough, pushing his way through a throng of breaktime extras, hailing him with a raised notebook and pen, was the short, scrawny figure of *Herald* reporter Phil Olsen. Tom waited while he caught up. He was in his standard rig of navy-blue suit, starched collar and cuffs, and red bow tie. A press ticket stuck out from the silk band of his straw boater but, even if it hadn't been there, the wire-framed spectacles, hawk nose and curl of knowingness on his lips marked him out as a newsman.

'I thought it was you, ya big Irish galoot,' Olsen said, extending a hand and pumping Tom's enthusiastically.

'If that's your latest line in flattery, Olsen, I'd try again.'

Tom couldn't help liking Olsen, despite himself. Talking to him could sometimes feel like walking a high wire, given his own need for discretion and the reporter's sharp nose for a story. But, unlike most of his ilk, Olsen was a man you could do a deal with and depend on, most of the time at least. A useful guy to know when you needed the dope on something fast.

'Aw, you're tough enough to take it.' Olsen batted a hand at him. 'I was thinking about you the other night, out at the Legion, Friday. Thinking I hadn't seen you at the fights in a while.'

'Can't be everywhere,' Tom made a beeline for the main gate, knowing Olsen would fall into step with him. 'And the nights are too damn hot for boxing anyway. All that sweat and hollering.'

'Got somewhere cooler to be, have you?' Olsen said, keeping

pace with him. 'Lucky you. Who is she? I hope you haven't dumped that gorgeous dame of yours? She's a keeper, that one.'

'I told you before, Olsen, Fay is no dame.'

'Oh right, she's a "missus", ain't she? *Mrs* Parker. Yeah, I almost forgot that.'

Olsen raised an eyebrow and gave a little smirk, and it took all Tom's restraint not to snap one back at him. Fay's unresolved marital status had been like a sword hanging over their heads when they both worked at Lasky. Now, they didn't have to worry about it so much, but the suggestion that there might be anything to be ashamed of always irked him.

Something in his face must've betrayed him because Olsen wiped the look off his face and hurried on. 'Sure, I know, I know. She's a class act, Tom. You're a lucky guy, no mistake. But, man, you missed a humdinger Friday. Even the bantie bouts. Rivers and Garber – you hear about 'em?'

Tom shook his head but Olsen was running on anyway. 'Jeeze, did they ever go at it. Whole place on its feet howling. Not to mention Griffin and Rubidoux in the semi. But the main event – Young Brown and Benny Vierra, for the championship. That was one torrid scrap. Vierra, he started off strong, lots of high-voltage stuff, cuts and jabs, but Brown just soaked it up and wore him down . . .'

Tom let him rattle on. Boxing was Olsen's principal enthusiasm in life, even if his daily beat was the movie business and everything to do with it. The longer he was spouting on about that, the further they got from La Marr.

But he knew that couldn't last, and it didn't.

'What's got you down here at Metro, anyway Tom?' Olsen said, changing the subject at last. 'You here on business? Got a juicy bone to throw me?'

Tom shook his head definitely. 'Not this time, Olsen, just dropping something off for a pal.'

'Oh, yeah? You're in the delivery business now? Anyone I know?'

'It's nothing you'd be interested in, Olsen.'

'I wouldn't be too sure, Collins. Wasn't that the great Mr Ingram's block I saw you coming out of? His name's worth a line or two any day. And, now I think of it, he's a countryman of yours, ain't he? Yeah, right, I get it. You Irish, you stick real tight, right?'

Tom knew saying nothing was as good as an admission. 'Sure we do, Olsen. And speaking of Irish – did you see what Van Court said in the *Times* about Jack Dempsey the other day? Said Willard's in training to take him on again? October or so. They couldn't really be going to let that happen, could they?'

'Can't see it,' Olsen said, heavy on the skepticism. 'Jess Willard's gotta have a glass jaw now, don't he? After the beating he took first time. Every punch Dempsey makes would be smack at it. I hear he's refusing to—' Something slotted down behind his eyes and Olsen stopped mid-sentence and looked around quickly, up and down the lot.

'Say, you wouldn't be trying to deflect my attention from something, would you, Collins?'

Tom snorted at that one. 'Don't you ever get tired of being so suspicious, Olsen? You know, I should be the one asking you what you're doing here. I mean, a pressman roaming free on a movie lot? They'd never allow that over at Lasky. I'm thinking, what? Maybe you gave your chaperone the slip? Maybe I should give them a call up front. Maybe you're so desperate for stories, you're sneaking on to lots now?'

Olsen was feigning a look of hurt. 'As if, Collins. I'm here by invitation, if you must know.' He dug in his vest pocket and pulled out a pass similar to the one Tom had been given. One thing stood out: it had the same shoot name, *Black Orchids*, printed on it.

'Looks like you're the one visiting Ingram, not me. What's going on, Olsen?'

'Goddamn nothin',' the reporter said disconsolately. 'I came in to see that actor guy, Connelly.' Olsen held up the pass again, and this time Tom saw the name. 'He's working on this Ingram flick, feeling his contribution is going a mite underreported, I guess. So, I offered to puff him up in the paper with some free column inches.' Olsen's expression was clouded with exasperation. 'Only, I'm guessing he must've gone and interviewed a case of Scotch himself before I got here. Because nobody'll let me within a mile of the guy. All they do is try to spin me some line about him being in no fit condition to meet a member of the press, like that's not double-speak for drunk as a skunk, and instead they give me some humbug about some crazy monkey or other. Sure, like I'm gonna swallow that one. God damn the mumbling old fruitcake.'

A chill ran down Tom's back, thinking Joe Martin would come to a sticky end if that story got into the papers. He offered Olsen a show of semi-sympathy. 'A monkey? They must think you're some kind of rookie, Olsen. Tough break, though. Do you think Connelly was going to dish some dirt?'

'Sure, from what he hinted to me in his cups a few nights ago. A great steamin' pile of it. Somethin' about this good-looking bean-eater, Samanego or Sama-*negroes*, whatever his name is, Ingram's so keen to promote. Said the kid's pinched a spread in *Photoplay* next month that he was up for. Old man wasn't happy about it. Not one bit.'

Again Tom felt the chill and tried to bluff his way through. 'I can see that wouldn't go down well.'

'You seen him on the lot this morning, Tom?'

'Who, Connelly?'

'No, the kid, Sama*negro*.' Olsen was delighting in getting the name wrong, inviting Tom to object.

'Here? No. I'm not sure I'd even recognize him.'

Olsen gave him a funny look at that. 'If you say so. He's quite the handsome boy, even by colony standards. Fairly drips off 'a him.'

Tom shrugged indifferently.

'Kid's still small beer,' Olsen went on. 'For now, anyhow. What I was really hoping for was that Connelly would make good on what he hinted about the bewitching Barbara La Marr – something nice and salty about Ingram's vamp of choice, so he said.'

This time Tom really had a struggle keeping his expression under control. 'Like what?'

Olsen shrugged. 'Like that girl's got more skeletons than cupboards to hide 'em in. Way more than that tub of adoring whitewash Adela Stinkpot Rogers ran about her last month. I've never seen so many sins wiped clean with a single sweep of the hand. My editor read it and offered a nice fat bonus to

anyone who could turn up something on her that'd stick.'
Olsen looked up again, assessing Tom with a penetrating gaze.
'Y'know, I really wouldn't mind splitting it, Tom, if you have
anything to sell.'

'About Miss La Marr?'

Something in the way Tom said it made Olsen narrow his
eyes, predatory.

'Yeah, *Miss* La Marr – her. Y'know, I wouldn't mind, but she
seems such a nice kid – in person, I mean. Ain't you met her?
All those parties you and your Mrs Parker go to. Host, even?'

Tom denied it as carelessly as he could but, again, the
knowingness rippled across Olsen's thin lips. He looked over
his shoulder quickly, eyes darting hawkishly about, before
leaning in, putting a hand on Tom's forearm and standing on
tiptoe to diminish the six inches between his mouth and Tom's
right ear.

'I heard something off a pal of mine 'bout La Marr last
week – would make your hair stand on end. Seems she's been
getting pally with some top people over City Hall way.' Olsen
stepped away a little, still on tiptoe, so Tom could better see
the obscene gesture he was making with his free hand. '*Real*
pally . . . jiggy-jiggy pally, like,' he continued. 'You know
anything about that?'

'No, I don't.' Tom didn't have to feign his distaste as he
brushed Olsen away. 'Now get the hell off of me, Olsen. Christ,
sometimes you make my skin crawl with all your muckraking.
How you sleep at night is beyond me.'

Olsen laughed drily. 'I have no trouble sleeping. And neither
does *Miss* La Marr either, I'll bet. All that mattress exercise.
And you should come down off that high horse of yours, too,
Tommy boy. You know the score. Live by the sword and all
that. If she dishes it out, she's got to be ready to take it in
return. She's the one getting rich and famous on the back of
it. Last time I looked I wasn't earning a grand a week like she
is. That's a heck of a paycheck. Enough, even, to spend on the
likes of you to cover her tracks, maybe?'

Tom did his best not to respond, but Olsen was not convinced.
Then again, he didn't need to be as, at that moment, two stone-
faced security guys in uniform ran up from behind and clapped

hands on Olsen, insisting he must leave the lot immediately. Olsen hollered at them, shook them off, brandished his pass, and insisted on his right to be there. To no avail.

Tom stood by, amused by Olsen's resistance in the face of the guards' blank impassivity, until they grew bored of his insults, grabbed him again, one on each arm, intent on ejecting him whether he was willing to go or not.

Still Olsen hadn't finished. As he was manhandled away, he looked over his shoulder, a mischievous grin on his lips, and called back to Tom: 'Like I told you before, Collins. You're a hell of a bad liar. But I won't hold it against you. Just keep me in mind next time you're looking to trade some quid pro quo, won't you? Don't you forget your uncle Phil, here. I'll be ready and waiting, OK?'

EIGHT

Half an hour later Tom was back at the office to pick up his car, head buzzing with thoughts about La Marr and her situation, and still feeling more than a little abashed for allowing himself to be bamboozled into going to see Samaniegos instead of getting on with the job Ingram had engaged him on. He fended off Mae's starstruck enquiries about Ingram and Metro and let her go get lunch, suspecting he might be gone most of the afternoon. La Marr had given him an address for Samaniegos at the Athletic Club downtown and told him she would call ahead and tell the young Mexican that Tom was coming to see him.

Waiting for Mae to return, something Olsen said about the fights came back to mind. It had been too long since he had seen his friend, and former partner, Thad Sullivan. Longer still since they had been out to see the fights together, which they had done so much while he was working at Lasky, regular beneficiaries of passed-on free tickets for the stars. He picked up the telephone and asked the operator to put him through to Central Police Station, and then another switchboard to connect him with Sullivan in the Detective Bureau.

Sullivan answered instantly, as ever seeming to confuse the notion of telephone with that of megaphone.

'Hey, Thad, there's no need to shout. It's me, Tom.'

The response was abrupt, devoid of the usual amiable greeting, and immediately dropped in volume into a breathy conspiratorial whisper. 'You've seen it, too, then? What do you reckon?'

'Seen what, Thad? What're you talking about?'

'The front page of the *Times*, of course.' By now Sullivan's voice was a strangled, fretful whisper. 'What else would I be bloody talking about?'

He could see there would be no point asking Sullivan for a simple explanation. So instead he asked him to wait while he went back into the outer office and plucked the *Los Angeles Times* off the desk where Mae had left it, folded neatly. He flipped it open to the front page. A story about a body found after lying for weeks undiscovered in a gully in wasteland out near Inglewood jumped off the page at him, being the most prominent. But he scanned the rest of the front page to see if there was anything else. He was perplexed, so he quickly raced through the story.

'Are you talking about this body in the Baldwin Hills, Thad? What's that got to do with anything?'

This time the reply was a muttered curse. 'Ah, for Christ's sake, lad, use the few bloody brains God gave you, would you?'

All of a sudden it dawned on Tom. The body. The length of time. There was only one thing Sullivan could be thinking about, and the thought of it made his blood run cold.

'Jesus, you mean . . .' But he stopped himself, knowing he couldn't breathe another word for fear that a switchboard operator might be listening.

'Jesus Thad, are you serious?'

'What do you think? Of course I'm bloody serious,' Sullivan said, sounding a little calmer now, if no happier. 'Look, we can't talk about this now,' he went on, 'not with every ear in this place out on stalks. When're you going to be in that office of yours, and I'll come see you? Or you let me know where you'll be later and we'll meet up.'

NINE

Tom spent most of the drive downtown weighing up the unsettling possibilities of Sullivan's telephone call. If the dead man was who Sullivan suspected, life could be about to get very difficult. But that had to be a long shot, and as neither had been directly responsible, it was hard to see how, in any serious kind of way, the trail could lead back to them. By the time he had ploughed his way through the heavy cross-town traffic, and found a place to park on Olive, he had satisfied himself it was practically impossible, and walking through the doors of the Los Angeles Athletic Club on West Seventh, he pushed the idea from his thoughts.

The club was one of downtown Los Angeles' more prestigious temporary addresses, a spot popular with the younger, more gregarious business crowd and on-the-up movie men seeking to bivouac in convivial comfort before settling somewhere suitably celestial out by the studios. Tom had been in and out of the club so often during his time at Lasky's that he knew the building well. Didn't even have to stop at reception, just tipped house detective Harry Halbert the wink and rolled on up in the elevator.

Keeping a suite on the seventh floor was certainly an indication of a man doing well, but the greeting Tom received did not exhibit the confidence normally associated with the male of the Hollywood species. He had to announce himself twice through the heavy six-panel door before the lock snapped back and the handsome Latin face he'd seen at the Oasis peered out quickly, before stepping back to allow him in.

Close up, Ramon Samaniegos looked like a man who had been born with the century, no more than twenty-two or twenty-three years old. Now he could see what Fay meant about him having the good looks of a young Valentino, enhanced by immaculate grooming and tailoring. The young actor ushered

Tom into the room with unexpected formality and grace. Yet, for all that, he also had a look of preoccupation and strain about him that spoke of trouble.

Tom got straight down to business, repeating what Miss La Marr had told him and asking what it was exactly that was troubling him. 'Whatever the problem is, she thought I might be of some assistance, Mr Samaniego.'

'Samaniegos,' the young Mexican corrected, pronouncing the final 'os' as if it were *osh*. 'But call me Ramon if it is easier. You're not the first person to struggle with my name. At Metro the pressmen all call me "salmon'n'eggs" – and worse – behind my back.'

Tom remembered the emphasis Olsen had chosen to put on it and didn't feel any better about his clumsiness. Despite Los Angeles' thriving Hispanic community, for a Mexican actor – no matter how good looking and talented – to rise in the industry was unheard of. Tom couldn't help suspecting that only Ingram's obstinacy and clout could have got this young man, and his surname, past the prejudices of casting departments and studio executives. Just as he had for Valentino two years previously and proved them all wrong.

'OK, Ramon, thank you. Like I was saying, if there's some trouble I can help out with right now, I will. And if not, I can probably advise you who to go to, or what steps to take. But you have to be frank with me. You have to tell me the truth.'

Normally it took more than that to convince a man to share his deepest fears and misgivings, but Samaniegos seemed to welcome the opportunity and quickly walked over to the neat mahogany table at the far side of the room and pointed to a copy of the *Los Angeles Times* on it.

'It is my friend,' he said, waving a hand at the newspaper. 'I am desperately afraid for him.'

He was doing a good job of disguising the quiver in his voice, but in the end his anxiety betrayed him. For Tom the combination of newspapers and movies only ever meant one thing. Unwanted stories leaking out from behind closed doors. The fear of career-destroying scandal. What Fay had hinted at the night before about Samaniegos's sexual proclivities resurfaced in his mind as he opened the paper and scanned the pages for an innuendo-laden headline, or a sniping sideswipe at some emergent Hollywood figure.

'Did the press boys get hold of something this friend of yours would rather go unreported?'

'No, no, you don't understand.' Samaniegos shot a look of exasperation at him. He pulled the paper back towards him, flipped it to the front page and prodded a finger at the biggest, blackest, most prominent headline splashed across it.

'This . . . *this* is what I'm talking about,' he said, pushing the newspaper into Tom's hands. 'Look, read it.'

Tom was dumbfounded. It was the story Sullivan had drawn his attention to earlier. The unknown body found in the Baldwin Hills. But how could the young movie star be linked to it? Especially if what Tom had been thinking about on the way over was a possibility. It didn't make any sense.

'I'm sorry, Ramon. I'm not sure I understand. Are you saying you know who this dead man is?'

'I hope not.' A small sob escaped the actor's lips, emotion getting the better of him at last. 'But I fear it is my friend. It must be, I think. It can only be him.'

'What makes you think that? I mean, even the police don't know who this guy is.'

'They say that but how can you be certain?'

Tom shrugged, not wanting to get into that, and pointed at the paper again. 'It says so right there.'

'And you believe it?' Samaniegos shook his head. 'They say they don't know and maybe that's the truth, but the people who killed him know who he is, don't they?'

Tom had to give him that. He decided to take a different tack. 'Does he have a name, this friend of yours?'

'Yes, of course, Gianni . . . Gianni is his name.'

'Gianni what?'

'Isn't that enough for now?'

'Well no, not really. Not when it comes to identifying a person, it's not. It's the first thing the police will want to know, when we go to them.'

Samaniegos waved away that suggestion with both hands. 'No. No police. That's impossible, you cannot mean that.' He moved the hands to his head, tugging at his hair violently. 'I knew I should not have confided in her, I knew I shouldn't.'

'OK, OK, let's calm it down a little.' Tom took the young man by the elbow and guided him towards an armchair. 'Look, why don't we sit down and talk about this. And you can start from the beginning.'

Samaniegos threw himself heavily into the chair, now placing his head in his hands despondently. Tom took the chair opposite, and sat hunched forward, elbows on knees, palms together, trying to be as encouraging as he could.

'Now look, Ramon, I'm not saying we *have* to go to the police. It's just the obvious place to start when a dead body is involved. But we don't have to do that straight away. Maybe not at all. It depends on how deep in you are. So why don't you start by telling me why you're convinced that this man, in particular, is your guy, Gianni. Were you out there in the hills with him?'

'No, no, nothing like that.' Samaniegos lifted his head abruptly, appalled by the suggestion. 'I haven't seen him for weeks. That is why I am so worried.'

'But you must have a reason for thinking it's him they're talking about. How else could you know that? Please, Ramon, you got to help me out a little here, give me something to work with.'

'Of course, forgive me.' Gathering himself a little, Samaniegos sat up straight, nodding. 'Gianni, he was . . . he was in trouble with some men. They wanted money from him and he didn't have any money. I did what I could to help him at first, I gave him what money I had. But it was never enough, and they wanted more each time and' – he heaved in a great breath of air – 'and, well, last time he asked, I said I couldn't give him any more, and . . .'

He halted to quell a catch of emotion in his voice. 'We had an argument about it. I said he had to recognize that it would never stop unless he stood up to them and he got angry . . . very angry, and he stormed out.'

Tom said nothing, waiting while Samaniegos struggled to get the next words out. Whatever his problem was, it had been building for a while – to the point where it was overwhelming him to give voice to it. But he swallowed hard and got there in the end. 'That was the last time I saw him.' He gave a small sob. 'Three weeks ago, or more.'

Tom thought about the report in the paper. From the brief description given, the body in the Baldwin Hills had been out there for at least that long, if not longer. Thad Sullivan obviously had reason to think it was there a lot longer – months, not weeks. But in this heat, who knew who long it would take a body to get into that state?

'OK, Ramon. I can see why you're worried. But you know as well as I do that Los Angeles is a big place and this guy out in the hills could be anyone. There's got to be something in particular that makes you think it's Gianni, right?'

The young actor looked up as if emerging from a trance. He tapped his forehead lightly with his fingertips in chastisement then stood up, shaking his head, and went back across the room to the table, looking for something. Failing to locate it, he strode over to the davenport, from which he snapped up an envelope that was lying on the cushion. 'You see, I know. I *know* it . . .' he began again with particular urgency. 'Because they told me. Shortly after the newspaper came this morning, this was left at reception for me – look.'

From the buff-colored envelope he removed two sheets of paper folded in half, urging Tom to take them. The first was an identical newspaper cutting about the story they had been discussing, cut out and pinned to the back of the letter he was now opening. On the sheet of paper was a large, crudely drawn black hand with a stiletto-type dagger plunged through it, with two or three droplets of what he supposed to be blood dripping from it. Scribbled across the top of the page, in an equally crude scrawl, was a threat: '*You're next, José.*' And, at the bottom, some more writing, a signature of sorts, clearly the product of the same hand: *La Mano Nera.*

'Is that Mexican?' Tom asked, uncertain.

'No, it is Italian, of course.' Samaniegos tutted. 'Gianni is . . . *was* Italian.'

Tom shook his head in disbelief. He had heard of such 'black hand' extortion letters before, in the newspapers and sensation sheets. But he'd never actually seen one – other than in a half-baked gangster movie once. He always supposed they were a myth. Or that they were confined to the big Italian immigrant communities of East Coast cities, where the so-called *mafiosi* preyed on the vulnerable and innocent among their own. But on the West Coast, in Los Angeles? His instinct was to laugh at the absurdity of it, but he could see from the look of fear on Samaniegos's face that he took it very seriously indeed.

'This is for real?'

Samaniegos gave him a scornful look. 'What does it look like? Yes, naturally, it is real. These people mean what they say.'

'So, you know who sent it?'

Again, the actor scowled like he was dealing with an idiot. 'Isn't it obvious? The people who killed Gianni sent it. Now they are turning on me.'

'So, do you or don't you know who they are?'

Samaniegos shook his head in bewilderment. 'No, I don't. Not as such. But they were blackmailing Gianni for months. He had nothing left to give them. So, they threatened to kill him. And that was the last I heard of him. Like I say, it is three weeks or more since I heard – nothing! And now this.'

'And this is the first time they've contacted you, yes? Directly, I mean.'

'Yes,' Samaniegos said emphatically. 'This is the first time.'

'And Gianni, is he a movie actor too?'

'No, a waiter, in a restaurant. He had no money. That is what I do not understand. Gianni had nothing, yet they kept after him all the same.'

'OK, Ramon, I think I get the picture. There's just one thing I'm struggling to understand. There's you, and there's Gianni – but where does this "José" fit in?'

TEN

The rest of the story did not take long to come out. How Gianni, a waiter in an Italian place on Figueroa, had caught his eye on a night out with friends some months before. How they too had become 'friends' – Samaniegos skirting the precise details of their relationship but leaving little room for doubt that it had been intimate and, on the face of it, loving. But the young actor was so deeply reticent about it himself, it wasn't always easy to tell.

'I don't use my real name when I'm . . .' He didn't finish the sentence but his meaning was painfully clear.

'Not even . . .' Tom paused, not wanting to offend him. 'Are you saying even this Gianni doesn't know you by your real name?'

'Yes.' Samaniegos dropped his gaze to his toecaps, like he was saying something shameful, and shook his head. 'What I mean to say is, I was baptized José Ramon Samaniegos. To my family I have always been Ramon. But I cannot be Ramon in this other world, in such places. If word got back to my parents, or to their priest . . . You understand? It would be impossible, the shame . . . So, I am José. Simply José.'

It didn't sound so much simple as sad to Tom. Sure, half of Hollywood did it, changed their names to something easier, more glamorous, more euphonious, more memorable. Somehow this felt different, but was it really? Not for the first time, he weighed the cost of keeping your deepest-self hidden from the world's gaze. Wondered, too, what it said about this young man that he could portion off such an essential part of himself.

'I'm sorry to hear it, Ramon. It sounds a tough thing to have to carry off. But sensible, I guess. Realistic. Given what's happening to you now.' He paused, thinking it through. 'The upside, from what you're saying, is that there's a chance that these guys, the blackmailers, they don't know who you are? Who you *really* are?'

Samaniegos didn't seem to have any doubt about it. 'I don't see how they could. Not yet. It is only this year, since I have been part of Mr Ingram's company, that I have had any success in movies. When I met Gianni, I was working as a dancer mostly – sometimes playing piano, or a singer, too. I'm certain he only knew me as José.'

'All this time?'

Samaniegos nodded, casting his eyes down again.

Tom held the crudely drawn letter up. 'So how did they get this to you?'

'Like I said, it was left at reception, this morning.'

'No, what I mean is, how did they know where to find you? You must have brought Gianni here, sometimes. Could he have told them?'

Samaniegos colored a little, like the thought had never occurred to him before, and Tom could have sworn he saw the beginnings of tears brim along his eyelids. 'No, I'm sure he would not have told them, not unless . . .' Whatever it was he was imagining, it was clearly violent as he plunged his head into his hands again, and began sobbing softly, repeating 'no, no' over and again.

Tom reached out a hand and gave Samaniegos's shoulder a reassuring squeeze. 'Look, I understand you're worried and that you're afraid now, too. But let me say this – you're making a tremendous lot of assumptions about Gianni and what's happened to him. And there's no evidence to back any of it up. Look at it from where I'm sitting, or any other outside point of view, and you'd see it's much more likely Gianni hopped a train out of town or something. He might even have told these guys that he got a good part of his money from you, just to get them off his back.'

'So, what? They just make this up?' He slapped the letter with the back of his hand. 'But that's crazy. Why?'

'It rattled you, didn't it?'

Now Samaniegos was offended. 'Gianni would never do that, not willingly.'

Tom examined the backs of his hands, flexed his fingers. 'Sure, but – willing or otherwise – you wouldn't believe what people will do when they're scared, and their back is up against the wall. It might not be what you want to hear, Ramon, but to be honest it's as good a reason for them coming after you like this as any. What you've got to do now is think of yourself and your own safety. No matter what happened to Gianni – and like I say, it could be nothing – the first thing we've got to do is get you safe. And keep you that way. So, this next question is important. Is there anywhere else they can connect you to in Los Angeles, other than here in the Athletic Club? Did you ever take Gianni out to the studio, for instance? To show him around?'

'No, never.'

'And what about the places you two used to go to around town. Could they know you from there?'

Samaniegos had said that he and Gianni occasionally visited some of the city's more daring haunts on the fringes of the old commercial area and how, during the 'revels' that took place there at New Year, they had been together at a masquerade. Things had taken a turn for the worse shortly after that – with Gianni receiving a letter demanding money, or else his employer would be told. Tom had heard plenty about these illegal masquerades where men and women with unconventional tastes could indulge them in relative privacy – the movie colony had always been somewhere people came to seek sanctuary from the forces of convention and moral stricture, a refuge for those who were different. The problem came when they ran up against the law, and a police force that exhibited no compunction in imposing it. At worst, the punishments for 'unnatural practices' were among the severest on California's statute books; at its pettiest, a city ordinance had been passed only months before making it an offence for a man to wear women's clothing on the streets of Los Angeles – punishable by six months in jail or a $500 fine.

Now, though, the young Mexican seemed shocked by the idea that he might be 'known' around town.

'No, that's not possible,' Samaniegos insisted. 'Perhaps I exaggerated before. We went to the masquerade only once. We knew of these places, but I am a private person, I could not live my life like that. Mostly all we did was go see movies together or dine in restaurants – even then not very often.'

'So what about these friends you told me you were out with

when you met him? Any of them be able to put the two of you together? Did you never go out to parties together?'

Samaniegos began to look a little overwhelmed by the thought his entire life was coming under examination. He consigned his head to his hands again rather than answer.

'Look, Ramon, I'm only asking because an unusually good-looking young guy like you, you know, it's not like you can pass unnoticed. And we need to know for sure who might recognize you. Now, Miss La Marr told me earlier that you are almost certain to get very, *very* well known in the coming weeks. That everyone at Metro expects this new *Zenda* movie of Ingram's will be a big hit, with lots of razzamatazz and publicity and all.'

'*The Prisoner of Zenda*,' Samaniegos corrected him, with no small portion of pride. 'Yes, Mr Ingram is certain it will be my breakthrough.'

'Right. Well believe me, Ramon, you're worth a lot less to these guys as Gianni's friend José with a few bucks to spare, than if they clock you as Ramon the new hot movie star who's blazing across the silver screen. If they think there's that kind of money washing around, they won't want to let it go. So, take a minute to think. Is there any other way they can connect you to the movies or the studio?'

Samaniegos slumped back in his chair. Now the spotlight was on him rather than his friend, it was all too much for him to take in.

'Come on, Ramon. Think.'

A dawning realization made Samaniegos screw his eyes shut and breathe out heavily. 'There is one thing, perhaps. *Photoplay* will have a feature piece on me in their next issue. About how I was plucked from nowhere, from the *barrio* even, to take a leading role in Mr Ingram's latest triumph. It is nonsense, of course, but excellent publicity.'

'*Photoplay*? Lots of pictures of you, then?'

'I imagine so, yes. But I have not seen the article yet, obviously.' At last a light seemed to switch on inside him. 'But if the pictures are of me in character, in my role of Rupert of Hentzau, I'm not sure anyone . . . Wait, look, you must see.'

Samaniegos jumped out of the chair and went to a chest of

drawers, pulling one open, then another, and extracting a sheaf of publicity photographs.

'Look,' he said, passing it over to Tom. 'I'm not sure anyone would recognize me from this.'

He was right. The head shots portrayed Samaniegos in the high, braided collar of an aristocratic military man, with slicked flat hair, a monocle in one eye socket and a heavily waxed mustache and goatee beard. The long shots of him in uniform, parrying a sword, sneering at a rival, were even less recognizable. Tom doubted the actor's own mother would identify him in that get-up.

'OK,' Tom said. 'That's something to be thankful for, I guess.'

'Unless they use this one,' Samaniegos said, handing him another publicity still – this a double-header of him both in character and out, with notes underneath about how the young actor with matinee-idol good looks had been transformed into a bad guy by the 'insurmountable genius of director Rex Ingram's vision'. The contrast between the two faces was indeed extraordinary. Tom's heart sank. He knew, if he were a magazine editor, that would be what he would choose to highlight.

'Well, let's just hope they don't have enough room on the page to use both. Either way we could still get lucky. These bad guys, judging by their handwriting here, there's a good chance they can't read much. Probably not *Photoplay* types anyhow.'

He said the words, yet they rang a little hollow. He knew how these things had a habit of somehow always getting in front of the people you least wanted to see them. Especially in Los Angeles, where movie puff mattered so much more than anywhere else. Their biggest hope still had to be that space might be at a premium in *Photoplay* next month, and that the pictures of Samaniegos in character would be the only ones they used.

Otherwise it could only be a matter of time.

'Look, Ramon. I think you've got a reasonable chance of getting away with this. But the one thing we do know is they've got a connection with you here in the Athletic Club. So, first and most important, we have to get you out of here – right now.'

'But that's crazy.' Samaniegos was horrified. 'I must move,

take my whole life? Do you know how hard it is to get a good room here—'

'Ramon,' Tom shut him down, 'I know it's a pain in the ass but there is no other way. Unless you're happy for these guys to be knocking on your door the rest of your life. Do you want that? Do you want to miss out on your big chance?'

Samaniegos swallowed hard and shook his head.

'Anyway, you don't need to give up your rooms here. In fact, it's better if you don't. So long as you can afford it. It'll confuse these guys more, and give us a chance, if you want, to confront them. In the meantime, have you got anywhere else to go to in town?'

'My parents' house on Hope Street? My uncle's on South Serrano?'

Tom shook his head and laughed. 'No, I think we both know that any chance of leaving them a nice hot trail to your family is a bad idea. In so many ways.' Tom scratched his head while he waited for Samaniegos to come up with a better idea, but he didn't.

'OK, look,' Tom said finally. 'We got to do this quickly if we're going to do it. So how about this? I know a guy runs a plush little hotel out in Venice. He's let me book people in under assumed names before, and he knows the need for discretion in anything he does for me. I know Venice isn't the most convenient. But that's exactly what we want right now. Somewhere for you to lay low, keep to yourself for a few days, while I look into what's happened to Gianni and figure out a way to get these guys off your back. How does that sound? OK?'

Samaniegos threw his gaze heavenwards and sighed. 'I suppose so. If you think it is really necessary.'

Tom held up the note again. 'Are you seriously telling me you don't?'

Samaniegos looked nervously around the room again and finally acquiesced more positively. 'OK, yes. You are right.'

'Good man. It'll mean you have to pack a small bag right now and come with me. I'll have someone come over later to pick up whatever else you might need and take it out to Venice for you – for discretion's sake. With luck, you'll only have to be there a short time, a week or two tops, until we can figure out a way to protect you and this newfound stardom of yours. And it'll keep all this nice and separate from the studio and Mr Ingram, too, which is more important than ever right now, Ramon, believe me.'

ELEVEN

At least the drive in from Venice was uneventful and he had a chance to sit back and properly think through what was going on. He had dropped Samaniegos off at the St Mark Hotel, which occupied a large corner lot opposite the pier with a fine shoreside setting. It was one of the few buildings in which the architectural ambition of Abbot Kinney's tribute – completed fifteen years before – to Italy's vaunted city of canals lived up to its billing, with pretentions to old-style grandeur and a sumptuous, slightly overstuffed interior that more than matched the promise of its richly detailed, elaborately arcaded, entirely fake Italian renaissance façade. There was even a nice cool breeze blowing in off the ocean to compensate the actor for having to abandon downtown and its oppressive heat. He left Samaniegos, still looking a little shell-shocked by the day's developments, in the hands of one of his older West Coast friends, Howard Standen, a genteel fellow he had got to know well during his time working security for Famous Players-Lasky. Someone he could trust absolutely and who, he could be certain, would be attuned to the bind the young actor found himself in. Howard and his partner Cyrus had been running the hotel together – a couple in all but wedding vows – for as long as he could remember, and he had absolutely no doubt that they had navigated a few similarly rough seas along the way.

Now, when he saw Thad Sullivan squeeze his massive frame sideways through the narrow door of the Turnpike restaurant, it was with almost as much relief as curiosity, and a sense that, for once, he might get to kill two birds with one stone. Tom put up a hand, waved him over, uncertain his old partner would spot him in the gloom that was such a contrast to the glare of the late afternoon sun outside. There hadn't seemed much point going back to the office, but Sullivan's suggestion that they meet here instead had surprised him – a dark corner not known for its food and definitely not a cop hangout. At least it was a shade cooler than outside, though even the torpidly spinning ceiling fans looked like they resented having to work in such heat.

'Jesus Christ,' Sullivan said gruffly, fanning his face with a hat so soaked even the wide silk band couldn't conceal the broadening ring of sweat around the crown.

'You're looking mighty overheated, old pal.'

'You're not wrong there,' Sullivan said gruffly, scraping a chair out from the table and sitting heavily into it. 'And there's few would bloody blame me. That's for sure. Jesus, what a mess.'

'Are we still talking about this Baldwin Hills guy? What's the big problem?'

'It's not one big problem, Tom. It's two. And they're both after my skin, the bastards.'

'For what? I don't get what you've got to do with it. You can't seriously still think it was Mikey Ross. That was months ago. He'd be dust by now, wouldn't he?'

Five months earlier, Tom had got himself into a pile of trouble over a murdered movie director and Sullivan had been dragged into it as well – unwilling witnesses to a deadly dispute out in Los Feliz between rum-runner Tony Cornero and two rivals trying to move in on his most lucrative patch. Al Devlin, a corrupt San Pedro cop of their acquaintance, and his sidekick Mikey Ross were both killed by Cornero's mob, but while Devlin's death had ended up looking like a suicide, Ross – or his corpse, at least – had not been seen since. Which in many ways for Tom and Sullivan, and the silence they were sworn to, was the best way it could stay for them. If only it would.

They waited while a waitress took Sullivan's order and refilled Tom's coffee cup.

'That's the bother, isn't it?' Sullivan said as soon as she was gone. 'This fella they found in the hills is not so much dust as shoe leather. It's like he's been dried from the inside out. Some animals been at him too, according to the doc. Barely got a scrap of clothing left on him. And nothing to identify him, other than a patch of suit coat he was curled up around.'

'Well, that's it, then,' Tom interjected. 'We're in the clear. Ross was wearing a black wool Ulster when Cornero's boys took him out. Surely, you're not going to forget that? So, it can't be him?'

'Unless it was blasted off of him, you mean. Come on, Tom, you're the one told me the shocking state he was in when they dragged him away. The lack of a coat doesn't rule anything out.'

'OK, but it doesn't prove anything either. So what's the problem?'

'Gab Ramirez is the damn problem. I told you before he's been sniffing around me like a bloody scent hound ever since Devlin washed up. Now, every time I answer the phone, his ears prick up. He even made a couple of cracks, within my hearing, about Devlin and the like. I'm telling you, Tom, he's got it in for me.'

Again Tom thought back to that night and how Thad's colleague Ramirez from Central had been out with Devlin trying to track him down, but had disappeared before the fatal shootout. How, even at the time, they had been unable to figure out whose side Ramirez was on, other than his own.

'But Ramirez has nothing on you, Thad. You know he hasn't, because you did nothing wrong. At worst you were in the wrong place at the wrong time and had to be a little selective about the truth afterwards.' Tom tried a grin, but it went un-appreciated. 'We both know this. We both agreed this at the time. All we have to do is stay calm, and quiet, and Ramirez will get bored and move on to something else.'

'But that's just it – he's already convinced he's on to something. Some dumb eejit by the name of Reynolds, from Inglewood County Sheriff's office, came in about the Baldwin Hills guy, and I thought I'd managed to palm him off. But goddamn bloody Ramirez got wind of it and now he's got the bit between his teeth again. All the more so because it looks like I was trying to play it down or hide something.'

'Play what down? I thought the guy couldn't be identified?'

'That's the problem. Nobody has a clue who he is or where he comes from, but that lousy patch of suit coat he was curled round – the only thing on him that survived – happened to be a pocket and it had only one thing in it. One bloody bastardin' thing!'

Sullivan was flushed so puce in the face, Tom was beginning to get worried. 'What? For God's sake, Thad, just tell me.'

'A piece of paper with my name and badge number on it.'

'Seriously?'

'Yeah.'

'And what's that supposed to prove?'

'That I knew him, obviously, and—'

'No, it doesn't.' Tom put a palm up to stop him. 'It only suggests that the guy knew you. Or about you, more likely. Either way, not very well.'

'But he had my badge number.'

'That's exactly what I mean. Why would anyone who knows you have your badge number? It sits in your wallet and only comes out when you flip it in somebody's face on a bust. I'm your best friend in the world and I wouldn't remember your badge number if you offered me a million bucks. I bet no one in your family could either, except Eleanor maybe, because she probably polishes the damn thing every night for you, straight after she's finished doing your halo.'

A mention of Sullivan's adoring wife Eleanor, the mother of his seven sons, was almost always worth a sheepish grin from the big man. But not this time. 'That's all fine, Tom, but it's the only thing they've managed to find out about him. The only bloody thing. And Ramirez is already threatening to bring the captain in if I don't play ball.'

'So, play ball. Tell them it's obvious someone from the department must have given the man your number – because who the hell else would know it? Why they might have done that, you do not – and could not – know. In fact, you're probably the least likely person to know. End of story. You know nothing more. Then tell them to go away until they've got something sensible to ask you.'

Sullivan didn't look convinced. 'Yeah, it sounds fine saying it like that maybe, but—'

'There's no "yeah, maybe, but" about it, Thad.' Tom reached across the corner of the table and put a hand on Sullivan's forearm. 'Look, Ramirez has a bee up his ass because he was the last cop on the force to see Devlin alive that night, and he knows Devlin was out to kill either you, or me, or both of us, at the time. I mean, we don't even know if Ramirez knew Ross, or ever connected him to Devlin, do we? And there's no way on earth he could have known Cornero was out there in Los Feliz that night. How could he? Like I said, keep telling him you know nothing, and he can't touch you.'

'Maybe, but he has clout, Tom. Ever since Lee Heath made captain, him and Ramirez have been tight as arse cheeks. If Ramirez wants to make trouble for me, he can. And I'm pretty damn sure he intends to.'

Tom could see this would keep going round in circles if he didn't steer Sullivan on to a new track. There was only one thing for it. 'For what it's worth, I've got a long-shot lead on who the dead guy might be, maybe. But you probably don't want to go showing any interest in it at the station, arousing even more suspicion.'

'A lead?' At least Sullivan was listening. He put down his glass, and eyed Tom intently. 'What're you talking about?'

Tom broadened out his smile. 'Well, you might not believe this, old pal, but I went out to see this new client today, only about an hour after I spoke to you earlier. Would you believe the shock I got when, the first thing he did, was point to the front page of this morning's *Times*, and say, "I think that man they found in the Baldwin Hills is a friend of mine" . . .'

TWELVE

I t was too hot to go to a movie or they would have caught the new Harold Lloyd at the Symphony. Instead they strolled hand in hand along Broadway, peering in store windows and laughing at the bounty on offer in the summer sales – men's fancy suits $26.50, women's Hudson seal coats (with collars and cuffs of natural skunk) $295, athletic underwear slashed to 85c, or false teeth as low as $5 – best set $7. It was thin entertainment but that didn't matter, it was a joy to be out in the cool evening air together and eventually they found themselves hungry enough to slip into a little cafeteria off Fifth where they feasted modestly on veal cutlets and Riverside salad and shared the highlights of their day amid the energizing hum of other people's conversations.

'You were right about Samaniegos,' he said to Fay. 'Man likes the boys – enough to get him into trouble.'

'Poor kid. I guess he wasn't just being quiet last night, then. Is that what Ingram wanted to see you about?'

'No, far from it,' Tom said, lowering his voice. 'It's Barbara La Marr he's worried about.'

Fay loved to hear the stories Tom brought home, earthier by and large than her own professional concerns. She laughed wildly when he regaled her with the story of how he saved Ed Connolly from the ape Joe Martin. That the famously eagle-eyed Olsen had missed the story seemed to particularly amuse her. Unlike Tom, for her a grudging admiration of his professional skills didn't extend to affection for Olsen. Her own day's news was that Clarence Brown had telephoned earlier to offer her a role in his latest movie, a light comedy.

Now she raised a gossip-ready eyebrow, but Tom was more intent on answering her previous point. 'Ingram doesn't know about this thing with Samaniegos. It was Miss La Marr asked me to look into it. Not a word to be breathed to Rex.'

'Are you sure that's wise? Won't he be upset if he finds out?'

Tom grinned. 'I don't see why. Miss La Marr's lawyer was in court so I couldn't go see him. All I did was send the boy out to stay in Venice while I look into it. If Ingram ever asks me, I'll tell him he should be grateful. I'm doing him a big favor. It would be disastrous for him if this got out about Samaniegos.'

Fay looked a little more thoughtful now and touched the side of her head gently, as if to check a lock of hair hadn't come loose.

'Poor man, to have to hide so much of himself.'

'I thought that, too,' Tom said. 'But it's really kind of hard to tell with him.'

'How do you mean?'

'Well, I better not go into too much detail, but tell me what you think of this? He told me when he's with a man he never gives them his real name. He's José, not Ramon. Even with a guy he's been seeing for months. Don't you think that's strange?'

Fay shrugged. 'Maybe he finds it easier to be himself if he's not the person who spends all his time hiding from it.'

Tom gave her his most perplexed look, and she scowled across the table at him, laughing. 'Oh Tom, stop pretending. You know exactly what I mean. Anyhow, would you take the risk? When it could land you in jail, or worse?'

Tom held his hands up. 'I honestly can't imagine what it must be like.'

'I'm sure I told you, I always half-suspected one of the reasons William asked me to marry him was because he was being blackmailed by someone he met.'

'You said he was trying to ensure he was never found out. I always took that to mean it was a blind, a cover for his family, or his firm. But that's not quite the same thing, is it?'

Tom and Fay had met on her very first day in the colony. She was the glamorous new signing at Famous Players-Lasky, just in from New York. He was the studio fixer assigned to show her around, take care of her every need until she settled in. Their needs proved so compatible that they had not spent many nights apart since. Other than during Fay's regular return visits to New York to visit her apartment in Manhattan and her husband William Parker, a charming man who had fallen to his knees in front of her one night, three years after they married, and confessed that he preferred to share his bed with men. His social standing, his position on the board of a venerable New York bank, ruled out divorce or scandal. But he did not want Fay's life ruined either and hoped she would pursue her own interests and ambitions, repaying her discretion in any way he could.

'The same? No,' Fay said. 'But he did admit he'd had a number of close shaves with some of the men he'd met, and a brush or two with the law, where his money was the only thing that saved him from exposure. I know none of that was pleasant or easy for him. It's a tough situation for anyone to find themselves in, Tom, and deserving of sympathy, don't you think?'

Tom nodded his agreement and polished off the last of his cutlet. It always amazed him that Fay never once displayed an ounce of resentment towards her husband, but only ever spoke of him with fondness and even a modicum of regret. True, his wealth allowed her to do pretty much anything she wanted to in life, and she had good reason to be grateful to him in so many ways. But he knew it ran deeper than that, too, and was glad it could be that way for her.

He felt her gaze on him now and, looking up, her glittering green eyes held his with intensity and honesty. 'William told me once his greatest regret was not being able to love me fully, or as much as he felt I deserved. It made me so sad, but then I think that, really, the greatest gift he gave me was this. The ability to be who I want, where I want, how I want. And to choose who I want to be with for the only reason that matters.'

Tom felt a quiet thump in his chest and responded the only way he knew how, leaning across the table and kissing her discreetly. 'Speaking as a co-beneficiary, next time you see him be sure to thank him for me, too, won't you?'

She laughed and they held each other's eyes for a few moments more while Tom wondered who he would need to thank for getting him to this precise moment in time, and decided it was too complicated to even think about.

THIRTEEN

'Hey, Tom Collins, come on in. It's good to see you. I heard you went out on your own. Well done, my friend. I imagine they must be missing you at Lasky's.'

Tom had only ever known two kinds of lawyers: the pinched, sour-mouthed, finger-pointing-pedant kind, and then there were the blond, athletic, impeccably manicured sons of the elite, the hale-fellow-well-met types who were never lost for a friendly word and likely as not would shake your mitt with one hand while stabbing you in the back with the other. Frank Drew was more of a one-off, a tall man with amiably large, square features, whose accent and bearing weren't of a man born to privilege yet who wore his $200 suit and shimmering silk tie like he wore everything else – as if he had a dozen more just like them in a walk-in wardrobe at home in some fancy white palace in West Adams.

His offices were suitably discreet: a suite of rooms on the second floor of a prestige block on Fourth and Spring, right at the beating heart of the commercial district. As soon as his secretary announced Tom's arrival, Drew flung open the double door to his office and ushered him in with the kind of enthusiasm that would make casual onlookers – though there were none – assume they had known each other for years. As it was, Tom had only worked with Drew twice before – on both occasions with miscreant actors from the Famous Players-Lasky studio in tow. And he had found him a lot more pragmatic and sensible than most of his ilk. A lot more likeable, too. Tom reciprocated the eagerness of his greeting, taking a seat and bringing him up to date with the world of private enquiries while Drew busied himself at a black lacquered Japanese cabinet by the window, spooning ice into heavy glass tumblers.

'I'd offer you a drink if it weren't for the dastardly provisions of the Volstead Act,' he said, giving Tom a wink and a grin over his shoulder and waving what looked very like a bottle of

Bushmills at him. 'So we'll have to make do with this special iced tea I have shipped in – all the way from Ireland, in fact.'

He handed Tom a glass chinking with ice cubes before installing himself in a high-back leather chair behind his desk. 'Your health, Tom – and to that of Miss La Marr, and her condition, which throws us together again.'

Tom must have blinked at that as Drew, in the moment of taking a slug from his glass, stopped and waved a hand, making a show of swallowing the whiskey with great pleasure before replying.

'Look, I know about the baby. In fact, I like to think I know all there is to know about the voluptuous Miss La Marr by now. What she is willing to let be known, at any rate. Which is far from everything. But let's get on with dealing with what we can, shall we?'

'I thought she was supposed to be coming in, too?'

'She sends her apologies – seems this heat is really getting to her. I spoke to her on the telephone this morning, which is when she told me she asked you to help out, too. Like I said to her, I was really glad to hear it.'

Tom nodded. 'To be honest, I'm not sure how I can help here. Miss La Marr and Mr Ingram said you would fill me in.'

'I expect they did,' Drew said, frowning. 'It's a pretty complicated situation, you know. Quite a few people involved. But I'll do my best to summarize.'

'A few?' Tom exclaimed. 'I thought we were just looking for a way to get this guy Deeley off her back?'

'Yes, that's what I thought too – until I met his lawyer, Hermann Roth. Do you know him?'

Tom shook his head.

'Count yourself lucky. This guy is a rattlesnake of the first order. A divorce specialist, and he has argued some big cases that I know of – and won. But that doesn't make him any less of a shakedown artist. He promises his clients big pay-outs, but at an extortionate price. And I fear he is capable of causing Miss La Marr a great deal of pain if we don't play ball. I tried to reassure her some, as my client, but I don't mind telling you, Tom, that I'm worried about this one. Far as I can see, Roth has all the cards, and he knows how to play them.'

'Which is where I come in, right?'

'Well, that's where you *were* going to come in. This morning, when I spoke to Miss La Marr. Unfortunately, things have taken a rather more serious turn since then.'

Tom didn't like the sound of that, especially when it was twinned with the look of consternation currently twisting Drew's amiable features into a grimace.

'Serious how?'

Drew took another sip of whiskey before pulling a keychain from his vest pocket, reaching down, and unlocking a drawer in his desk. He drew out a file and placed it face down on the tooled leather desktop, sighing heavily.

'Serious like you wouldn't believe, Tom.'

Drew was right. It was hard to believe that anyone, even a woman of La Marr's supposed notoriety, could find herself in such a pickle. Not that it was her fault. It took the best part of twenty minutes for Drew to lay it out. The fact was that Deeley's divorce petition was just for starters – all the more so when Drew had thrown back at Roth La Marr's insistence that the so-called marriage to Deeley could never have been legal in the first place, because she had never gone to the trouble of divorcing the husband before him.

Roth was having none of it. He had bluntly informed Drew that if he insisted on going down that road, he would have bigamy charges brought against La Marr instead. Which would mean not only a bigger scandal but jail-time as well. And when Drew had tried to backpedal from that position, Roth had pulled the rug from under him again, saying that if La Marr didn't move to settle, Deeley would file a new petition for divorce on grounds of her infidelity – this time with no fewer than seven named correspondents.

'Seven?' Tom gawped. He could see that she would have no shortage of admirers falling at her feet, but even so. 'Is this guy for real?'

'That's what I said to him,' Drew snorted grimly. 'But he very aggressively insisted that he meant every word of it. One of the problems for us is that it's been over eighteen months since she was with Deeley.'

'Even so.' Tom laughed. 'She'd still have to be a quick worker. Any names?'

'A couple of teasers. But Roth's playing his cards close to his chest. He says some of the names are dynamite. Guaranteed to get headlines coast to coast. But those he's holding back on, for now – presumably so we won't have grounds to lodge a petition to injunct. There's Jack Dougherty, who she was seeing but split with. And Ingram, of course.'

'Ingram? No way.'

Drew narrowed his eyebrows. 'Why're you so sure about that?'

Tom sat forward in his chair. 'Because I saw them together yesterday, and they just didn't act like that. If anything, Ingram seemed rueful for having hired her at all – and, before you ask, *not* in a jilted lover kind of way. It's just a gut feeling but—'

'No, that's good for us. Roth could be in danger of over-playing his hand with the big names. If we can prove the spuriousness of even one of those names, we can argue to a judge that Deeley's petition is vexatious, and that he has included the name of every man she's ever met solely in order to drag her name through the mire. Of course, Roth says that's not so. He says he's got evidence of extramarital endeavor in every instance.'

'But that's crazy. He'd have to have been in league with Deeley for months to gather enough evidence to make that stand up.'

'Again, that's what I said. Roth just dared me to challenge it. In fact, what he actually did was give me three days to make an offer to settle or he'll file the petition regardless and release all the names to the papers.'

'Three days?'

Drew held his hands up. 'Sure. He knows his threat is stronger with Hays in town, gunning for trouble, and her new movie coming out.'

Tom breathed out slowly, still trying to take it all in. 'So, a settlement is what he's really after, right? Did he say how much?'

'Not yet and – between you and me – I'm not sure it matters. I doubt La Marr's got the kind of dough he thinks she does.'

'And what's she got to say about all this? She never mentioned any of it to me.'

'Me neither,' Drew said, exasperated. 'This all comes from Roth, and honestly, I'm pretty sure she knew nothing about it. Roth only stuck the idea of the new divorce petition to me this morning, and I didn't speak with her until she called shortly after. She didn't take the news well. I was actually quite concerned. She said she was feeling unwell and put the phone down. Then her maid came on the line and said she was OK.'

Tom cursed beneath his breath and looked around the office. In his own mind he had enough of it already and began to rise from his chair. 'Frank, I sympathize, I really do, but as far as I can see, you'd be better off hiring a few more lawyers, or calling the cops at a push. I really don't see how I can be of any help. If I understand rightly, what you're asking me to do is track down five guys we don't actually know the names of, to see if they've slept with La Marr or not. In three days?' He shook his head. 'Did you actually hear yourself say that? If you did, you'll know how crazy it sounds.'

'Unless we can figure out some other way.' Drew was on his feet now too, but still smiling. 'Look, Tom, I'll be honest, I'm in a bind here. Professionally, no way can I afford to be seen to be made a fool of by a snake like Roth. I know you're a good man, and Miss La Marr seems to think you're capable of anything. She won't be happy if she thinks I let you get away.'

Tom shifted uncomfortably on his feet. 'I told La Marr I don't do rough stuff.'

'Of course not,' Drew said hurriedly. 'I didn't mean it like that. But the way this is shaping up, we need you on our side. Please, as a favor to me, sit down and hear me out. I could help you, too, you know.'

Tom sat back in the chair. 'How do you mean?'

Drew spread his hands wide, palms up, on the desk. 'I can recommend you strongly to my clients who need enquiries services. Compared to the other saps doing your job round here, you're miles ahead. Smart guy, you know your stuff. It'll be a good chunk of business, Tom, especially if word gets around. Would make a difference to a man starting out on his own. And it'll make me look good too. So, come on, what've you got to lose? This'll be finished in three days either way. How about it?'

Tom could see it was a good offer, one that could help make his business into what he wanted it to be. Might even mean he could take on another investigator and have the capacity to run more than a handful of cases at a time.

'Whether we get anywhere with Roth or not,' Drew said, stretching out a hand, 'I get plenty of people looking, and you know I'll be as good as my word.'

Tom didn't need to be asked again. He grasped the extended hand and shook it warmly. 'I'd be a fool to say no to that.'

'OK, great, that's settled then. So, any ideas?'

'Just one. Do they know about the baby yet?'

'No, thank heaven. Not that I'm aware. Why?'

'Just wondering if that was the axe Deeley really wants to grind, even more than the money. But it doesn't sound like it. Do we know who the father is? Is it this guy Dougherty?'

'She says not.'

'But she hasn't said who is?'

Drew shook his head. 'No, not a chance. Said that to me straight. She knows who the father is but he sure as hell never will. And no one else will, either. She seemed particularly determined about that. And she doesn't get knocked off course easily, as you probably noticed.'

'Hard not to.' Tom nodded. 'But, look, we can probably assume the father's one of the people on the list. Someone who might not want it known either.' Eyes down, he ran his hand through his hair, thinking. 'You know, I can spend a few days asking around about who La Marr's been sharing her bed with, sure. But I'm thinking it would make a lot more sense to talk to the only man other than Roth who knows those names.'

'Deeley?' Drew said. 'But there's no way Roth will let us anywhere near him.'

'Not you, maybe. But Roth doesn't know me from Adam. Neither of them do. And Roth's hardly moved in with him. If we got an address for him, I could knock on his door later, talk to him. Just a conversation. About names, what proof he has, how much he's after.'

'You'd have to keep my name out of it,' Drew emphasized. 'Legally, I can only deal with Roth directly once he's approached me.'

'Sure, and maybe if Roth is as much of a rat as you say, Deeley will have clocked that too. You never know, we might be able to offer him a better deal.'

FOURTEEN

The address given for Deeley in the legal papers was care of Roth's office but, being an actor, he wasn't so difficult to track down. A couple of calls to two casting men of his acquaintance and a cross-check with a cashier at Mack Sennett's studio, where Deeley recently played a small part in *Molly O*, led Tom to a rundown frame house across the river in Boyle Heights. He sat in the Dodge a while, watching the place, huddled like a runt between two bigger properties, the front yard encompassing nothing but dirt and trash cans and a small pile of sun-bleached shingles left over from some long-since repair. Nobody came or went.

His knock on the door raised no one either but, hearing the sound of a gramophone, he followed the porch round the side and was surprised to find, in a backyard coolly shaded by a stand of pines, eight or nine people lolling in various attitudes of extreme intoxication. A scattering of empty jugs, cups and wraps were evidence enough of an all-day party, the only ones left standing being a couple waltzing out of time to the strains of a woozily wound-down 'Kleptomaniac Rag'. Solely, it seemed, in order to keep each other upright. Not one of them had sufficient awareness to spare to become alert to his presence.

Tom cranked the handle on the gramophone and the music shrilled back up to its intended tempo. The waltzing couple did nothing to adjust their own barely perceptible rhythm but one woman, of indefinable age but well-muscled around her bare arms and sprawled in the chair nearest to him, fluttered her eyes open and smiled sleepily at him.

'Did you get me anything, sugar?' she slurred, her voice and accent redolent of Mississippi mud.

'Not me,' Tom said, amiably. 'But Ben Deeley, is he around?'

She closed her eyes again, waved a hand dreamily towards the fly-screen on the open back door, snickering to herself. 'Benny Boy, couldn't take the pace.'

Tom went inside. The small kitchen was in much the same state as the garden, bottles and glasses on every surface, zinc ashtrays piled high with stubs, stacks of squeezed-out oranges and lemons, and the solitary remnants of someone's drunken efforts to make a sandwich, still intact apart from two large bites. The living room, running front to back, was also empty, but for a fat man lying curled in a corner, snoring fitfully. Leaving only one other room downstairs, at the front. The door was open a crack and Tom stuck his head in, saw a man face down on the bed wearing only a white vest, shorts and socks held halfway up his calves by a pair of blue silk garters.

From what Tom could see of him, it was Deeley all right, the half-profile that wasn't buried in bedsheets matching a photograph he'd seen, and the build corresponding to his casting description: stocky, mid-height, mid-forties, black hair receding at the temples. It was not easy to square the seedy, unshaven figure flat out before him with the intensely nurtured glamour of Barbara La Marr, or how they could ever have shared a bed in a place like this. Maybe it wasn't she who had risen so high over the past eighteen months, but Deeley who had fallen low. She did say straight out that he was a drunk and nothing he'd seen so far had contradicted that, least of all the booze-sodden snore emanating from him now.

Spying a clutch of envelopes on the filthy stub-burned table beside the bed, Tom sidled over, shutting the door gently behind him. The letters settled it, bearing Deeley's name at this address. He leaned over the bed, whispered the man's name into his ear and gave him a firm shake, but he got no response other than a squeak of sagging bedsprings. He tried again. Nothing. Not even a grunt to interrupt the snore.

Tom sat on the edge of the bed, flicking through the envelopes, eyes widening when he noticed one bearing the letterhead of Roth's Third Street office. But the contents proved innocuous, standard terms of business and a copy of the contract Deeley had signed, agreeing to pay Roth's unspecified fees plus a swingeing fifty per cent of any settlement made. There was also a reference to a draft advance of $250 enclosed.

Tom shook the empty envelope only to confirm his assumption that the check had already been cashed and had, in all probability, both prompted and funded the party which, judging from the date on the letter, could have been going for the best part of two days. He shook Deeley roughly again, but to no avail. He thought about filling a couple of jugs with water and splashing them over him, but after a two-day bender he knew, in all probability, that would have little or no effect either. There was no point hanging around here, the man would be out cold for hours yet.

Instead he slipped the letter into his pocket and let himself out the front door, certain of two things now, at least. If Deeley was tapping money from Roth already, he had to be broke, which made him, potentially, flexible. And if Roth was advancing him funds in anticipation of a big score, he had to be pretty certain of Deeley's ability to deliver.

Later, while they were shutting up the Oasis at the end of an unusually quiet night, when Fay had let everyone go home early, she put a hand on his forearm, a look of mischief firing up in her eyes.

'I was talking to Marion on the telephone today. She asked to be remembered to you.'

'Really?' Tom said. There was only one Marion in Fay's life – Marion Davies, a startlingly beautiful woman, and a fine actress, looked down upon by many in the colony for her scandalous connection to the press baron Hearst, whose bludgeon-like efforts to promote her career cast a spreading stain over her talent and reputation. Fay, though, was a fast friend in regular contact, and they had worked together on screen a handful of times. He liked Davies a lot, too – a partiality Fay never failed to tease him about.

'Don't pretend to be surprised, Tom Collins, I've seen the way you two giggle and mew at each other.'

'Only because we share an interest. She's as big a fan of yours as I am.'

Fay had to laugh at that. 'Hmnn. I think there might be more to it than that . . . but look, what I meant to say is it reminded me of what you were saying about La Marr last night.'

'You didn't say anything to Marion about . . .' His heart did a minor skip at the thought.

'La Marr? No, of course not. You know I would never be so indiscreet.' Fay shot a dagger of offended disbelief at him. 'It was something she said a couple of months ago, actually. About La Marr, if I remember rightly. We'd been to see that dreadful Arabian thing she did with John Gilbert – though *she* was quite good in it – and Marion spat out some barb about the company La Marr was keeping, and how she'd better watch out or she'd be in danger of becoming more notorious than herself.'

'Isn't La Marr notorious enough for Marion already? I mean, that article in *Photoplay* said it all, no?'

'Yes, but Marion's is a different kind of . . . an altogether different *quality* of notoriety, if you like. Don't you see?'

'You mean more high ranking?' As the image of Ben Deeley snoring off his cups that afternoon came to mind, he thought she certainly couldn't go much lower.

'Yes, I think that's exactly what she meant. Like she thought La Marr had made some powerful new connection. But dangerous, too, maybe.' She hesitated, as if afraid of saying too much. 'Oh, I don't know Tom. I didn't even note it at the time, other than to assume it must have come from Hearst himself – because Marion mentioned something about elections and City Hall in the next breath, and we must've moved on.'

'You think she maybe meant it was a politician?' All he could think of now was the list Drew mentioned, and La Marr's insistence on keeping not just her pregnancy but the baby's paternity under wraps, too.

'Honestly, she didn't say as much. It was so throwaway, really. But you said your friend Olsen was prowling around Metro, and it occurred to me that maybe that was why. You said he was acting oddly, didn't you? And you got a sense it was La Marr that he was really after. Might that be why? His is a Hearst paper, isn't it?'

FIFTEEN

Once again a studio pass was ready and waiting at reception. Tom made his way through the studio's thronged, cacophonous avenues, convincing himself that being out on his own had its advantages, until he reached the *Black Orchids* stage and was pulled back to the present by its eerie stillness. It was as if a veil of hush had been drawn over this one spot. The door to the main stage yielded to his push, but the vaulted interior was as vacant as a ruined cathedral, nothing but laid-up platform scaffold, spotlight rig and stacked flats in the vast echoing space, and a galaxy of dust motes tumbling and drifting in the sunlight shafting down from the muslin-swathed roof glass.

Over at the compound, it was almost as quiet from the outside, though he found plenty going on inside the warren of bungalows and linked cabins. Ingram's office door was wide open, the director ensconced in a leatherback chair, his nose in an outspread copy of the *Los Angeles Times*, his long legs stretched out in riding boots resting on a massive carved walnut desk that looked to be of considerable antiquity. The frown of intense concentration on Ingram's forehead dissipated when he looked up, and he smiled a welcome, waving Tom in with his free hand and swinging his heels to the floor.

'I came over via the stage – it's like a ghost town over there.'

'Sure, we finished the last of the retakes yesterday – thank God,' Ingram said. 'It won't stay empty for long. Vidor's got a big one, due to start shooting in a couple of days' time – *if* he promises to stick to the budget this time.'

'And will he?' Tom raised an eyebrow. The director King Vidor was getting a reputation in the colony for overspending. And while he might never have been allowed to splurge to the level of a Von Stroheim, it was a major red flag for every studio head.

'I imagine so. At the eleventh hour. He'll hold off signing

anything until then, just to needle the money men. Not that he'll stick to it. A point comes in every shoot where you've spent so much the studio can't afford for you not to finish. I realized pretty damn quickly on *Four Horsemen* that *that* is the moment when a director feels most in control. Despite all their yammering, there's absolutely nothing the hand-wringing bastards can do about it at that stage. There's no better feeling in the world – *true* creative freedom!'

Despite the glint of mischievous good humor in Ingram's eye, Tom could tell he meant every word of it. Yet again he thought he wouldn't like to be the one trying to stand in this man's way. Whatever direction he was going in.

'Not that we're going to have freedom of any kind round here if this shifty little finagler gets his way.' Ingram stabbed a finger at the photograph of William H. Hays splashed across the front page of the *Times*, the headline blaring out his arrival on the West Coast the previous day at the Pasadena railhead, and his overnight stay at the home of a wealthy local Republican.

'All hail the censor, all hail the destroyer of cinematic art,' Ingram barked, making a mock military salute. 'Who the hell does he think he is? A lousy politician coming to tell us how we should and shouldn't make movies. The man wouldn't know artistry if it struck him in the face and roared its name at him. Or morality for that matter. And now they want—'

He broke off, scrambling to retrieve a ball of paper from the wastepaper basket. 'Would you credit what they sent me this morning?' he said, uncrumpling what appeared to be a Metro management memo and stepping round to hand it to Tom. 'Now they're saying it'll be an actual breach of contract if we don't turn up for this luncheon they're giving him, tomorrow, at the Arts Club. The goddamn nerve of them. I mean, I already said I'd go. Why do they feel the need to threaten me again? They're just bending over and sticking up their asses for him. It beggars belief.'

Knowing there was nothing he could, or wished to, add to that, Tom said precisely that. In the silence, Ingram appeared to realize he had been ranting. He shook his head, disguising his embarrassment by snatching the memo from Tom's grasp and lobbing it back into the waste basket again, cursing beneath his breath. Moving behind the desk with a weary sigh, he deposited himself in the chair, signaling Tom to occupy the one opposite. 'Truth is, what's really upsetting me is that Hays is saying one thing in public and another behind closed doors. The official line is "Hays finds no horrors in Hollywood" but in private – well, we've already been told he's going to insist at this lunch tomorrow that any and all instances of moral turpitude, among the people we employ, must be reported to management from now on. And that he's actively looking for suggestions as to who he should make examples of and ban from screen work. Can you believe the cheek of the man? I tell you, nobody's going to stop me giving him a piece of my mind when I *do* go tomorrow.'

Ingram paused long enough to look like he was still debating the wisdom of that in his own mind. 'Which, sorry as I am to say it, Tom, makes it all the more important that we are not the ones who hand him what he's come here looking for. Someone to hang out to dry.'

Tom nodded in agreement. 'Everyone's saying it, now. Hays is not going back until he's found someone.'

'I will not allow Miss La Marr to be that person.' Ingram's features softened and a smile ran across his lips. 'By God, were we ever lucky we got those shots in the can when we did. She says now she can't cope with this heat. Expects it's only a matter of days before the baby comes.'

'You spoke to her?'

'This morning. She sounded tired, but I suppose you would expect that.'

'How many other people do you reckon she might've told?'

Ingram batted his concern away. 'No need to worry. I wondered about that too and asked her straight out. She said she thought we – Alice and me, that is – should know that, what with *The Prisoner of Zenda* premiere so soon, she might not make it to New York with us. But she's already done all the magazine publicity for that, so if it's a smash they won't be pursuing her too hard, at least not this week or next. If all goes as expected, she ought to be able to manage an appearance or two after that, and we can work around the rest. She's so keen to act the part.' Ingram leaned forward, elbows on the desk. 'You know, I can't bear the thought of *Zenda* being sunk because of this. I need it to work. So many people say I can't have another hit like *Four Horsemen*. That it was a flash in the pan. But in so many ways, *Zenda* is the superior movie, and I am so much better a director now. As for *Black Orchids* – I'm confident it is a work of such dark cinematic artistry as the world has never known. I couldn't bear all that to be marred by a tawdry scandal trumped up by the press.'

'You'd better hope Miss La Marr holds her nerve, then,' Tom said, amused by how, in Ingram's eyes, her pregnancy was now the press's fault. 'It's sure to be tough for her. It won't be easy, you know, keeping her little bundle of joy, the new light of her life, in the dark like that.'

'You don't think she can do it?'

Tom shrugged. 'So long as she keeps her mouth shut. Like you, the biggest problem I can see is the timing. The two problems together could really sink her.'

'You saw Drew then?' Ingram asked, tentatively.

Tom nodded. 'It's a mess, to be honest. When he started telling me about the other guys—'

'Other guys?' Ingram put a hand up and rose from his chair. 'OK, hold on there. I'm not sure I want to hear this. As far as I can see, with Hays on the warpath, the less I know the better. All I want to know is can it be kept quiet? Can we stop it getting out? Are you able to tell me that?'

Tom could have laughed at the idea, but he stifled it. 'You know I can't do that. There is no certainty about this kind of thing. This Deeley, he looks like he needs money, so he could get her into a mess of trouble, and she'll need a lot of luck to get away with it, frankly, because his lawyer's an even bigger rat than he is. But, you know, there's always hope. It's not impossible.'

Tom offered to fill him in on the details but again Ingram flatly refused.

'Thanks, but I meant what I said. I don't want to know any more, for now. I wouldn't want to love the dear girl any less. She's such a beautiful soul, and for me the power she has lives on the screen, not in shoddy reality. So, you get on with it, Collins, if you don't mind, and do what you can for us so I

don't have to listen to those money-monkeys upstairs tell me
they were right all along about hiring her. I couldn't abide that,
really. It would kill my spirit. Just send your bills to me, care
of the studio. I'll be heading to New York from Saturday. I'll
let you know where I'm staying so you can telegram me with
anything urgent, OK?'

Tom agreed to do that and stood up to go. Ingram rose too,
sticking a paw out across the desk to grasp and shake Tom's
hand vigorously and with real feeling.

'Don't forget,' he laughed, 'harp to harp, I'm relying on
you to prove them wrong and save not just my honor but my
sanity, OK?'

Tom laughed too. Despite Ingram's unwillingness to listen,
it was hard not to be won over by the man's charm.

'By the way,' Tom asked, unthinkingly, 'have you heard from
Ramon Samaniegos in the last couple of days?'

Whatever way he said it, Ingram stiffened and pulled his
hand back, alarm sparking up in his eyes. 'What do you mean?
Why should I have heard from Ramon? Don't tell me he's in
some kind of trouble as well.'

'No, no. Of course not,' Tom said, shielding himself with a
gesture of mock surrender, desperately hoping to undo the
mistake, and the damage, with a double bluff and a look of
blank unconcern. 'I'm just asking after the kid. He seemed
pretty wound up the other night at the Oasis, remember? Said
he was looking forward to the premiere. Reckons he'll hit the
big time with it. What do you think?'

Ingram relaxed visibly and threw his eyes heavenwards.
'Sorry, I guess all this rumor and suspicion flying around is
getting to me more than I realized. Damn that man, Hays. If it
weren't for him, we'd be managing all this with only a quarter
of the worry.'

'I don't doubt it.' Tom breathed an imaginary sigh of relief.

'It's not the biggest part, of course,' Ingram said.

'What's that?' Having banished Samaniegos to the back of
his mind, it took Tom a moment to realize Ingram was returning
to his original question.

'Ramon, man, his part,' Ingram said a little impatiently.
'It's not the biggest but it is memorable. He's done everything

I hoped he would with it, and a little more. So, yes, I do believe that, with my name attached, my backing, he has every chance of becoming a major star with this. Maybe the new Valentino, like they're saying. Or better. Something with depth. You never completely know with these things, but he could crack it wide open with this one, if the public take to him as I think they will.'

Tom was walking out of the block when he saw a slim figure in a light grey coat flit down the corridor opposite and ease quietly, almost suspiciously, through a dressing-room door. All he could see was the back, but he was sure it was Ed Connelly. Tom went after him and knocked on the door. Answering the call to enter, he squeezed in, saw the old man hurriedly stick a quart bottle of something amber into a drawer.

'Mr Connelly, remember me? Tom Collins. We met at the Oasis the other night. And I helped drag that ape off you the morning after.'

Connelly eyed him suspiciously. He was four sheets to the wind already and his memory was clearly as addled as the rest of him. He drew himself up to his full height and would probably have cut quite a dash if he hadn't been swaying. 'I thank you, sir, most sincerely. Although I couldn't honestly say I remember your heroic efforts. I was experiencing a very considerable degree of shock at the time. God damn and blast that ape.' Out from his unbuttoned coat cuff, Connelly popped a heavily bandaged hand, the dressing badly soiled and clearly unchanged since it was first applied. At the same time, he used his free hand to pull down the collar of his shirt to reveal a half-ring of purple bruising on his neck. 'They're lucky I don't file a suit against them, for reckless endangerment. Take them for everything they're worth.'

Tom bared his teeth in sympathy and nodded towards the bandaged hand. 'Are you sure you shouldn't get that seen to, Mr Connelly? It really doesn't look so good to me.'

But Connelly mistook his concern for something more sinister and fixed him with a rheumy eye again. 'Are you working for the studio, sir? I trust you're not here checking up on me. Well, let me tell you, I have funds to employ neither a doctor nor a lawyer, sir. Or you can be sure I would have both at my side right now. And not because I have anything on *my* conscience. No, sir. You can go tell *that* to Mr Hays for nothing, let me tell you.'

He was swaying in his seat now and, from the venous state of his eyes and the bloom of purple on his nose, Tom could tell Connelly probably hadn't been anywhere near sober for days. Looking round the tiny dressing room, he wondered why he hadn't been moved on already, since shooting had stopped. Was he just hanging on here, for want of anywhere else to go?

He tried to put the older man at his ease, insisting that he was working for Ingram and not the studio. Once he'd got that out of the way, Connelly relaxed enough to pull his bottle from its hiding place and offer Tom a swig. Which, for the sake of keeping the man companionable, he accepted. 'I bumped into that reporter Olsen on the lot the other morning. Said he was coming in to see you, Mr Connelly. I guess the interview never got done, what with the incident and all?'

It was distaste that fired up behind Connelly's eyes now. 'Are you talking about that obsequious streak of misery from the *Herald*? I haven't seen him in weeks.'

'Really?' Tom said. 'He told me he'd come by to give you a boost but he was having trouble tracking you down. So, you didn't have an appointment with him that day?'

Wariness wafted off Connelly as strongly as the whiskey in his pores, as if he thought he was being accused of something. 'Well, as I said, I did meet the fellow a few weeks ago, at a club I occasionally visit downtown. And he asked if he might stop by some time for a formal interview. I told him *Black Orchids* wouldn't be in the theatres for months, but he was unusually insistent and, yes, now you mention it, the next day I think I did ask reception to arrange a pass for him. But he never dropped me a line to confirm it, and it quite slipped my mind until you mentioned it.' Connelly paused to take another swig from the whiskey bottle. 'I can't imagine why.'

'Well, like you say,' Tom said, declining the proffered bottle this time and getting to his feet. 'It was probably the shock, or something. Take care, now, Mr Connelly and, if you'll take my advice, be sure to pop into the studio clinic and ask the nurse to change that dressing on your hand. They'll do it for free, if you ask.'

As he was passing reception, Tom couldn't stop thinking about Fay's idea the previous night about Olsen, and how maybe he hadn't really been looking for Connelly at all, and how maybe it was La Marr he had in his sights all along. It was beginning to make more sense to him now. But why would Olsen go to so much trouble? It was such an elaborate set-up. He was deep in thought when he heard his name being called and he looked back and saw the desk clerk waving at him, calling him back.

'Mr Collins, your secretary was trying to get hold of you. She said it was urgent, but Mr Ingram told us you left already. I really think she wants you to return the call, sir. Can I do that for you?'

SIXTEEN

I t was Mae all right. Her voice was such a frenzy of excitement he had to ask her to repeat herself at first.

'. . . Two cops, I said. Plain-clothes guys. They tried to force their way past me into your office when I said you weren't in.'

'Did they say what they wanted?'

'No. But, even if they had, I wouldnt'a given it to them. They were coming on way too strong.'

'What did you do?' Tom said, the whirr of possibilities in his mind momentarily stalled by a vision of Mae standing, arms out, fierce, blocking the progress of two burly bulls. 'You said they tried to force their way in.'

'Hah! Sure, they did.' Mae laughed, triumphant. 'I told the one in charge I'd have his badge if he took a step further.'

'And that stopped him?'

'Too right – when I told him I was District Attorney Woolwine's cousin . . . or his wife's, rather.'

She waited a beat for that to sink in before chuckling again and continuing. 'I read a society piece about Mrs W. in *Los Angeles Life* magazine over lunch, so I had a few details to blind him with, like calling her "cousin Clara" and the like. It was enough to make him think twice and turn right round.'

'Jesus, Mae, you've got some nerve.'

'Nah. They walk in, all they see is some dumb girl behind a desk. They're expecting a walkover. Doesn't take much to knock 'em off course.'

There was truth in what she said but there was more to it than that, too. She was utterly fearless.

'Well thanks, Mae. But next time, if there is a next time, don't take any chances, OK?'

'What could they do to me? They had no right to be there, and they knew it. They sure were keen to talk to you, though.'

He couldn't help laughing again and shaking his head at her pluck.

'So, did he leave a name – the guy in charge?'

'Uh-uh. That was the oddest thing. I asked him and all he said was he'd catch up with you later. Then he hung a thumb on the other guy and they walked out.'

'Can you describe him to me?'

Tom had only encountered Sullivan's colleague Ramirez a couple of times before, but the man Mae described to him – a stocky, sallow, pug-faced man, bald beneath his hat – matched that memory more or less perfectly. Going on what Sullivan had said earlier, he could just about see why they might want to talk to him. But to try to break into his office? That did not sound right, at all.

'I'm guessing you aren't so keen to talk to them, right?' Mae broke in on his thoughts. 'Should I hold the fort for now, or do you want me to close up in case they come by again?'

He only had to think that one over for a second. 'No, we're staying open for business. We have nothing to hide and, even if we did, I wouldn't want them to think I was rattled. I've got to go see somebody, but I'll be back in an hour, two tops. If they come back before then, don't stand in their way. Ask them if they have a warrant and, if they do, tell them our clients have a right to confidentiality and they can only search the place with me and my lawyer present. Otherwise they'll have half the movie-studio lawyers in the colony breathing down their necks. Are you OK with that?'

'Sure,' she said, like she was relishing the prospect of a second round already. 'This is the most excitement I've had in months.'

The desk clerk didn't have a problem with him making another call. Not even when Tom glared at him and said he needed it to be private. He simply smiled politely and retreated to the far end of the counter and engaged a random colleague in conversation. Tom looked at his wristwatch, waiting to be put through, getting angrier by the second at Sullivan, who clearly hadn't been telling him the whole truth about his problems with Ramirez. But the person who picked up the phone in the Detective Bureau said Sullivan was out on the job and had no idea when he would be back. All Tom could do was check the shift times and leave a message for him to call as a matter of urgency.

Out on Romaine, the sun was more intense than ever, the glare bouncing off the sidewalk, the air so oppressively hot and still not a soul could be seen on the deserted streets leading off in any direction. Even under the shade of the canopy, the black leather seat of the Dodge scalded through the cotton of his suit pants as he sat in, searing the heels of his hands as he reflexively lifted himself up to avoid the heat, and again when he clutched the steering wheel. All he had to do was get moving, he told himself, get some air circulating, as the anger and frustration built up inside him – but even the motion of the car once he got going seemed to do nothing to ease the oppression of this particular afternoon, the noise and heat of the engine, the metallic tang of hot exhaust fumes serving only to raise his temperature and make his circling thoughts angrier still that fate seemed determined to deal him another blow, just when things were going so well again. What the hell had Sullivan let slip to send Ramirez sniffing around in his direction? The not-knowing was only making matters worse.

He found a shady spot to park on Gower right outside his building, but he didn't go straight up. Instead he went to the drug store on the corner and got himself a glass of ice water, then another, sitting chin on fist at the counter rehearsing the arguments he had himself outlined to Sullivan a couple of nights before to convince himself that Ramirez really couldn't have anything on either of them. And that the visit to his office had been nothing but a fishing expedition, the actions of a man from whom he had nothing to fear. Eventually it worked, the tight-ness in his chest began to ebb away and, going into the bathroom, he splashed enough water on his face to finally get his tempera-ture down and his breathing back to normal. Ramirez had nothing on him or Sullivan. Couldn't have anything on him or Sullivan. He'd been a fool to be rattled. All they had to do was stay calm and it would pass.

It wasn't until later, around five, that the call came through. Mae had been strangely distant most of the afternoon. Evidently relieved to see him walk in the door as seemingly cool and collected as ever, she had worked away quietly in the outer office, silent other than to put calls through from clients and potential leads. Already they had got their first referral through from Drew, a gem importer downtown convinced one of his cutters was pilfering stones but unable to prove it. Just the thought of tackling something different in a new arena that had nothing to do with the movie business gave Tom a boost, a much-needed dart of renewed hope and purpose.

Then, around four thirty, Mae tapped on the door and popped her head round.

'Got a minute?'

'Sure.'

He looked up at her, waiting. She was hovering uncertainly, half in, half out the door, an uncharacteristically awkward expression clouding her features. He invited her to sit and she did, but on the edge of his desk rather than on the chair, her back half towards him, hands clasped between the dress fabric covering her legs, looking over her shoulder like she was about to flirt with him, though he knew it wouldn't be that.

'You liked how I handled those guys, yeah?'

'The cops? Yeah, sure I did. That took real gumption, Mae. I doubt I could've handled it so well myself.'

She smiled to herself, pleased with that. 'I didn't get scared, you know. Only angry. All I wanted was for them to get out of here.'

Tom shrugged happily. 'Good for you. I was thinking about it after. You don't back down for anyone, do you? Not Mack Sennett. Not those cops. If they needle you, that's it.' He smiled and winked at her. 'I guess I better watch out. You're not about to ask for a pay rise, are you?'

'No.' She smiled, more softly this time. Then thought better of it. 'Leastways not yet.'

He laughed again. 'So, what is it?'

She shifted around a little further, her arm ramrod straight from the palm of her hand on the desk to the shoulder on which her chin now rested, head inclined slightly, eyes wide with enquiry. 'I guess I wanted to know if you think I could do what you do?'

The question didn't exactly floor him, but almost. He had to blink a few times, let the muscles in his face and neck go slack for fear of giving the wrong impression. In the end it had to be a question. 'Running an enquiries business, you mean?'

She shook her head, leaned closer to him, her voice intent and hopeful, eyes scrutinizing his face for any sign of doubt. 'Working it, I mean. Like you. Out there. Asking questions. Getting in scrapes. Helping folk. I think I'd be good at it.'

Every thought crowding in on him was screaming no, and yet, at another level, he couldn't see a reason – other than experience, like his own long hard years in uniform, or any training whatsoever – why she wouldn't be good at it. Or some of it at least. She had a way about her that could charm birds from trees, a quicker brain than his own, and seemed genuinely to be afraid of nothing.

'Maybe you would, at that,' he said, trying to be as noncommittal as possible. But that wasn't how she took it.

'Seriously?' She half screamed with glee and, clapping her hands together, slid off the desk and stood in front of him, laughing, expectant. 'Will you let me? Will you—'

Which was precisely the moment the clamoring telephone bell cut through the electric air. In truth he was relieved, unsure of how to take that conversation forward anyhow. He grabbed the apparatus, listened a moment, then asked the caller to hang on for a second. Mae was already reaching for the door handle, her face a picture of hope deferred. He put a hand over the mouthpiece, whispered to her.

'Look, we'll talk about it some more, I promise. But I have to take this, it's about those cops.'

SEVENTEEN

The Hib was already heaving when they got there. In the circumstances, it was reassuring. The fierce buzz of after-work chatter, the sharp scrape of cutlery on plates, the clinking of glasses and bottles at tables, the intermittent hoots and roars of mirth drowned out all likelihood of being over-heard, even by those at the tables closest by, despite the majority of customers being cops, their women friends or fellow Irish in the know. No other joint in the Los Angeles area flouted the laws relating to the sale of alcohol quite so egregiously, or so raucously, as the Hibernian. Not even the Prohies dared cross this line.

Huddled together over a small table in one of the gloomier nooks by a wall, Tom and Sullivan avoided the subject at hand until the whiskey was brought over to them in a small clear glass jug. Thad wafted a nostril over the rim before accepting it from the waiter, only letting him pour the shots once he was satisfied it was barrel fresh and 'proper'. All it took was a single fierce slug before Tom piled in, letting go of his pent-up anger with a growl.

'What the hell is going on, Thad? Gab Ramirez, turning up at my office, threatening Mae, trying to force his way in? What are you not telling me? How did he even know where to find me?'

At this, Sullivan met his eye at last, his lip curling. 'You're listed in the directories like anyone else, aren't you? And he's a cop for chrissakes. It's his goddamn job to find people.'

'You know what I mean.'

'They didn't hurt the kid?'

Even through his anger, Tom had to laugh. 'Mae's not one for scaring easy. The way she told it, Ramirez was lucky to get out of there with his skin still on.'

Sullivan raised a dubious eyebrow but Tom ignored it. 'That's not the point, is it? Anyone else but her might've folded, and then those monkeys would've been all over my business, big time. That's not on – and you know it. So you'll forgive me for asking you again, what the hell were they doing there?'

Sullivan shifted uncomfortably in his seat, as if the chair itself was trying to put the gripe on him, then drained his glass and poured another for himself and Tom.

'C'mon, Thad. What's going on?'

Sullivan didn't respond but looked over his shoulder slowly, around the room at the mass of dining, drinking humanity that filled it, and for a split-second Tom wondered if he had actually heard him over the din. Then the big man leaned in across the table, his huge shoulders brushing the smoke-stained wooden wall they were huddled against.

'I messed up, Tom.' His tone was one of low, rumbling confession, not far short of a sob, and it sent a snap of chill fear trickling down Tom's spine.

'What are you talking about?'

'I thought I was doing the right thing, and now I think I might've messed it up. For both of us.' If the catch in Sullivan's throat was lost to the hubbub around them, there was no missing the swallow he made while saying it, rippling over his big Adam's apple like a bad omen.

Instinctively Tom jerked back, fixing Sullivan with a hard stare.

'Both of us?'

Sullivan reached out, grabbed Tom's upper arm and pulled himself closer until his mouth was just inches from Tom's ear. 'A snitch of mine told me a while back Gab Ramirez was as crooked as the day is long. Not just kickbacks but running his own deal. Said he was scooping up all of Devlin's trade out of San Pedro.'

Again, Tom wanted to pull away but Sullivan's grip was inescapable. 'I always thought it was wrong he was out there the night Devlin went after you. I wanted to be sure he wasn't a threat. So I made a few enquiries. On the quiet like.'

Sullivan paused to chew his upper lip. 'Or so I thought.'

The chill on Tom's spine slithered round into his gut and coiled there, a slow pulse of ice. 'What are you saying, Thad?'

A regretful look clouded the big man's eyes. 'I don't know

how he got wind of it, Tom. But it's why he's coming after me, for sure.'

Tom felt Sullivan's grip slacken and pulled his arm away. 'And me too, by the look of it. For God's sake, Thad! I told you not to pick at that scab. The one thing you had to do was leave it alone, and we were in the clear. Jesus Christ, what have you done?'

Sullivan was trying to shush him. Out the side of his eye Tom noticed people at the tables around them looking over now, drawn by the heat of his anger.

'Look, nothing's changed,' Sullivan was saying urgently, between gritted teeth to keep the volume low. 'I'll admit, I'm worried about my own situation. But it's like you said, the guy's got nothing on *us*, does he? He only went after you to rattle me. He knew it would get back pronto. It's me he's putting the squeeze on.'

Tom shook his head, unconvinced, and forced a deep breath out of his lungs, thinking hard. 'There's got to be more to it than that. I mean, this Baldwin Hills guy. How did he tie you to that? How the hell could he even know about Mikey Ross? Unless one of Cornero's boys blabbed.'

They both knew how unlikely that was. Sullivan shrugged, doing his best to look unconcerned, and failing. 'Like you said yourself, Tom. We don't actually know that he does know about Ross. He's never said the man's name to me. Devlin's sure. But never Ross's. Not once. I mean, it could just be a fluke. Or a shot in the dark, at best. He was casting around for something to hit me with – and what a bloody gift that note was. It scared the shite out of me, Tom, you saw that. But the more I thought about it after, you were right. It's the last thing anyone would know about me.'

Tom looked up sharply. 'You think it could be a plant? A frame-up? Would he do that? Is he smart enough?'

Sullivan's eyes widened at the implications. 'Jesus, you mean he could've set it up with Reynolds from the off?' He gasped to himself, his mind appearing to run away with the idea. 'I didn't see it that way before. But it'd explain a lot, wouldn't it? How it's the only thing left on the body. How he came to hear about it at all, like.'

Tom was still thinking it through. 'And why he feels he can ride you so hard over it.'

Anger was sparking up in Sullivan's eyes, his face flushing red already, a field-full of furrows forming on his brow. 'The bastard,' he grunted, bunching his fists.

Tom put a hand out, grabbing him by the forearm. 'There'll be plenty of time for that later, Thad. But you've got to keep it to yourself for now. He still has you in a bind. Don't lose sight of that. The main thing is, for Christ's sake, don't give him any more shit to throw at you.'

Tom let go and pushed the empty whiskey glass towards Sullivan. He picked up the jug, but there was barely a trickle in it. He raised it in the air and signaled for another one.

'You never know, if he thinks he's got you on the run, he might get careless,' Tom said. 'Let something slip.'

Sullivan wasn't convinced by that. 'Maybe. If he doesn't have me up before the board first.'

The waiter arrived with the fresh jug. Sullivan didn't bother checking it, but poured, downed his drink in one and filled his glass again.

'What I don't get,' Tom said, 'is why you're worth the trouble to him? Has he really got so much to hide?'

Sullivan snorted like he'd just been insulted. 'My guy said Ramirez was Devlin's main line into Central. His link to all the downtown rackets. Gab wouldn't want that known, especially if he's in the middle of trying to pinch them all for himself. Like I said, I must've spooked him, asking around.'

Tom had to stop and think about that one. 'The rackets?'

'You know I don't like to badmouth the department, Tom. But they're all at it. Ever since Cryer was elected mayor. It's like everyone's suddenly piling in for a slice. I told you before, this new Vice Squad, it's like Ramirez and the rest are just running the show for themselves.'

'Ramirez is in Vice? You didn't tell me that.'

'No?' Sullivan looked like he thought Tom should have known that anyway. 'I'm sure I mentioned he moved over as soon as Heath made captain. Like I said, those two are tight as all hell.'

'So, what's he doing investigating a murder?'

Sullivan shrugged. 'That's what I asked. All I got told was to shut my trap and answer the questions.'

'Jesus, Thad. You better watch your step with this guy. There's something really not right going on here.'

Sullivan threw his hands up. 'Why do you think I've been so worried, man. If Ramirez gets his way, I'll be out on the sidewalk, toot sweet. I mean, how will I support my boys then, Tom? I'll never be able to look Eleanor straight in the eye again.'

The sudden look of despondency on Sullivan's face shook Tom back a step towards sobriety. 'That's not going to happen, old pal. Not now we know what the bastard is up to.'

He rubbed his cheeks with both hands, clasped one of them round his chin and tried to wipe the fuzziness of the whiskey from his jaw. An idea was beginning to come to him and he could do with being able to think straight. Or maybe just one more drink would help it along.

'I was thinking, maybe we can work this other thing of mine to your advantage. The Italian kid I was telling you about? If what we're thinking is true, the last thing Ramirez would expect from you is a theory about who the dead guy might be, right?'

Fay laughed when she saw the gleam in his eye when he came in through the door. She was lounging with a book in her hand on the butter-colored chaise at the far end of the living room, looking like a goddess, the French windows thrown open to the balcony in scant hope of catching a cooling breeze.

'You have got to be kidding me, Tom Collins. You stay out drinking whiskey half the night with your cop pal, and you think you can waltz in here looking like a tomcat. I can smell the liquor on you from over here.'

And yet, there was a fondness in her voice, a glint in her eye, too, perhaps.

'I guess I better hit the shower,' he said.

'Sure, and the spare room straight after if you don't want a sore head in the morning.'

Tom attempted one last charming grin, all the more so for being lopsided. 'I'm willing to risk it if you are.'

'You try it and you'll have that sore head right now.'

EIGHTEEN

He could have run the distance from Fay's to Ingram's place on Sunset. It was less than half a mile. But he had barely rubbed the fog of sleep from his eyes when the telephone rang, and he knew he'd need the roadster if things were as bad as they sounded. That, and the heat of the day was already intense, though his wristwatch read only eight thirty.

Turning on to the curving dirt driveway, the house looked an incongruous residence for the industry's most successful young director and his movie-star wife. A neat cedar-shingled bungalow that couldn't have contained more than a handful of small rooms, set in a grove of five or six similarly unpretentious dwellings, all charmingly laid out in the spacious, well-maintained grounds of another, larger house set right on the Boulevard.

Tom knew of the place by reputation. Canary Cottage, described by some as an artist's colony, was the vision of one Jack Donovan, whose reputation went before him as a man of big ideas, if smaller accomplishments, and who strove to combine the creative gifts of architect and actor. As Tom pulled up out front of the rustic-looking dwelling, he could see how its artsy atmosphere might have appealed to Ingram as a single man freshly arrived in Hollywood. But he wondered how long the newlywed Mrs Ingram would be willing to stick it out, especially if more and even greater success would soon be heaped upon them, as her husband anticipated.

As he switched the engine off, the front door was opening. Alice Terry's uncertain smile of relief and concern blocked out everything else.

'Oh, thank heavens. That was no time at all.' She was outside now, grasping his arm as he stepped down from behind the wheel, pulling him towards the entrance and whispering confidentially all the while, though there was no one obviously within earshot. 'Thank you so much for coming, Mr Collins. I really wasn't sure what else I could do.'

'It's fine,' Tom said. 'You said Mr Samaniegos is actually here with you? Is he . . . is he all right?'

Terry laid a hand gently on his forearm, as if he might be the one in need of reassurance. 'Don't worry, Mr Collins, I know all about this now. Barbara – Miss La Marr, I mean – telephoned me a couple of hours ago and told me everything, She said she simply couldn't cope with it herself just at the moment, and so she sent Ramon over to me. The poor dear, he's in such a state. Nothing I say seems to be of any consolation to him.'

Inside, the house was more richly appointed than the cabin-style exterior suggested. Most of the deceptively large living space was taken up by extravagantly carved, opulently upholstered antique furniture. From the walls hung faded tapestries and curtains of damask and velvet, drawn to keep out the harsh sunlight, which looked to have been brought in straight off one of Ingram's sumptuously stylized movie sets. As his eyes adjusted to the dim-lit interior, Tom caught sight, on one of three capacious settees arranged around the oversize stone hearth, an anxious-looking Samaniegos, his face pale with trepidation.

'What's up, Ramon?' he asked. There didn't seem much point in pussyfooting around. 'Mrs Ingram here tells me you're pretty shook up over something.'

The young actor's eyes were brimming with tears as he reached out to shake Tom's outstretched hand.

'I'm so sorry, Collins. I'm really am. I tried your office, but I guess it was just too early for you to be there and I panicked. I didn't know where else to come but here.'

'So, what's the problem?' He glanced at Alice Terry again. 'You've told Mrs Ingram about your situation now, right?'

Samaniegos nodded, embarrassed.

'So are these guys putting the bite on you again? Did someone track you out to Venice? Have you had to leave the hotel already?'

It was too many questions, he knew, but he wasn't in any mood for subtlety.

'No, I mean . . .' Samaniegos hesitated, reselecting his words, steadying himself. 'No, not as such. I went back to the Athletic Club this morning.' He held up a hand to forestall Tom's objection. 'I went very early, and in the back way, so no one would see me. I needed some of my own clothes, my own . . . *things*,' he said. 'One of the bellboys said there was a message for me at the desk. It was left in last night, they said. They don't know who by. But it's . . . it is as you feared.'

Samaniegos pulled a manila envelope from his jacket pocket. On the front his name was scrawled in black ink, in what looked like the same crude hand they had seen before. Inside was a sheaf of papers, mostly the cover and six pages ripped from the edition of *Photoplay* magazine that had hit the streets the day before, predicting a meteoric career for rising star Ramon Samaniegos as a result of the soon-to-be-released sure-fire hit, *The Prisoner of Zenda*. Tom flicked through the pages. Occupying almost the whole of one spread was, exactly as he had feared, the double-header publicity photograph highlighting Samaniegos's remarkable transition from boyish aspiring star to sneering military aristocrat. Pinned to the cover was a note featuring the same mix of crudely scrawled symbols as before – the black hand, a heart pierced by a dagger dripping blood. But more explicit this time, directly threatening, the name José angrily blotted out with jags of black ink and substituted by a superscript of inch-high capitals:

> We know who you are, ~~Jose~~^{RAMON}
> $2000 – pay it or die like your friend

Tom shook his head at the rotten luck of it. 'I'm amazed these guys read anything, let alone fan magazines. I think you were unfortunate there, Ramon. But at least we were ready for this. And if they left it at the club, it's a cert they don't know you've moved out yet.'

Samaniegos put his hands up to his cheeks. 'Reception could have told them.'

'No, I made sure of that. I told them you'd only be gone a few days, and if anything needed forwarding, my office would take care of it. My girl Mae's been checking every morning. But you got to it before her today, I guess.'

Tom sat down on the adjacent settee, rubbing the heels of his hands on his trousers. 'Honestly, Ramon, I can see why you'd be upset – frightened, even – by this. But I think they could have played into our hands here. Now that they've made an explicit threat to your life, we can take this to the police. And by coming here and telling Mr Ingram and Miss Terry about it, there's not so much they can blackmail you with.'

Whatever reassurance Samaniegos wanted, that wasn't it. Again, he flatly refused to involve the police. 'No, it's impossible. My career would be finished. The movie would be finished.'

Tom had been aware of Alice Terry's presence behind them in the room all along, but now she came forward and sat down beside Samaniegos and took his hand in hers.

'I'm not sure that would be a wise move, Mr Collins. Not for dear Ramon, and certainly not for us. In the sense of the movie, I mean.'

'OK, so . . .' Tom looked at her askance then, realization penetrating the lingering fuzz of last night's alcohol, he looked around the room. 'Speaking of which, where is Mr Ingram? Are you telling me he still doesn't actually know about this?'

'No, he left for the studio early this morning.' Terry had the good grace to look embarrassed. 'Not that Rex would disapprove. I mean, we have many friends who are . . .' She trailed off, failing to find the right words. 'It's just that, honestly, I'm not sure how well Rex would take this right now. He's oppressed enough already, what with Miss La Marr's condition and being forced to get involved in all this sucking up to Hays. He's been in a foul humor these past few days. Frankly, I'm glad he left early today. I'm not sure I could have coped with it if he'd been here for this.'

She exhaled heavily, as if thinking she'd said too much, and turned to Samaniegos, smiling sympathetically. 'Honestly, I'm not blaming you, darling. You do understand that, don't you? I know this is none of your doing. It's just that Rex can be so temperamental, as you know. And if he thinks the movie is under threat—'

Such was the level of anxiety in her voice, Tom couldn't help being concerned by it himself. 'Is there something I'm not seeing here? Something you're not telling me?'

The last question was directed at Samaniegos, but it was Miss Terry who answered for him: 'I fear you haven't seen the worst of this situation, Mr Collins.'

She gave him a meaningful sidelong glance and indicated he should look again in the envelope. Sure enough, inside was what appeared to be a glossy photographic print that had caught on a pin when he had pulled out the rest of the pages. He withdrew it now and was unable to disguise his shock at what he saw: an image of two naked men engaged in copulation and a third standing by, clearly aroused but in the moment only looking on, observing.

'Jesus, God,' he said beneath his breath, struggling to keep the irritation out of his voice. 'Tell me you didn't know about this, Ramon.'

But Samaniegos was unable to tell him what he wanted to hear. Instead the young actor looked away, such an intense sense of shame and humiliation radiating out from him that Tom's incipient anger drained away to nothing almost immediately. The kid was not only mortified, he was terrified.

'Is this your friend, Gianni?' Tom asked, pointing to the only man facing the camera full-on, an expression of bemused horror invading his face.

Samaniegos appeared almost cowed by the question. 'Yes,' he said eventually. It was little more than a whisper.

'And that's you lying down, is it?' Tom couldn't be entirely sure. The face was directed away from the humiliating lens, captured in hazy mid-grey tones.

Samaniegos nodded, unable to meet his eyes.

'Well, that's something, I guess,' Tom said. Only someone who knew Samaniegos intimately would be able to identify him with any degree of certainty. 'I know you're probably thinking it's real obvious that it's you, Ramon, but I'm not sure anyone would recognize you from this.

'Would you?' he said, passing the photograph to Terry.

She coughed, as if unsure of whether to laugh or not. 'Not as such,' she said, dragging her eyes away from the most readily identifiable part of the photograph.

'And this other guy? Do we know who he is?'

Samaniegos shook his head. 'I think he said his name was Marco, but that's maybe not a real name. I never saw him again.'

'And the photographer?'

'He just burst in and was gone again. I never even saw his face.'

Tom cupped his chin in his hand. 'Do we know how many snaps he took? Are there any other photographs?'

Samaniegos said he only remembered one flash going off. 'It all happened so quickly. I don't see how he could have taken another.'

'All right, so did you see the camera? Was it a big one, like the pressmen carry?' Tom held up bunched hands either side of his face, mimicking the action. 'Is that why you couldn't see his face?'

Samaniegos thought about it, then nodded quite definitely. 'Yes, I think that must have been it.'

Tom nodded too. 'Sure. Those cameras take two photographs, one each side before the film holder needs changing. So, there's a good chance there was more than one.'

'I remember only one – from the flash going off, but . . .' Samaniegos looked embarrassed again, like he was forcing himself to an admission. 'But yes, I'm sorry. Gianni did say that there was another picture, just as . . . bad.'

Tom could hardly believe his ears. 'He knew there was a photograph? Why the hell didn't you tell me that?'

'Because . . . because . . .' Samaniegos was so flustered he could barely get the words out and Terry was making big eyes at Tom to ease off. In the end, the actor heaved it out anyway. 'Because I hoped they would . . . that they would go away. OK? How can you blame me for wanting that?'

Samaniegos was on the verge of tears.

'I'm not blaming you for wanting it, Ramon. I'm blaming you for not telling me. As you can see, it's not exactly irrelevant to what we're fighting here.' Tom shut himself up, scratched his head furiously. It wasn't just that he was a little hungover. He had every right to be annoyed. He looked over at Samaniegos, who was staring up at him now, wide-eyed, bemused.

'The point I was trying to get at, Ramon, was how the hell did Gianni know about the photograph in the first place?'

'They must've shown it to him, I suppose.'

Tom's jaw didn't drop exactly, but his mouth did fall open a couple of seconds. 'Hang on. You told me, on the way out to Venice, it was all done through letters and money drops. Now you're telling me Gianni actually met with these guys?'

That was not something Tom had heard of before. Blackmailers usually went to enormous lengths to hide their identity – for obvious reasons. 'You're saying Gianni knew who the blackmailers *were*?'

Apparently, Samaniegos had no answer for that. Tom glanced across at Alice Terry, got nothing but a shrug and a shake of her head in response. He held the photograph out in front of Samaniegos's downcast eyes. 'So, what? You're telling me now that this isn't the first time you've seen this pic? Have I got that right, too?'

Samaniegos didn't lift his eyes from the floor. 'Gianni had it with him last time I saw him. When he came to ask for more money. He said there was another picture, too. Said he saw it, and that's why he wanted the money. To get them both back for us, and the negatives. He needed the money to settle with the men, but I didn't want to give it to him. I didn't think they would stop. I didn't think they would hand the negatives over.'

'How much did he ask you for?'

'He . . .' Samaniegos licked his lips like his mouth had suddenly gone dry. 'They wanted five hundred dollars.'

'Five hundred?' Tom whistled. 'Where in hell did he think an ordinary guy, a dancer, was going to find that kind of cash?'

'That's why I was worried . . . You see now why I am so concerned for him?'

Tom nodded vigorously. 'Sure, I do. And I don't doubt that you have good reason to be. But you should have told me this from the outset, Ramon. If they've got something on you, something concrete, *visual*, like this, it puts a whole new complexion on things.'

Samaniegos was so painfully at a loss for words that Miss Terry seemed to feel obligated to say something on his behalf. 'Is there nothing you can do, Mr Collins? You must see how resorting to the police is impossible for us just now. If it were to come out with Mr Hays in town, I don't dare to think what might happen. It is all so unfair.'

The plea in her enormous blue eyes was like taking the glare of a stage light full on – so intense, Tom had to look away and gather his thoughts again. He blew out a long blast of air, not so much from his lungs as the depths of his conscience.

'Look, if you're determined not to bring in the cops, it's hard to say. You only have two choices: face up to these guys, wait to see what happens if you refuse to play ball, and ride out the consequences should any come. It's either that or hand over the money, pay these guys enough to make them hand over everything they've got, once and for all.'

Samaniegos's head popped up instantly. 'You really think they would do that? Give it all to us? I'll pay anything they want so long as I know Gianni is safe and well.'

Tom shook his head. From everything he'd just heard, there was less reason than ever for the blackmailers to have killed Gianni. The likeliest thing now had to be that he'd ratted out Samaniegos and skipped town to get himself clear of the mess.

'Look, I know this all seems bad, Ramon. And I'm not going to say it's not. But I've come across this kind of thing before. And these shakedown artists, you know, they tend not to be killers. They're driven by greed, by money. It's not good business for them to go killing people. They just want to scare you, or Gianni, enough to get you to pay up. And then pay up again. And again. It's not in their interest to kill the goose that lays the golden egg.'

He rummaged around in his head for another way to put it. 'Look, the truth of it is you're barely recognizable in this photograph, so Gianni is really the only thing that connects you to it. They're not going to want to get rid of him for that reason alone.'

'That's got to be good, Ramon.' Miss Terry put a comforting arm around his shoulder. Samaniegos leaned into her, hope welling up in his eyes. For the first time Tom appreciated just how bad the kid had it for this man, Gianni. His was the face of a man in love, and suffering for it. It was just a shame Gianni might not be the man to deserve it.

Tom picked up the photograph again. Wondered what it was he could see in Gianni's expression, in the way he was looking at the camera. It wasn't something he'd really considered before but, now, his thinking had changed completely. The fact that Gianni had met the blackmailers really rankled with him. That raised questions. Questions that had to be asked. Even if they were painful.

'Look, Ramon, please, I realize this is not an easy thing to ask. But you've got to understand, I have to.' He waited until Samaniegos lifted his head, curious now. 'Did it ever cross your mind that maybe Gianni was in on this?'

He heard Terry draw her breath in sharply, but he kept his gaze on Samaniegos, whose face slowly went a shade redder, from his throat to the tips of his ears, as he digested the question. 'How do you mean, *in* on it?'

'You know as well as I do what I mean, Ramon.' There was no point beating about the bush. 'Surely, it must have occurred to you? Asking for all that money. Producing a photograph like that—'

'No, of course, it did not *occur* to me,' Samaniegos said angrily, cutting him off. 'Gianni was my friend, my . . .' He paused and gritted his teeth together, enraged that he even had to think twice about what he would say next. 'My friend and . . . as you have seen so humiliatingly in that photograph, Mr Collins, he was my lover. Yes, my *lover.* Of course, I never suspected him. Do you seriously think I could be this worried and concerned about the welfare of someone I thought could betray me in such a fashion? How dare you!'

Samaniegos was on his feet now, furious, a different man, apparently intent on either quitting the room or throwing a punch. Tom put a conciliatory hand up and urged him to sit back down.

'Look, that's not what I'm getting at, Ramon. You love who you want, I'm easy. All I care about is getting you out of this fix you're in, so you can get on with your life with whoever you want to goddamn love. But, come on, let's not forget you're the one who was holding out on me about this. All I want – all I *need* – is to be sure of how well you know Gianni, and how much you would rely on him.'

Samaniegos didn't look convinced, but he sat down again, and took the hand that Terry extended to him, gripping it tight in both of his.

'So you never suspected him?'

'No!' Samaniegos sighed in exasperation. 'For heaven's sake, why would I? We weren't just . . . we were close, really close. He was every bit as shaken by this as I was. You know, to him I was a dancer, making a living. OK, so I was living at the Athletic Club, but he knows how money comes and goes in this business. He agreed with me, you got to make the most of the good times.'

'And you're absolutely sure you didn't let anything slip? You didn't share your dreams and ambitions with him – you two being so close and all?'

The anger came rushing back. 'What are you suggesting?'

'I'm not suggesting anything, Ramon. All I can see is you're being scammed in the rottenest way possible and I'd like to straighten that out for you. But, like I said before, you have to be honest with me. And I'm frankly disappointed that you haven't been. OK?'

'OK, yes. But you asked me about all of this before.'

'Yes, and I had no reason to think otherwise then. But whichever way you look at it, and whether he intended to or not, Gianni was doing the blackmailers' work for them by showing you photographs and asking you for money. And I can't help thinking that if I'd been lucky enough to get a break like you did, sign a contract that would make me a star, I'd have been so happy I'd want to talk about it with the person who means most to me. Now come on, Ramon, be honest. Didn't you feel that just a little?'

Samaniegos blushed to his roots again, but perhaps this time from anger. 'Yes, I did. A lot more than "a little", if you must know. But I also knew I had to be careful. You don't understand, Mr Collins, in this world . . . in *my* world, everyone knows the value of discretion. No one asks questions because everyone knows the cost of discovery. It is difficult, even very painful at times, but completely, entirely, totally *necessary*!'

Even while he admired the man's spirit, Tom was determined not to let him slip off the hook. 'So, even when you got your contract, you kept it a secret from Gianni? You had all that going on behind his back? You said nothing?'

Samaniegos was getting flustered again. 'Well, no, of course not. He knew I was happy about something. But it's not like we spent all our time together. We were not living together. I suppose Gianni must have noticed something, but I don't remember a specific occasion when he did.'

'And what about these photographs? You told me first you used to go to masquerades together, then you said you only went the once, when this happened? Which is it? Lots of times or once?'

Samaniegos threw up his hands in frustration 'OK, so maybe we went two or three times. I don't know. I cannot remember exactly. But you are missing the point. We were close, I trusted Gianni. What's in that photograph . . . that bordello, it was horrible. It was never supposed to happen like that. I did not even want to do it, but he did. Just the once, he said. It should never have happened—'

'So, what you're saying,' Tom interrupted sharply, 'is that it was Gianni's idea, to go to this place, this bordello?'

'He said it would be fun. And now—' Samaniegos broke off, choking up again, emotion getting the better of him. 'All I wanted you to do was find him for me.'

And I might just do that, Tom thought. I might just do that, yet.

NINETEEN

One of the guys on the City desk at the *Herald* gave him a bead on Olsen and it sounded about right enough to be worth a look. Three minutes later he was pushing through the polished wood and etched-glass double doors of a French place on Aliso, packed even at this hour by mobs of diners sitting at cane tables or standing at the counter chowing down on enormous sandwiches, the air heavy with the aroma of roast meats. He spotted the reporter sitting alone at a table in the back, an empty plate pushed aside to make room for the notebook he was jotting in and a stack of evening editions by his elbow.

'Still working, Olsen?' Tom scraped a chair out from the table and sat into it opposite him. 'I thought all you *Herald* boys knocked off early.'

'Not a chance, Tommy boy,' Olsen said, betraying no surprise at his sudden appearance. 'Some of us are so wholly devoted to the first amendment we barely put our pens down when we sleep.'

'Some of your stuff sure reads like that, Olsen, I'll grant you that.'

The reporter chuckled and put his hands up. 'Ever the charmer, Collins. Y'know I had a feeling, after our brief encounter the other day, it wouldn't be long before I'd see you again. So, what's behind this uncharacteristic attack of conviviality? You decide there's something I can do for you, maybe?'

'Sure, just taking you up on that offer you made me.'

'You know me. Generosity is my greatest fault. I'm always willing to help out a brother if I can. Do I have to guess what it's to do with, or tease it out of you?'

'You could let me get settled first.'

'Well, if you're staying, you better have something to suck on – seeing as how you're paying for the both of us now.' Olsen laughed and called across the counter to an extravagantly mustachioed man surveying the throng with a proprietorial air.

'Hey, Frenchy, can I get another of your dipped-beef beauties for my pal here.' He turned back to Tom. 'Don't argue with me on this. My fame as a connoisseur of the sandwich is growing daily, and the beef here is the best in the city – except maybe over at Coles, on a good night.'

Tom had no intention of objecting. Since he stepped in the door his stomach was swooning from the meaty enticements emanating from the kitchen.

'Fine by me.'

Olsen took him at his word and let him settle, chattering on about the upcoming championship wrestling bout between Walter Miller and Johnny Meyers at the Athletic Club, and how he'd been up to the Mercury Gym that morning to see the world champ fresh in from Chicago and already training.

'Meyer's a heck of a grappler, Tom. You know that. But to see him in action close up – it's a sight to behold. That double wrist lock of his – there's just no getting out of it.'

Tom had never been much of a wrestling fan. Boxing was the interest he shared with Olsen and, not for the first time, he wondered what was at the root of a skinny little guy like Olsen's obsession with big, brutal sports that, most likely, he'd never been into the ring to try out for himself. But there was no denying the man's encyclopedic knowledge, and he let Olsen rattle on, grunting responses at appropriate moments, while he got to grips with the juice-dripping heaven-in-bread that had been placed in front of him, a straight shot to paradise for a man with a yawning gulf in his gut.

'It's gonna be a heck of a match, Tommy boy. Y'know, I could talk to Charley Kappen at the AC. See if we can get you in ringside with us press boys, if you want?'

Tom didn't reply immediately, savoring the last of the soft, juice-laden bread as it slipped like liquid velvet down the back of his throat, then wiped his fingers and lips, sitting back and sighing with profound carnal satisfaction.

'Thanks for the offer, Olsen, but maybe save a treat like that for someone with a keener appreciation of grappling than me. Anytime you fancy a rematch with one of these sandwiches, though, count me in. My God, that was good.'

'I told you.' Olsen laughed. 'This member of the fourth estate don't lie. At least, not when it comes to the important stuff. So, now you're sated, y'gonna tell me what brings you down here?'

Tom made a happy gesture of surrender. 'Sure, like I said, I just want a lead on something. You've been on the city beat so long I thought you'd be the man most likely to know – given your longstanding interest in the seamier side of life.'

'Seamy, me?' The reporter grinned. 'Whatever can you mean?'

'Oh, you know, those stories you sometimes run about cop raids on the swish bars and bordellos downtown, and the guys who frequent them.'

'What about 'em?'

'Well, you'd know your way around those joints, some at least, wouldn't you? In a professional capacity, I mean?'

Olsen's principal response to that was a raised eyebrow. 'I would've thought you'd have to, too, Collins, given the business you're in. There're a lot more swishes in movies than on my beat.'

'Well, yeah, sure, we come across it every now and then, for sure,' Tom said, on the back foot now. He'd been hoping to keep the movie connection at bay for a minute or two at least. But he should have known Olsen would see through that straight away. 'Same as any other sphere, I guess. And once upon a time I knew my way round every vice den in New York, when I was a cop back East—'

'Oh, for pity's sake, Collins,' Olsen broke in. 'Would you shut up being so coy. It doesn't suit you. We're both grown-ups here and we ain't talking ancient history. So, just spit it out. Who d'you want to know about – and why?'

Tom put his hands up again, knowing Olsen always had him pinned as a lousy liar. 'OK, OK, you got me. But it's not so much a who as a where. You ever came across a joint called the Butterfly Club?'

Tom wouldn't have sworn he saw Olsen's ears prick up like a hound's, but it felt that way. And there was no mistaking the way the reporter's eyes darted swiftly sideways before returning just as quick to hold him in their spotlight glare.

'OK, yeah, maybe that does ring a tiny tinkling bell. Why would you want to know?'

'Can't you tell me something about it first, maybe?'

'Sure, I can. Like that it's no place for beginners, Collins. I can tell you that much.'

'How do you mean?'

'I mean, if it's the place I'm thinking of, you wouldn't be going there by accident. You'd have to be in the know. And if you had brains enough to be in the know, you wouldn't be going there at all.'

'Sounds like you know quite a bit about it.'

'Only by reputation, I assure you – and it's all bad. You want chapter and verse, I can't help you. But I do know it's run out of a rackety old place over East, between Hewitt and Rose.'

'Near the old Water Department building,' Tom said, recalling Samaniegos's description. 'That sounds about right.'

'No,' Olsen said, with enough vehemence to make Tom look up again. 'There's nothing right about that place. It's called the Butterfly Club to attract the unwary, but it's known to every pro-freak and pervert downtown as "the flutter-by" – meaning not only the obvious, but also that you better not hang around too long there or you'll get hurt. It's a shakedown joint, pure and simple. You go in there looking for a good time, you're likely to come out with the worst time ever snapping at your heels.'

Olsen drew a breath while he let that sink in and Tom felt the reporter's eyes roving his face as he sunk his own gaze to the floor in thought. It was as he'd suspected from the off. Samaniegos and his pal had been the target of a deliberate squeeze. But what were they doing in such a dive in the first place?

'If it's so notorious, how come people go there?'

Olsen shrugged. 'You tell me. Why does anyone go in these places? It's not like fruits have a monopoly on stupidity when it comes to being led by their dicks, is it? There's got to be ten times more straight-up brothels than bordellos in this town and a fair share of clip joints among them, too. Doesn't stop every kind of fool going in them and getting stung.'

Olsen was proving more sympathetic to the plight of the unwary than Tom had expected, but at the same time he was steeling himself for the question that inevitably had to come. And it did.

'So, not that I'm one to assume anything, Collins, but what does this have to do with your visit to Metro the other day? Was it one of Ingram's boys got caught out? Or Ingram himself, maybe?'

'Ingram?' The anxiety on Tom's face was instantly eclipsed by the surprise that came with the mention of that name rather than Samaniegos. He laughed out loud. 'You're kidding me, right? You newspaper guys have only just shut up about how he and Miss Terry got married in secret making their last movie. Now you think he's a swish to boot?'

It was enough to convince Olsen he was backing a loser. 'Wouldn't be the first to have it both ways,' Olsen said, defensively. 'And it's not like he didn't introduce that powder puff Valentino to the screen. *Four Horsemen of the Apocalypse* was full of that kind of depravity.'

'You must've seen a different movie to the one I saw,' Tom said. 'Even you'd have to be pretty desperate to try and cook up a scandal from that. But, just for the record: No, that's not why I was over at Metro the other day.'

'So, who's in trouble then, Collins? Come on, I've given you everything you asked for. Quid pro quo, remember. Grease the goddamn wheel, why don't you.'

'I'm paying for your dinner, aren't I?' Tom said, laughing again now. 'That's the price you quoted me. Anyhow, you haven't told me who runs the place yet. If it's so well known, it's got to be someone with connections, right?'

Olsen scowled and shook his head again. 'Like I said, I only hear stuff. Guy running it is new in town, they say. Italian goon, out of Chicago, I think. Calls himself a "fruit trader", if you can cope with the irony of that. But it's the local fruits he makes his money from – squeezes 'em dry.'

Tom laughed coldly. 'Sounds like you've been rolling that one round in your mouth for a while, Olsen.'

'Sure. Waiting for someone like you to come along and give me a chance to use it. Are you gonna?'

'Maybe, eventually, if I had a name. You got one?'

Olsen drew his breath in and checked the room again. 'A few of 'em, as you'd expect,' he said, leaning into the table. 'But Vitale's the name I hear most often. And something else that goes right along with it is that you really, *really* don't want to go introducing yourself to this guy. I mean it, brother. You do *not* want him putting your name in his ledger. This one's vicious, a real animal, with a taste for hurting folk bad, and enjoying it, too.'

Tom pondered that. Olsen had a hack's natural tendency to exaggerate but he had to have good reason to be laying it on so thick. 'So, he's got to be connected,' Tom said. 'Or at least protected? To run a house like that and get away with it, right?'

Olsen looked uncertain. 'I suppose there's got to be somebody, the way he goes about business with such impunity. Some say he's connected with the Italian mob back home. But Chicago is a long way away when you're operating out in the open like that on Charlie Crawford's patch. You don't go doing that without some serious muscle behind you.'

'Crawford?' Coming out of nowhere obvious, the introduction of Los Angeles's most prominent racketeer into the conversation hit Tom's hopes like a rabbit punch. 'Crawford's not backing this guy, is he?'

Olsen shrugged. 'Can't see it. This Vitale's built quite the rep in the short time he's been here, so there's no way Crawford doesn't know he's out there. But, like I say, word is the wop's thumbing his nose at him. Paying nothing. Not to Crawford and not to Crawford's rotten pals in City Hall.'

Olsen almost spat the last bit at him, but Tom knew it was knee-jerk. It was like Sullivan said, ever since Mayor Cryer was elected, rumors had been rife about the city administration's corruption. Olsen's paper was by far the most vocal on the subject.

'Can't be long before he's brought to heel then, right?'

'That's what folk have been saying.' Olsen nodded. 'But this guy Vitale, he's gotta have something cos he's still out there and he's making not just Crawford but the whole of the City Hall gang look bad. Weak even. So, like I say, this Vitale, he's not one to go up against, Tommy. He really is not.'

'Thanks for the warning, Olsen. If I can return the favor, let me know.' Tom reached for his hat to go, only to be halted by a raised hand from Olsen.

'Hang on a tick, brother. You're welcome for the tip but, now

I think of it, maybe there is something you can help me with. Speaking of City Hall and all.'

'City Hall?' Tom was genuinely surprised.

'Sure.' Olsen's sharp eyes were roving Tom's face like a bird dog flushing game. 'I thought you might have heard some whispers while you were over Metro way the other day.'

Tom was glad he didn't have to fake it. 'What is it with you and Metro just now, Olsen? If you'd stop speaking in riddles, I could maybe figure out if I've got anything for you. But as it is—'

He broke off, made a baffled gesture with his hands.

'Aw, forget it,' Olsen said, sounding weary for the first time Tom had known him. He broke a piece off a bread roll in the basket and, reaching across the table to Tom's plate, sopped up a pool of juice and popped it in his mouth with a gap-toothed smile. 'I thought my ship was comin' in when you turned up. But all you got on your mind is some swish. Which is pretty much the opposite of what I'm after.'

'Yeah?'

'Yeah. I been chasing it down for weeks, trying to put some legs on it. Seems one of our esteemed civic leaders was doing the naughty with one of Metro's young ladies. But I can't make it stick. When I saw you out there the other day, I thought that might've been something. But apparently not. So much for the pulchritudinous Miss La Marr. The "girl who is too beautiful" . . . my ass. Though, I must say, she does possess one hell of an ass.'

Olsen seemed momentarily lost in reverie and Tom struggled to keep his face straight. Every hair zinging up the back of his neck screamed at him to get off the subject pronto in light of what Fay had said to him the night before, but he couldn't let the opportunity to learn more slip by.

'Seriously?' he heard himself say. 'La Marr? What's she got to do with City Hall?'

Olsen batted the question away. 'Long story, old man. But you know how exercised we at the *Herald* get about our so-called anti-corruption mayor's glad-handing, back-scratching, contract-mongering, Crawford-shielding, utterly morally bereft administration. We do everything we can to paint them black, but nothing seems to stick. I thought I got a big sniff, that's all.'

Tom saw his chance to back off and decided to take it. 'You reckon all that's true about Cryer, then? He's got the whole city sown up? Even the rackets?'

Olsen gave him his most disparaging stare and snorted like he could see straight through him but didn't mind. 'Come on, Collins. Even you ain't that green. If Cryer really wanted Crawford gone, don't you think he'd be dust by now? Sure, these politicians say all the right things to get the votes. Like the so-called Vice Squad that Cryer and his puppet-master Kane Parrot set up. And what does that turn out to be? A bunch of licensed goddamn bag men in uniform collecting dues from every whorehouse and keno game in town.'

There it was again. What Sullivan had been saying about police corruption and the rackets flared up in Tom's mind even as he laughed under his breath. The idea of Olsen, who frequented every dive in the city, wanting to lead a moral crusade was bizarre to say the least. If the restaurant hadn't been so obviously dry, Tom might've thought he was drunk, he was getting so het up.

'Goddamn reform ticket.' Olsen was prodding a finger at him now. 'Cryer, Parrot and all their cronies, they're like every other crook you ever met. Only in it for themselves, so they can do what they like and take what they want – *screw* who they want – and roll over the little guy every time. I look at Cryer, all I see is a guy on the make. Plain as the stupid goddamn nose on his plug-ugly face.' Olsen laughed, then almost as an aside to himself. 'Jeez, can you imagine what that kid would look like?'

Tom had no idea what he was talking about, but there was no doubt the reporter was genuinely feeling it.

'I never knew you were so public spirited, Olsen. I'm not saying I can promise you my vote if you ever run for office, but . . .'

'Yeah, very funny, Collins.' Olsen rose from the table and gathered his papers. 'Just remember, it's your taxes they're stealing. And mark my word, you watch *your* nose when it comes to that Butterfly spot, or they'll slice it right off for you.'

TWENTY

I t was right on the edge of the tenderloin, a few blocks south of Chinatown. A spot once throbbing with the life of the original pueblo but long since obliterated by the sprawl of warehouses, offices, factories, freight yards, printworks and flophouses that overwhelmed those narrow, dusty streets with the coming of the Southern Pacific Railroad depot. Few if any stores or residences remained now, and most of those that did were boarded up and crumbling, holding out for a speculator's better price, or by night hosting the city's less salubrious trades, red lamps flickering enticement from upper windows. Only the venerable old Walton Hotel at the far end of the street held out any hope of sanctuary for the travelling salesman or company agent who might find themselves unwarily seeking lodgings in the area, though even that was looking battle-worn these days.

Tom parked on the corner, in the shadow of the old Water Department building, giving him a good view down Rose and most of its approaches. At the far end of Second he could see a locomotive slowly clanking out of the depot, across the center of Alameda, the long-drawn-out tail of freight cars full to brimming with fresh Southern California produce, bound first for the port at San Pedro and onward to God knows where.

He had already driven by the building he was watching further down on Rose. A dilapidated two-story with an ornate mission-style roof and a boarded-up storefront window that must have been, once, in better days, some storekeeper's pride and joy. Now it looked disconsolate and lonely, dwarfed by the bigger, blanker edifices all round, a steel bar padlocked across the doorway, peeling-paint shutters closed against the late evening sun on the upper windows. It might have looked abandoned were it not for the twin columns of gaudily painted butterflies fluttering up either side of the doorframe and arching over it. No mistaking the promise of that, come sundown.

For now, though, it was a little early for the city's revelers to be on the march. Darkness was the trigger for that. This was the hour when preparations were made, owners and staff arrived for work, prepared, restocked, and cleaned if so inclined. The streets shimmered in the in-between stillness between day and night, with few passers-by to take notice of a tall man sitting in a cherry-red roaster reading his evening paper in the failing light. He pulled his copy of the *Herald* from his pocket and settled down to wait. One article immediately drew his eye:

WILL HAYS WOOS CITY HALL

Will H. Hays, modern high priest and human dynamo selected by the motion picture industry to lead it out of the wilderness of censorship and other ills, today demonstrated that a prophet is not always without honor in his own country . . . the 'little Napoleon of the movies' electrified his audience at the Chamber of Commerce luncheon held in his honor at the Alexandria Hotel, pledging the industry to a program of better pictures and higher standards of art, morality, and education . . .

Tom wondered if this was the luncheon Ingram had been complaining about. But, reading on, he saw Hays was scheduled to be given another – from which the press would be excluded – to leading lights of the movie industry at the Hollywood Arts Club the following day. Which sounded more like the one Ingram said he would be attending. Hays, Tom reckoned, being the consummate politician, was simply making sure he got the city fathers, the money men, on board first.

Mr Hays stood in the center of the Alexandria ballroom behind a long table at which sat Mayor Cryer, attorney Kent Kane Parrot, president of the Chamber of Commerce John D. Fitzpatrick, leading figures in the production end of the motion picture industry and the city's most prominent bankers and businessmen . . .

Tom couldn't help noticing the reporter gave Kent Kane Parrot, the man Olsen had named as Cryer's puppet-master, second billing on the list of attendees, ahead of the Chamber of Commerce chief, though as far as Tom knew, Parrot held no official position at City Hall. Now that was power. He wondered how much dirty money was changing hands behind the scenes. As Olsen said, with the rumored levels of glad-handing and straight-out bribery in City Hall just now, you'd wonder which way the dirty money would be flowing at a do like that. Was Hays being greased by them for keeping the city's biggest industry alive, or would Hays be oiling City Hall on the studios' behalf, encouraging them to keep what they said about the movie colony positive? Not that the newspaper report threw any light on that. It was all the usual puff, quoting Hays's high-flown rhetoric at length:

> 'The American public is the real censor for the motion picture, just as it is for the press and the pulpit. The people of this country, of course, are against censorship fundamentally – against censorship of the press, against censorship of pulpit and against censorship of pictures. But just as certainly my friends, is this country against wrongdoing – and the demand for censorship will fail when the reason for the demand is removed . . .'

The man sure had a gift for flummery. But did he mean a word of it? Or was it all, like Olsen said, so much applesauce served up for the gullible to swallow whole. One thing was certain: it was the folk on the ground, the ones who made the movies, who were in his crosshairs.

> 'There is one place and one place only where the evils can be eliminated and the good and great advantages of motion pictures retained. That is at the point where the pictures are made. And it can be done then and there, make no mistake. There is no zone of twilight in the matter. Right is right and wrong is wrong, and men know right from wrong. The corrections can be made. Real evil can and must be kept out. The highest standards of art, taste and morals can be achieved, and it is primarily the duty of the producers to do it.'

TWENTY-ONE

Tom cursed and stepped down from the auto into the street. In the failing light he'd caught only a fleeting impression of the guy, but it was enough to make him pause: a hulk of a man and mean-looking with it – a huge sallow head on heavy shoulders, giving him a bearish hunch that was accentuated by the easy, wide-swinging arms of a man used to having a physical advantage over others. Butterfly was one thing this guy most definitely was not.

Tom ran through his options and failed to find more than one: walk up, knuckle the door on some pretext or another, and elicit an answer as to whether this was the Chicago tough Olsen had told him about or someone else entirely. He was making his way along the sidewalk, about to embark on the plan, when he saw another figure enter the street, this time from the opposite end. Something in the man's gait made Tom stop and take an interest in the shopfront beside him, study the painted sign for the Hamilton Cornice Company on the wall. Out the side of his eye, he could see this one was much younger and slighter than the other, no more than mid-twenties, wearing a loose-cut suit in a green fabric that seemed to float on the roll of his hips as he hurried along, hands in his pockets despite the anxious expression on his face of someone late for an appointment or work. As he drew nearer, Tom made out the olive, sharp-cut features, the longer-than-average black hair and, with a jolt, recognized him as the man in the foreground of Ramon Samaniegos's blackmail photograph.

Well, that was a hell of a turn-up.

All he knew now was he had to get to the door before him. Looking around with enough sham confusion to attract attention, Tom fixed his gaze on the doorway of the Butterfly Club across the street and snapped his fingers demonstratively in what he hoped looked like a gesture of sudden realization. He crossed, quickening his pace and pulling the brim of his hat down, feeling the young man's curious gaze upon him now. He was determined to get to the door first – without meeting his eye.

'Looking for something?' The tone of the enquiry was not uncurious but with a sharp edge, like he was impatient for Tom to get out of the way.

Feigning surprise, Tom turned. 'Oh, hello,' he said, forcing a note of hesitancy into his voice. 'Yeah. The Butterfly Club. I'm guessing this is it.'

'Not so hard to figure, huh?' The boy looked up, scanned his face, an expression rife with amused skepticism. 'But I think you've got the wrong idea, mister. The kind of butterfly you like won't be the kind they got in here.'

He tried to push past to the door, but Tom stepped round just enough to block him, smiling broadly as he did. 'You don't say? Well, you might be right about that, but I'd like a look inside anyhow, Gianni, if that's OK with you.'

The young man blanched visibly.

'Your name *is* Gianni, isn't it?' Tom asked again, moving in closer now, using his height.

'You ain't been in before.' The young man's voice was an octave higher now. 'Who the hell are you? A cop?'

'No. I'm a friend of José's,' Tom said. 'Or Ramon, if you prefer. You remember him, don't you? And how fond you said you were of him.'

The young man's eyes lit up with a realization that he tried but failed to disguise. He glared at Tom, then said something in Italian that didn't need to be understood and tried to duck around him. But, again, Tom matched him step for step, blocking his way.

'Poor Ramon's been worrying himself sick over you. Thinks you've been bumped off by some shakedown artists, Gianni. Some lowdown scammers who put the squeeze on you and left you dead for the crows and dogs to pick at. Know anything about that?'

'No. And I don't know no Gianni. Or Ramon. Or anything else what you're talkin' about. Get out of my way.'

The sneer was still there but Tom could see he was rattled, trembling beneath his coiled-up posture of defiance. Again, Tom blocked his way, this time grabbing him by the shoulder and pushing him back.

'Get off me, you ain't no cop.'

'Which makes this your lucky day, Gianni.' Tom reached inside his coat pocket and pulled out a business card and held it up in front of the young man's eyes. 'That's how worried he is, Gianni. It never occurred to him you could be in on the squeeze yourself. He liked you *that* much. No, he *trusted* you that much. Couldn't even convince himself, so he had to go and hire me to figure out what was going on. I can tell you one thing – he'll be so devastated when I tell him about you, I don't reckon he'll be visiting you much in pokey.'

For some reason that really seemed to get to the young man. His shoulders sagged of a sudden and he looked up at Tom, a plea in his eyes now, which were brimming with tears. Whether they were fake or not was too early to judge.

'Ain't nothing I can do about it. Or you. Like I said, you ain't no cop.'

Tom tucked his business card in behind the handkerchief in the top pocket of Gianni's jacket. 'I'm not,' he said. 'But some of my best pals are. So you better start talking, or I'll drag you by the neck over to Central and have you up before a judge for extortion.'

'No, please. Please. That won't do nobody any good,' Gianni stammered. 'If the papers get it, he'll be finished. Look, I tried to stop 'em. Honest, I did. I really like José. I told 'em I'd work off the money myself. I even pretended he'd left town, so they would leave off. Until they saw that goddamn magazine. Who'd you think got a beating then, huh? Not José. No, I did. Me. Just like I'll get a beating now if I don't get in there quick. So please, do what you like but I gotta . . .'

He was cut off by a noise from inside the building of a chair or table scraped roughly across a floor, and a heavy, creaking tread on a stair. Was it descending? Now the young guy's face switched from scared to undisguised terror as he blanched and struggled again to escape Tom's grip.

'G-Get away now, for God's sake,' Gianni said, his voice a strangled whisper. 'He'll kill me. He'll kill both of us if he sees me talking to you. He's crazy, I'm not kidding.' The kid wriggled even more until Tom tightened his grip on his suit so much there was no more room to squirm. He shoved his face into the boy's.

'Who is he?' Tom demanded under his breath. 'A name, now, or I take him down here and now and tell him what you told me.'

The boy's eyes widened further. 'You seen him, right? That's not going to happen.'

Tom ignored him and held his grip, unmoving, the sound of the tread pausing on the stair like a boom within their silence. 'His name, now. Or that's it.'

'Vitale, for chrissakes,' the boy gasped desperately, tearing at Tom's wrists now, the creak of floorboards getting louder as footsteps approached behind the door.

Tom dropped him and stepped back, half-turning from the door just as it swung abruptly inwards and the hulking figure he had seen go in earlier poked his massive head and shoulders out the open doorway.

'A block down that way, yeah? That's great. Thanks, pal,' Tom said, casual as he could, to Gianni, who was patting down his crumpled suit lapels and brushing a hank of hair back from his eyes. Tom pretended not to take much notice of the man-mountain glaring out at them. The guy was even bigger than he'd reckoned. Six-five or -six at a pinch and, hunched under the doorframe as he was, seeming almost as broad. A dark sweep of iron-grey shadow conferred an anvil-like quality to his jutting jaw.

'I'll be on my way then,' Tom said, tipping his hat finally to Vitale, and walking away, up Rose Street, in the opposite direction to where his motor was parked. He could always double-back down Second and Alameda, but no way was he giving that brute a chance to challenge him by turning back, or even know which direction he was really heading in.

He didn't even look round when he heard the sounds of angry interrogation break out behind him, and what he knew could only be the whimpered pleading of Gianni. He just kept on walking until he rounded the corner on to Second and slackened his pace, stopping only to consult a storefront window to confirm for himself in reflection that he really had got away with it unscathed. He was more convinced than ever that they would need to move quick and smart now if Samaniegos was to have any hope of ever savoring his newborn stardom.

TWENTY-TWO

L it up on all sides with an electric declaration of its own
self-importance, the red, terracotta-tiled campanile of City
Hall glowered above Broadway and the surrounding
thoroughfares, steadfastly refusing to move out of Tom's line
of vision as he made his way down the incline on First towards
Central Police Station. Again, now, everything Olsen had said
to him about Charlie Crawford and his City Hall cronies was
turning over in his mind as he found a place to pull in amid
the clutter of patrol cars parked out front of the oppressive,
granite-faced building and entered via the arched doorway
that echoed almost exactly the three arches leading into City
Hall itself.

The front desk was humming with activity – marks and
gulls standing in line to report robberies and run-ins, patrolmen
frog-marching drunks to the cells, streetwalkers slumped
moodily on benches awaiting bailout or the slammer. Tom
headed for the stairs. He had seen it all before. Too many
years in blues himself, and never so relieved as the day he
shrugged that uniform off for the final time and took up
Zukor's offer of nice, easy security work at his movie studio
on the sunny West coast. Maybe it hadn't worked out entirely
as he had hoped, but he'd had some great years. And whenever
the days began to grind now, he only had to think of those
tougher times for the bright side to come back into view
again.

He wasn't prepared, on entering the detectives' high-ceilinged
squad room, for the pallor that had taken hold of his old friend's
features, or the hollowness in the eyes that lit up just a flicker
on seeing Tom enter the room.

'You took your time.' Sullivan roughly kicked out a straight-
back chair towards him, opening his desk drawer and removing
two glasses and a half-empty liquor bottle.

'Nice to see you, too, ol' pal,' Tom said, sitting heavily into the chair and surveying the sea of desks around him – unoccupied other than by a handful of stragglers on the far side of the room, hands behind heads, heels on desks, making the most of a quiet patch on the late shift.

'Powers, is it?' Tom nodded at the bottle's diamond-shaped label as Sullivan handed him a glass. Prohibition or no, he could always be relied upon to have a bottle of the very best Irish to hand. 'Father Doran been grateful again?'

This at last brought a twitch of a smile to the big man's lips, but it died as soon as it reached them. 'Make the most of it. Might be the last in a while, way things are going here.'

'You'd better ease up on that relentless optimism of yours, Thad.' Tom emptied his glass in one gulp, relishing the ferocity of the liquid heat that bypassed his belly and went straight for his soul instead. 'And there was me thinking I might be the bearer of good news.'

'Oh yeah?' Such was the skepticism in the curl of his lip, the very idea might have been anathema to Sullivan. 'How do you make that out, then?'

Tom took another look around the squad room and leaned in towards him, cradling his glass in both hands, elbows on knees, confiding. 'Well, I know it was a long shot, anyway, but you can rule out my guy as your Baldwin victim, for a start. I can say with absolute certainty, it wasn't Gianni's body they found in that clump of cactus.'

'And you know this, how?'

'Because I got a hook into him earlier, alive as you like, swanning into a swish club down on Rose. I got talking to him, too. Enough for him to admit putting the squeeze on my client. Thing is, he was only the bait in the set-up. Another guy, a real shark, he's the one I got to figure out how to get to back off. Looks like it won't be easy, either.'

'And that's all you've come to tell me, is it?' Sullivan said with a scowl. 'Does it really look like I don't have troubles enough of my own?'

'No, for God's sake, Thad.' Tom put a hand up. 'I was only trying to help. I don't see why you can't still use it, or something like it, as something to throw at Ramirez.'

Sullivan said nothing, just grunted an acknowledgement and

turned his face away like he could care less. Tom told him anyway, about his visit to the club on Rose Street, and what Olsen had said about the guy who ran it, Vitale. Sullivan expressed no surprise or interest, just shrugged his shoulders and muttered something crudely unhelpful about men who love men and what they should get in the way of payback.

Tom shook his head impatiently. 'Last time I looked I was the best pal you have in this town. So, I know you better than that, Thad. And if you're sitting here with a glass in your paw and not too busy to shoot the breeze anyway, is it really so much to ask? Just tell me who I should have a word with about getting a joint like that shut down. Whatever you might think about the guys who go there, no one deserves to have their life threatened like that. Except maybe the guy who runs it, by all accounts.'

Sullivan blew out the air from his lungs, taking so long about it that Tom really was beginning to wonder if he had meant what he said. Then he gave his glass a swirl, emptied it, and held the bottle up to offer Tom another slug.

'I'll tell you one thing for nothing. Unless this fella's gone and killed someone, you've come to the wrong place. Ever since Chief Oaks was appointed, all that kind of thing's been handled by the new Vice team. Which, if I hear right, means it isn't being handled at all, other than to drive the old rack-eteers out and replace them with new ones – mostly Charlie Crawford's boys, as I'm sure you know.'

'Yeah.' Tom threw his eyes heavenwards. He'd been hoping for something new. 'I heard something to that effect all right.'

'Well, in that case you probably know too that if this guy is operating openly enough for someone like you to find him, and doing it from an identifiable location, he's going to have protection from somebody. And, as there's pretty much nobody left downtown now but Crawford, it'd have to be from him. Which means Vice aren't going to do a thing about it, other than go and collect their weekly dues from this guy and maybe give him the sniff that some private man called Tom Collins is looking to cause trouble for him.'

'Jesus, Thad. Are you serious? You won't take an interest in saving a guy being screwed over by some animal?'

Sullivan didn't like that. But he wouldn't rise to the bait either. All he did was pour himself another whiskey.

'So, what is it you're saying I should do?' Tom pressed on. 'Go direct to Crawford? You reckon if he knew what was really going on, he might be convinced to put a stop to it?'

Sullivan was mid-gulp, and if it hadn't been for the nationwide shortage of fine whiskey, he might have spat the rest of it out, such was his amusement at the idea. As it was, Tom had to slap him a couple of times on the back to help get him over it.

'What's so goddamn funny?'

'What're you planning on doing? Walking right up and telling Charlie Crawford he's running a bad house for queers. The man has a finger in every crap game, brothel, casino and speakeasy in the city, and what he doesn't own he takes a slice off. Do you really think he's going to give a damn about one swish who might or might not've got hurt. Jesus, that's the best one I've heard in years.' Sullivan descended into another wheeze of laughter. 'And to think you used to call yourself a cop.'

Tom just stood there, color rising in his cheeks, feeling like a chump. Maybe Sullivan was right. Maybe he was being naïve. Maybe he'd been off the streets too long to deal with an ape like this Vitale guy. Why not just give the guy what he wanted and hope he went away? Only problem with that idea was he wouldn't go away. Not ever. One thing Tom did know for certain from his time in uniform was that this guy wouldn't stop until he'd bled Samaniegos dry.

'So, what, we just give up?'

'Ah, don't go takin' it like that, y'eejit,' Sullivan said at last. 'Look, I'm sorry I said that, Tom. We both know you were the best cop I ever met. But just because Crawford wasn't born on the streets doesn't mean he isn't from them, in the only place that matters – in his heart and soul. And, God knows, for all his two-hundred-dollar suits and diamond stickpins, Crawford has a sewer for a soul and a cold black stone where his heart should be. The only thing he respects is money and power, and the only way to get at someone like that is through one of his own kind.'

'So, you're saying we shouldn't even try? Because the only man I know of his kind is Tony Cornero, and I don't think we want to be asking any more favors from him, do we? Especially not right now. Not in the current circumstances, right, Thad?'

'I'm not sure it'd give him any more hold over us than he has already.' Sullivan grinned ruefully at him. 'But that's not my point. You're thinking like someone who doesn't have friends in high places, Tom. I meant people at the other end of the scale. It's not called the City Hall gang for nothing, you know. All those movie friends of yours, the ones who flap around in high circles? Surely the studio this fella you're working for must have some clout. Someone who can have a quiet word in the mayor's ear, or to one of his cronies. Who do you think fills Cryer's war chest come election time? The bloody studios do.'

'Thanks, Thad, but that doesn't get me any closer. You have an exaggerated idea of my circle of influence. And if the studio got wind of this, that'd be the end of my guy. Easier to dump a problem than deal with it, especially with Hays in town.'

Sullivan spluttered in frustration. 'Well, weren't you only telling me the other day about your man Rex Ingram and how you were doing some work for him? He must be one of the most famous men in the world right now. Why don't you get him to have a word with one of his friends on high?'

'He's only a director. He might be famous, but he has no clout outside the studio. He's a blow-in to this city, just like you and me.'

'Ah, get away with you. Money always talks, same in this city as any other. A word in the ear with the right man. That Kane Parrot, he's your man. They all say he's the power behind the throne. Now you can't tell me you can't get access to him.'

'Kent Kane Parrot? How in God's name, if I can't get to Crawford or Cryer, am I supposed to get to a man like him?'

'Sure, isn't his wife working on that film you were telling me about, *The Prisoner* of something or other, for Ingram?'

'His wife? What are you talking about, Thad? Have you gone stark staring mad? What would Kent Kane Parrot's wife need to be doing working on a movie? She'd be out there running charity drives – or probably the charities themselves, more like.'

'It's true, I'm telling you!' Sullivan's whispered umbrage came at him like a rush of elephant's breath. 'Why would I make such a thing up? I saw it for myself, back in March or so. There was an almighty row, at a fancy house out Hancock way. Neighbors called it in, uniforms attended. Captain Heath called Krause in a big hurry, told him to bury it, pronto. I went down there with him. Turns out it's Kent Kane Parrot's place, the woman in question was his wife – they were in the middle of a divorce. What a spitfire she was. Fine-looking woman, and, to be honest, I felt sorry for her, married to him. But she said something about having to get to the studio for some movie she was working on, under a different name. A pen name, like. I heard it again just recently, connected to this Ingram fella of yours. It must be because she sounded so Irish. Ah, it's on the tip of my tongue . . . it won't come. She does the story, the words, I know that. Mary something . . . I know that much.'

Tom's head was spinning. 'Mary O'Hara?'

'O'Hara! That's it, exactly!' Sullivan looked like he'd won a prize. 'You couldn't get more Irish, could you?'

Tom couldn't do anything but wheeze out a cough of disbelief. 'You're seriously trying to suggest she's Kent Kane Parrot's wife?'

'I'm not suggesting anything, it's an irrefutable fact.'

'But I was talking to her myself only a few days ago.'

'Well, there you go – who better to ask, then?'

'Fay told me she was divorced. We were talking about it . . .' And he remembered she said O'Hara was coy about saying who her ex was. But Sullivan was rattling on anyway.

'She probably is divorced by now. Like I say, this was back in February or March time. I tell you, there was no doubting she wanted to get away from that scoundrel as soon as she possibly could. Is it any wonder she felt the need to use a pen name?'

TWENTY-THREE

He spent the morning racking his brains over what to do about this Vitale. With Hays in town, the safest bet for Samaniegos had to be to try and play for time. But Vitale really didn't look like the playing kind and Tom knew he would need not just a plan but a backup too, if he was going to tackle him. Maybe find another way of putting pressure on him. He was also undecided about what to tell Samaniegos for now, if he said anything, about his friend Gianni. He could see it might do more harm than good telling him what he had discovered, and forcing the young actor to face the truth. Especially when nothing had been resolved yet. But balanced against the ongoing agony of not knowing, would it really be worse? And who was he, anyway, to decide what Samaniegos should or shouldn't be told about his life?

In the end, instead of making a decision he turned his attention to a sheaf of overdue accounts that Mae had left on his desk to check. He wouldn't honestly have cared if most of them paid up or not, if it weren't for the pressure of having to pay his own bills and the fact that his clients tended to have money to burn in any case. The good thing about working for movie folk was they thought nothing of paying him well. His last big payday, a job for Mack Sennett, had funded the first six months rental on the office, and went a fair way to meeting Mae's salary costs, too. There was still quite a bit of that roll left, sitting in the bank. If only every payday could be like that one. For a while checking the rows of figures seemed a welcome distraction. But still the jangle of the telephone came as a relief.

'Mr Drew's office for you,' Mae called from her desk outside. She barely had to raise her voice. Tom picked up the extension and plucked the earpiece from the prong, eager to tell Drew about the odd conversation he'd had with Olsen the night before.

'Hey, Frank, I was trying to get you this morn—'

But the voice that broke in on him was not Frank Drew's. 'Mr Collins? This is Mr Drew's secretary, Joan. Mr Drew is on the way over to Miss La Marr's house and he would like you to join him there as soon as you possibly can. If you get there before him, he asks, will you please ensure she talks to no one until he arrives.'

Joan sounded like she was reading the message from a note and, sure enough, she was unable to afford him any more information other than to insist it was a matter of urgency and give him an address up in Whitley Heights.

It was barely a mile away. He could zip up there and hold the fort until the lawyer arrived. He grabbed his hat and ran out, telling Mae he'd be back shortly, keen to get there before Drew. And he would have, had it not been for a snarl-up on Wilcox that delayed him long enough to leave him only just pulling up outside 6672 Whitley Terrace as the attorney did so, too, in a snazzy-looking yellow Buick.

Both men reached the elaborately wrought white iron gate at the same time and automatically shook hands. From this vantage point only the red-tile roof of Miss La Marr's residence was visible, it being on the vertiginous downward-sloping side of the street. A steep set of steps descended to the house, which was nestled in a crook of the decline in a garden rampant with fragrant eucalyptus, manzanita and sage.

'Sorry to call you out, Collins.' Drew pulled a handkerchief from his pocket, wiped a slick of sweat off his face. 'Roth's gone and spilled to the papers, but I don't know how much. I was hoping we could get here before them but—'

He pointed towards three other autos parked on the bend in the street and was about to say something when an explosion of gaiety – a mix of coarse male laughter and at least one woman's voice – echoed up the hillside from the house below.

'Looks like they got the jump on us,' Tom agreed, standing back to allow the lawyer to start down the stairs ahead of him.

Like the house, the entrance was modest in size but with pretentions to grandeur, a heavy, carved-wood frame encompassing a nail-studded Mediterranean-style oak door. It was opened by a woman in a white apron who Drew addressed familiarly as Irene, and Tom assumed to be Miss La Marr's maid. She took their hats before showing them through, whispering something about 'robes' to Drew that Tom couldn't quite catch above the sound of her mistress's seductive tones emerging from the living room.

Tom saw what she meant as soon as they entered. La Marr was ensconced, feet up, like the Queen of Sheba on an extravagantly cushioned daybed. A coral pink turban tipped with an egg-sized green glass gem and a flamingo feather drew the eye up and away from the oceans of flowing silk robes in which she was engulfed. She could have been pregnant ten times over and nobody would have spotted it unless she got up and moved. Even then it would probably be doubtful. Before her, in the tastefully appointed room, three men sat on a long settee, enthralled. All of them had the slightly underfed air of pressmen, shirts grubby round the collar, suit cuffs scuffed, elbows shiny and shoes not. And they all held notebooks and pens in their hands, yet none were scribbling. Rather they were smiling in rapt attention as La Marr regaled them with one of her tall tales, something about being kidnapped by a man on a horse. Tom felt their resentment bristling as the new arrivals interrupted the story and forced them to look away from the source of their beguilement.

'Ah, Mr Drew – and Mr Collins – how nice, we've been expecting you.' La Marr waved them in regally, as if they were freshly arrived supplicants seeking an audience. It was only then that Tom recognized the third reporter along, whose face had been obscured by the other two leaning forward. Phil Olsen clocked him at the same time and his eyes all but popped as his mouth opened. A second later his expression was one of brow-wrinkling disappointment as he shook his head and tutted deliberately to himself before sneering above the heads of the others. 'Jeez, Collins, you rolled me good this time. I never had you down for such a bluffer. Remind me never to play at the same table as you again.'

Every gaze in the room now darted between the two men, wondering what was going on. Tom looked at Drew, whose eyes flashed a silent interrogation, and shook his head.

La Marr was quick to fill the silence. 'Are you and Mr Collins already acquainted, Mr Olsen?' she asked, eyes sparkling at the palpable tension between them.

But Olsen only laughed like a man admitting he'd been bested. 'Sure we are, ma'am. Old pals. Collins here takes me for a ride every now and again – don't ya, Collins?'

Tom said nothing but grinned and gave Olsen an apologetic shrug as he made his way to the other side of the room. This was Drew's show and he didn't want to get in the way. La Marr had moved on in any case and was addressing the reporters again.

'I imagine you gentlemen know Mr Drew here, too, don't you? He's my attorney, and he says he doesn't want me answering any of your questions about whatever it is you've come to see me about today. What an old spoilsport he is.'

She laughed in a way that would have made any other woman seem coquettish or arch but with her somehow added to the overall allure. Was it any wonder he'd been putty in her hands at the studio, Tom thought, at the sight of three hard-bitten Los Angeles pressmen tittering at her like tenderfoots.

Drew, meanwhile, tucked his shoulders back and jutted out his chin. 'That is correct, gentlemen. I'm here to tell you that whatever poison Mr Roth poured in your ears this morning, it has no foundation in fact, and if you print a word of it or refer to it in any way on the pages of your newspapers, you will have a writ on your desks in the morning seeking substantial damages for libel. To avoid any confusion, I have dispatched written notices to that effect to your editors as well.'

None of the newspaper men was remotely flustered by this. It was a standard play they heard every day of their working lives.

'What is it you think Roth's told us, Frank?' said the man in the middle of the three, laughing and winking at his two colleagues. Dexter Doheny, a reporter for the *Times*. Tom remembered his former boss, Charlie Eyton, having a tussle with the man over some looming scandal at Famous Players a few years back. The other one, Harry Carroll, Tom knew as one of the *Examiner*'s newsmen.

Drew was having none of it. 'Can't go repeating defamatory statements, now, can we Dex, because you might be tempted to quote me. Now, gentlemen, as no complaint of any kind has been filed against my client by any party, you are, as you know, prohibited by statute from making malicious reference to any such nonexistent complaint. Do I make myself clear, or do I need to show you the cease order I have in my pocket, which I intend to lodge with the court as soon as I return downtown. You know you cannot hope to get anything into print before then.'

The three pressmen groaned, and in one move stood up together, throwing their hands up and complaining about wasting their time coming all this way out of town for nothing. Drew turned on his heel and, leaning over, said something to La Marr that couldn't be heard above the hubbub. He then turned back to the newsmen and, holding his hands up for quiet, addressed them again.

'Miss La Marr is, however, willing to take a question or two from each of you on the understanding that if she declines to answer any of them for the reasons outlined already, the fact that she declined will be held to be strictly off the record. OK?'

The three newsmen paused, looked at each other curiously, and promptly sat down again like obedient puppies.

'Looks like he's not such an old spoilsport, after all, eh boys,' La Marr mewed from her daybed. 'Come on, then, give it your best shot.'

What followed was not so much a question-and-answer session as a shrewd information-gathering exercise on Drew's part. Tom had to admire the lawyer's tactic: the newspaper men asked their questions, he stepped in and forbade his client to give any but the most innocuous answer, and at the same time got a clearer idea of what, and how much of it, Roth had already told them. Not as much as he had threatened, Tom concluded, although one of Olsen's questions thrown in, about Miss La Marr's friends at City Hall, did seem to stall her a fraction more than others, though her hesitancy didn't seem to resonate with anyone else in the room and he wondered if it might have just seemed that way only to him. After a few minutes, the reporters realized what was going on and began to complain again, Doheny getting irked and coming right out with the question they'd all been wanting to ask.

'Oh, come on Miss La Marr, let's stop pussyfooting around. Ben Deeley says he has more than one co-respondent he can throw at you. What've you got to say to that?'

La Marr visibly blanched, her lips opened, yet nothing emerged as her mouth flapped, searching for words that refused to come. Plenty of time for Drew to step in angrily and instruct Doheny to shut the hell up and forbid La Marr to say another word.

By then she had recovered enough to joke. 'He's clammed me up proper this time, boys. Any other topic I'd chat the whole day through. But look, you can't come all the way out here for nothing, so here's a zinger for you. My new movie *The Prisoner of Zenda*, directed by the great artist Rex Ingram, has its premiere in New York real soon, and already the preview boys out there are calling it the movie of the year, and yours truly as the sensation of the season. So here's a quote for you: 'I've never looked better than I do in all those silks and furs boys . . . and *out* of 'em! What a knockout!'

She laughed and the three reporters relaxed again. Carroll salaciously suggested, 'So you gonna show us some of that vamping now, Miss La Marr?' The gesture he made, like he was pulling a shift down his shoulder, prompted yet more laughter all round.

'I guess you'll have to wait boys.' She beamed at them. 'But some things are worth the wait, am I right? You can quote me on that, too. Now, you all run along or I'll get my lovely Mr Collins here to show you what happens when a gentleman refuses to leave *this* girl's rooms when he's asked.'

Again they all laughed and began to gather their jackets and leave. By now Drew was offering to show them personally to the door, his impatience getting the better of him. Only Olsen hung back, supposedly to offer some joshing final thanks to La Marr, while jotting down something in his notebook. On his way out of the room, to Tom's surprise he extended a hand to shake. 'No hard feelings on my part, Collins, you big mauler. But you owe me now.' Tom felt a piece of folded paper slip into his palm as he shook, and Olsen, chin dipped and brows raised meaningfully, gave him a knowing look. 'You really do, boy.'

Once they were gone, Drew thanked Tom and said he needed a moment in private to discuss some business with La Marr, so Tom excused himself and left. By the time he mounted the steep stairs back up to street level, his limbs feeling twice as heavy in the leaden afternoon air, the newsmen were gone. He took a moment to get his breath back and admire the surrounding houses, built in the past four or five years but already looking like they had inhabited the place a lot longer, like some ancient hilltop community that came into existence naturally, perched on the slopes of this rocky outcrop with views in all directions.

A gust of hot hillside air brought him quickly back to earth. Like the fug of male lechery he'd been breathing in for the past hour, it left him feeling restless, with no desire to go back to the office. He took the note Olsen had slipped him from his pocket and unfolded a page torn from the reporter's notebook:

Meet me at the Wienerhaus downtown tonight at eight, or, I promise you, I'll dig out who your swish client is and plaster him over the front page.

Just the possibility of Olsen finding out about Samaniegos sent a chill down his spine, despite the cloying heat. He knew it would almost certainly be an empty threat, and that in Olsen's warped way of seeing things he probably respected Tom even more now that he thought he'd been bested. But even so, Tom didn't want to risk upsetting the reporter too much. He liked Olsen, for all his faults, and he'd always been his most reliable source of information about how things really worked in the city – as opposed to how the newspapers and movies chose to portray it. He didn't want to lose access to that. He would have to go mend some fences. He only hoped the price wouldn't be too high.

Climbing into the Dodge, he realized he'd forgotten to tell Drew about his meeting with Olsen the night before. All the more relevant now, he reckoned, but he was loath to go up and down those steps again. And Drew had been clear he wanted to be alone with La Marr. Tom pressed the starter button, thinking it could be covered by a telephone call, or he could call in to Drew's office later. In any case, something else was forcing its way back into his mind as he followed the steep and twisting avenue back down towards Franklin. At the intersection at the bottom he spotted a small new cafeteria open and pulled in across the road from it. At the counter he ordered a glass of ice water and a short coffee and asked if he could use the telephone. He knocked back the coffee, savoring its aromatic kick, then double-clicked the prong. He had intended calling Mae to check for messages, maybe even tell her to take the rest of the day off, it was so damn hot. But instead he found himself asking the operator to put him through to a Venice number. It took a couple of minutes for the St Mark reception to pick up and more to put him through to Room 403.

'Ramon, we need to talk some.'

TWENTY-FOUR

He had rarely heard a man happier than Samaniegos when he told him Gianni was still alive. Still, he kept the details thin, told a bunch of straight-out lies about where and how he had found him, and told the actor to stay safe out in Venice until he could figure a way to get the real bad guy out of his hair.

'I was thinking the best thing for now could be to pay him off, Ramon. But he looks a rough sort and we have to find a way of guaranteeing it's a one-time deal. Otherwise there's no point. Either way you have to stay out of Los Angeles for a few more days. It is the only way we can be certain of keeping you safe and your name off the front page.'

That seemed to do the trick. Samaniegos, half laughing, half crying, promised he would. They arranged to meet up to make a plan and he put the phone down. The truth was, agreeing to pay was the only clear choice they had right now. If they could stall Vitale and delay payment until Hays left town – and Hays was due back on the Los Angeles Limited and headed for New York by the end of the weekend – there was a lot less chance of it blowing up in their faces. If nothing else, it would give them breathing space.

Tom hung up and looked around the cafeteria, at its smattering of happy, relaxed people fanning the heat away from their necks and chattering over coffee, eggs and oozing slices of pie. One or two were sitting alone, hunched over tables, eating mechanically, looking bone tired, like they had just come off a twelve-hour shift somewhere. The thought of jumping in the roadster and shooting out the mile or so along the Boulevard to see Fay, sitting out together on that broad balcony, enjoying an iced drink in the shade, the sea air adding a hint of salt to their lips, flitted through his mind like the ghost of a pleasure postponed. He grabbed his hat, left a couple of dimes on the counter and walked out the door.

*　　*　　*

It was the best part of two hours later when he stepped out of the elevator at Drew's place and instantly got the sense that something was not right. The lawyer's secretary, Joan, so upright and composed the last time he had visited, rushed out of the office doorway looking flustered, and took a step back in surprise when she saw Tom.

'Oh, Mr Collins, you're here already,' she said. 'You'd better go straight in.'

He hadn't called ahead to tell them he was coming over, so that in itself was unexpected. Inside he found Drew in a state of even greater upset than his secretary, bent over, sweating and red-faced, picking scattered file folders and documents off the carpet around his desk. His jaw flopped open when he looked up and saw Tom standing there.

'I only just asked Joan to call you.' There was a haze of puzzlement in his expression, like he had gone through some terrible ordeal seconds before.

'Must've felt something in the air,' Tom said. 'I was passing, thought I'd drop in.'

'Did you see Roth on the way out?'

'He was here?'

Drew shook himself like he was trying to wake from a nightmare, a dazed look still in his eyes. 'Jesus, was he ever.'

He invited Tom to sit and he went to the drinks table, poured a couple of shots from the nearest bottle and knocked one straight back before handing the other to Tom and refilling his own, fingers trembling.

'I think I overplayed my hand,' Drew said, 'and it blew up on me, badly. When I got back, I sent a boy over to Roth's with a strongly worded note threatening to report him to the California Bar for his underhand methods with those press boys, saying it amounted to malpractice. I thought it might make him think twice before trying on anything like that again. Some chance. A half-hour later he turned up here, burst right in, screaming hellfire, ripped up the note in front of me and threw it in my face. He had an amended complaint in his hand, listing the names of the co-respondents. You wouldn't believe it, Collins.'

'Try me. I can get straight on to it.'

Drew shook his head. 'You'd hardly credit it. Daugherty obviously. Ingram too, like we guessed. Me.'

'You?' Tom thought back to how Drew had behaved around La Marr: protective, courtly almost at times. How he had stayed behind after everyone else left. It didn't seem so entirely implausible.

'It's crazy, obviously,' Drew said, without much conviction. 'Then Roth demanded $25,000 to settle and he wouldn't file the petition. It's . . . it's tantamount to blackmail And twenty-five grand. Where in hell does he think she's going to find that kind of money?'

'From the studio, maybe?' Tom was not as shocked by the amount as Drew obviously was. He'd been there before. People always thought movie studios had bottomless reserves of money to tap. Which some undoubtedly did, though in reality most of them teetered on a financial knife-edge half the time.

Drew looked up, sheepishly. 'I'm afraid I lost my head at that point. I told him we knew how much he was screwing Deeley for on the settlement, and that his actions in relation to my client amounted to extortion. He went completely loco, screaming at me to stay away from Deeley, hurling my own papers at me. Then he stomped out, saying we had less than twenty-four hours to pay or the complaint would be filed at twelve noon, tomorrow, and he'd have the press boys primed to meet him there so the news can make the evening papers.'

Still a little shell-shocked, Drew slumped back in his seat.

'He must have some pretty solid proof if he thinks he can get away with behaving like that. Can he pull it off? Has he got the goods?' Tom stood up this time and poured a couple of shots, handing one to the lawyer, telling him to knock it back in one again. It seemed to have the desired effect. Drew pulled himself together and sat forward again.

'The names are there to guarantee headlines. Or at least to guarantee a panic response from us. What proof he has, I don't know. Except for one. He claims it is rock solid. Shoved the evidence right in my face.' He swallowed hard, a note of horror creeping back into his voice. 'I mean, scandal-wise, I don't think it could be any worse. It's sure to go coast-to-coast. I don't see how we could stop it.'

'So are you going to tell me who it is?'

Drew looked uncertain, then climbed out of his chair and went to the door to make sure it was fully shut. 'If this gets out—' He broke off, fished his handkerchief from his pocket again and wiped a fresh slick of sweat from his cheeks and brow. 'It's not just Miss La Marr will be ruined, Tom, or even Ingram . . . She'll bring the whole goddamn city down with her.'

Sullivan couldn't quite believe his eyes. His day had been tough enough and frustrating as all hell already, chasing down a pair of elusive bunco artists who'd boosted a succession of doddering oldsters for every dime they possessed in an elaborate investment-scheme scam. He and his occasional partner, Detective Dirk Krause, had caught a lucky break from a money man of their mutual acquaintance and, over three days, tracked the bunco boys to a hotel on Figueroa and were about to make the bust – only to discover the rooms abandoned, curtains still flapping from an open window to the fire escape, nothing but an empty suitcase and a horribly stained union suit left for them to take into custody. The clincher came when Krause – never one to accept such eventualities dispassionately – treated the hotel manager, who'd tipped the pair off from reception, to a bloody and probably broken nose. Which, however satisfying in the moment, was exactly the sort of thing Sullivan knew could waft back on him, too, though he hadn't laid a finger on the fat little schmuck, tempted as he might have been.

What he couldn't credit now was that the repercussions could come so quick. There on his desk already, barely two hours since the fateful punch, was a sheet of yellow notepaper demanding he present himself in Captain Heath's office before he finished for the night. He had only come back in to sign off his shift – and Krause's, having left the fool to cool off in a speak over on Flower. Sullivan checked his wristwatch, figuring whether he could get away with leaving it until the morning, weighing the balance between the ameliorative effects of an overnight delay and the distinct possibility of vexing Heath further by failing to turn up on command. He looked at the time again. Almost eight, so Heath – never known to put in a longer day than necessary – would almost certainly be gone anyway.

Sullivan mounted the stairs wearily. The old brick building absorbed heat like a rock in a desert and the captain's office was up on the top floor, at the far end of a long airless corridor that felt all the longer for keeping you from your fate. He knocked on the door of the outer office and was gratified not to receive a call to enter in reply. He tried the handle. It wasn't locked so he looked in, saw Heath's secretary had gone for the day, and sidled in, intending to leave the yellow sheet there with a note on the back to the effect that he had answered his summons but to no avail.

He was leaning over the desk writing it when he heard a sound of voices inside Heath's inner office and saw through the ground glass panel the shadow of a figure approaching the door. He cursed low and floridly under his breath, grabbing the note, straightening up and preparing to make his excuses to Heath as the door opened. But it wasn't the captain who filled the doorframe as he emerged. Rather it was Gab Ramirez, a look of intense surprise breaking across his sullen features.

'Jesus, Gab,' Sullivan wheezed, his shoulders instantly relaxing. 'Ye nearly put the heart crossways on me, there. I thought the captain was gone home. He's still inside, is he?'

Ramirez made no effort to reply but remained, glaring at him, from exactly the spot where he'd frozen on seeing Sullivan, blocking the doorway into the gloomy interior office. Now he flicked a long glance back over his shoulder, as if seeking permission, muttered something and took a couple of steps back, inviting Sullivan in with a sweep of his hand.

'You'd better come on in, I guess.'

As soon as he crossed the threshold, Sullivan knew something wasn't at all right. A manila file of papers was spilled untidily across the floor in front of the captain's desk, behind which he saw, with increasing puzzlement, nothing but an empty chair. He turned quickly to confront Ramirez, who was standing fully aside now, a grin that was more like a snarl spreading across his face. Too late, Sullivan felt a sudden rush of air behind him, the sound of someone coming at him hell for leather, no chance even to raise a shoulder to deflect the blow that came flying at his head, not even to feel any more than the blitz of pain hit home before a brutal blackness collapsed in on him, around him, under him, falling.

TWENTY-FIVE

'You owe me, Collins.' Olsen was really beginning to lay into him. 'Especially when I was so nice to you when you came looking for information for your pansy client. Then what do I find? You've been lying to me and going behind my back. It's not right buddy. It's not on.'

They were standing in a corner in the dingy, low-ceilinged back room of the Wienerhaus on Seventh, the small airless space crammed with loud, half-drunk German types, the stench of dried-on sweat, tobacco smoke and beer – all that could be got here – intense in the windowless space. Tom had already endured forty minutes of Olsen's tetchy reticence in the drab Teutonic restaurant outside, the reporter uncharacteristically tight-lipped while they sat and he worked his way through some kind of pork and dumpling stew, while Tom contented himself with a schnitzel and a green salad. Only now, after a couple of schooners in the hidden back room where a locally brewed beer was available, under the counter, had he begun to loosen up.

'You've got to give me something,' Olsen complained. 'Or I won't think you're my friend no more.'

'It's not like you've been a hundred per cent with me, either, Olsen,' Tom said. 'If you'd said from the outset that La Marr was the story you were chasing down, I might've been able to help. But you didn't.'

Olsen shot him a look that could have felled a moose. 'Man, I as good as told you that the other night, and you said nothing. Zilch. Zero.'

'Maybe that's because I didn't know anything then.'

'Oh, come on Collins. You have me down as some kind of pushover now? Look, I know you fooled me once, but I ain't *that* stupid. You couldn't wait to pump me when I asked you about La Marr's City Hall connections. I thought you were trying to steer me away from your swish. Only I know better now, don't I?'

'I swear, Olsen, on my life. I was as much in the dark about that as you were. I knew nothing about a City Hall connection.'

'So what the hell were you doing up at her house, today?'

'Wasn't it obvious? Drew got a tip-off that this lawyer Roth had spilled the beans to you guys. He called me and asked me to get up there to make sure she said nothing before he arrived. You gotta believe me, I had no idea *you* would be there. If I had I'd have thought twice about turning up myself, wouldn't I?'

Olsen didn't look remotely convinced, but something Tom said made him raise an eyebrow. 'Drew thinks this only came out yesterday?' There was a deep skepticism in his tone.

Tom shrugged and held a hand out to Olsen. 'Look, I'll give you whatever I can. But it's got to be off the record. Totally off, and I mean it.'

The reporter smiled. 'OK, Collins, you got it.'

'Shake on it.'

'Say what?'

'You heard me. Shake on it.'

'Jeez.' Olsen sighed like he was deeply insulted. 'Anyone would think you were the one who'd been hard done by here.' But he shook Tom's hand regardless. 'Off the goddamn record, OK.'

'OK.' Tom nodded. 'First I heard of this was while I was working on that other case I told you about. I know Drew from way back. On Monday he asked me in, said he needed help. La Marr's ex is looking for a divorce and this guy Roth is a shark and Deeley was only after Miss La Marr's money and all that – you know it already, right?'

'Sure.' Olsen nodded.

'So Drew said Roth was making all sorts of demands or he'd file a vexatious claim fingering seven well-known names as co-respondents. He gave out a couple of movie names as examples but kept the rest to himself. Roth said once the claim was filed the damage would be done, you boys would be all over it and Miss La Marr would be finished. So Drew wanted me to look into it, on the quiet like, to try to find out if there was any truth in it. But I didn't get very far – and then you guys got to know everything today anyway.'

'Is that it?'

'What more could there be?'

'Are you stupid or something, Collins?'

'Not that I know of.' Tom shrugged.

Olsen shook his head in disbelief. 'How long is it since you bumped into me at Metro? I told you the other night I've been chasing down this story for over a week. And you seriously think Roth only let this cat out of the bag yesterday? He'd been feeding us a line for weeks. On an exclusive basis, of course, or so he said, trying to get me to do his legwork for him. Then, I turn up yesterday and find those other two hacks there alongside me. And you to boot. The goddamn shyster. If it wasn't such a humdinger of a story, I'd sling it back in his face and do one on him.'

'You think it's true then?'

'You don't? With her reputation for putting it about?'

Tom ignored that. 'How would I know? Look, you didn't get this from me, OK? But like I said, Roth didn't give Drew the names either, apart from a couple. She laughed at them. Doug Fairbanks, for Christ's sake, yeah?' He watched Olsen's reaction; the name was clearly no surprise to him. 'It's too stupid, only there for the headline. Same with Ingram. I mean, who's going to believe it? Fairbanks is Mr Faithful and Ingram only just married. It's laughable.'

Olsen screwed up his mouth, making a strange shape with his lips. 'Some people will believe anything if you put it in print. Especially of movies. Sodom and Gomorrah's got nothing on most of 'em.'

'Roth kept back the other names, though. Made no mention of City Hall.'

'Sure, that's cos it's his ace card. He knows we *really* can't run that one unless it's true.'

'You mean you know who he's talking about?' Tom caught the barman's eye and stuck up two fingers, got a nod in reply.

'Course I do. You mean you don't?'

'He wouldn't tell Drew. Messing with his head, probably. Hoping to drive a wedge between him and Miss La Marr.'

Olsen nodded like he knew the tactic well. 'She wouldn't say either?'

'Not a word.'

'Jeez.' Olsen sat back, stretched and gave the back of his head a double-handed scratch. 'So Drew was working in the dark? He didn't even know when we were there this afternoon?' Olsen sounded almost admiring.

Tom nodded his head. 'Not a thing . . . until tonight.'

Tom watched as the realization of what he'd said sank in and made itself evident in the rising color in Olsen's cheeks. 'Hang on a second—'

But Tom cut in, determined to make him see what had happened. 'I only just found out myself. Roth went around to Drew's this afternoon, went totally loco. Smashed up his office. Demanded Drew make the payoff within twenty-four hours. Otherwise, he said he'd file an amended complaint tomorrow and tip you guys off.'

Olsen sat back, eyes narrow behind his wire-rims, face flushing red with anger. 'The shyster bastard. He's trying to sell us all out. After all the goddamn footwork I did for him on this.'

'How do you mean?'

Olsen was about to say something but checked himself. He looked Tom straight in the eye, reached a hand out and put it on his shoulder. 'I got to know we're talking about the same thing here.'

'What else could it be?'

'So what's the name?' Olsen said, his eyes roving Tom's face now. 'You tell me.'

'Oh, come on, Olsen, who else could it be?'

'Plenty. You tell me first.'

Tom tried to wriggle out of saying it but Olsen, suspecting another trap, was adamant. He would not budge. Tom was forced to cough it up.

'Mayor Cryer,' he said, like he was laying out his hand for the biggest draw ever.

'Mayor Cryer,' Olsen echoed, like he was almost disappointed. But there was relief there too at the confirmation. 'Roth told me last week that La Marr was dangling Cryer on a hook all last summer. Said the fool was totally besotted with her – though, to be fair, I can see if she turned that on me, I wouldn't be saying no either.'

Olsen looked round and over his shoulder again, making sure nobody was paying them undue attention.

'I said I needed proof, so Roth wafted a couple of letters in front of my nose. I got excited thinking maybe they were the real McCoy – y'know, lovey-dovey billets-doux from Cryer or some such. But Roth wouldn't hand them over. Said they're from some floozie nobody's ever heard of – Rose Arbor, like that's a real name – saying she was at a party and saw La Marr go in a bedroom alone with Cryer. And that when she went in the adjoining room with another guy – who, by the by, Roth says was Kent Kane Parrot – she could hear them at it like jackrabbits.'

'Jesus,' Tom said. 'That's quite the detail.'

'Is that not what he said to you?'

'To Drew,' Tom corrected him. 'Drew doesn't tell me everything. He only mentioned one letter. Said it was "extremely prejudicial" and didn't give me details. But that one letter would do it, wouldn't it?'

'Don't get overexcited,' Olsen said, only to be interrupted by the waiter bringing over the two foaming schooners. Olsen went at his like a man who'd been in the desert for a week, then wiped his mouth with the back of his hand and leaned in closer. Tom didn't touch his.

'Look, you got to see now, it's not La Marr I'm even after here,' Olsen continued. 'Although, the way she plants stories all the time, she sure sets herself up for it. What matters here, to me, is that the *Herald* most definitely did not support Cryer for mayor. So Hearst's as good as put a bounty on his head, and his whole administration with it. The reporter who brings Cryer down, well, that'd be some coup. Which is why I'm keen to reel this one in. But Roth knows it, and too goddamn well for my liking. He'd been feeding me crumbs, getting me to do all his checking up for him. In the end, it's me's gotta make it stick if we're going to print it and, to be honest, there are bits of the story that still stink like fish. Not least of them this Rose Arbor. I can't get a line on her anywhere. And if it comes to it, what jury's going to take a name like Rose Arbor seriously? Unless Roth hands over that letter to us along with the girl – and we can get her to swear out an affidavit – it's gonna fail.'

'Rose *Arbor*?' Tom said. He knew of an actress called Rose
Arthur who'd been known to trade her favors for a break or
two. But he wasn't about to tell Olsen that. He pushed his beer
towards the reporter, said he'd had a couple before he came in.
Olsen took it, saluted him, and took another draft before
continuing.

'So it seems nobody's ever heard of Rose Arbor. She's not
with any of the casting agencies and mostly all I get is giggles
when I ask around. Did a name ever sound more made up? I'm
telling you, you take on someone like the Mayor of Los Angeles
– especially with a ball-breaker lawyer like Parrot fighting his
corner, you got to have your story copper-fastened ten times
over – or you'll get screwed in the ass ten times over more.
Maybe even end up dead in a ditch.'

'You think they'd go that far for Cryer?'

'Sure I do, if it took that. I guess they'd get Crawford to
handle it for them. But even if Cryer only took us through the
courts, Parrot's the most brutal attorney in Los Angeles.
Everyone's terrified to go up against him. He's got most of the
judges on his payroll, and he as good as runs the goddamn
police department. You must've heard that from your pals on
the force.'

Tom nodded. 'I did, now you mention it, and only a couple
of days ago at that.'

Glass in hand, Olsen leant in again. 'See? Would you fancy
your chances going up against him?'

'I guess not.'

'And now you tell me Roth's already trying to sell us down
the river to Drew. Did he even mention a figure?'

Tom shook his head, avoiding the direct lie. 'I guess he
must've to Drew, but not me.'

Olsen seemed too incensed to notice. 'Jesus, man, what kind
of fools does he take us for?'

'A fool who doesn't have an inside man on the other side,
like you do now. Seems to me, it's not just you guys either.
Roth's trying to play us all for suckers. Maybe that's the
story you should be writing, Olsen. Maybe Drew might even
be willing to make it worth your while.'

Tom knew instantly he had overstepped the mark.

'I'm gonna pretend you didn't say that,' Olsen said. 'You forget I'm a man of honor. If I had the moolah from every time I've been offered a few hundred to stay schtum about something, I'd be . . .' He hesitated. Tom couldn't tell if it was for effect, or just the effect of the beer. 'Well, maybe not rich exactly, but I'd have a lot more dollars to my name than I do now. It's not what I'm after. I won't be happy until I see Cryer, Parrot and that whole rotten gang brought down.'

Tom leaned back in his chair, his hopes of turning Olsen against Roth receding ever further into the distance. La Marr and her interests seemed to have got lost in the conversation. 'OK, I'm sorry, Olsen. I didn't mean to offend your high moral principles. You got to understand, from the layman's point of view, they don't always come across so clear-cut. All I can see is, if any of this gets into print, La Marr is pretty much doomed. What's your high moral take on that?'

Olsen gave him a skeptical look. 'You never heard the expression "no news is *bad* news", Tommy boy? Vamp like her, she'll make a mint and love every minute of it. This thing hits the headlines, she'll be the most famous woman in America.'

'The most notorious, anyway.'

'You think there's such a big difference?'

'Sure I do. You ask Roscoe Arbuckle – he's had the difference kicked outta him.'

'Oh, come on, Tom. It's not like she went out and murdered anybody.'

'Neither did he,' Tom said finally. 'And look where it got him.'

The first drops of rain fell as he eased the Dodge out on to Eighth and headed West, and it came down steady the rest of the way. At last some relief from the heat. Tom kept the windows open all the way, his head still spinning from what Olsen had told him which, coming on top of Drew's revelations, had acquired a semi-apocalyptic quality in his mind by now. He had thought Drew was being overly melodramatic when he said the scandal could bring down the city. But it was hard to see now how exposure wouldn't fatally wound Cryer and his administration, and how the inevitable press frenzy wouldn't wipe out La Marr and Ingram and maybe even the whole of

Metro with it, if it kicked up enough dust. Tom had tried to argue with Drew, that the last thing Roth would want to do is actually play his ace card. That they should stall and call his bluff and see what happened. But Drew had seen something in Roth that afternoon that scared him – a greed to have his way at any cost.

Drew's parting words to Tom – 'She doesn't have the money' – were still going round in his head as he finally, wearily, turned on to Sunset. At that moment a lightning flash far out to the West over the ocean lit the street jaggedly for a second and he thought he saw Sullivan's ancient Ford parked a few spaces down from the canopied entrance to the Oasis. He shook his head, too tired for any more trouble. But as he pulled alongside it, he saw it was someone else's flivver and he breathed a long sigh of relief. He had enough on his hands with La Marr and Samaniegos. The problem of Ramirez, and the past that threatened to come back to bite him, could be held off for a few more days yet, he prayed.

TWENTY-SIX

It might have been the early hour, but Drew had that slightly dazed look about him of a man who hadn't got enough sleep. Or any sleep even.

'We . . . I mean, *she* hasn't got the money, Tom. Not twenty-five grand, at any rate. We're going to have to fight it. She actually *wants* to fight it. And I think maybe we can win it.'

Tom scratched the back of his hand. 'Are you sure that's wise, Frank? Or even possible?'

Drew squared his shoulders, looking a bit more bullish. 'Sure, why not? Is there something you know that I don't?'

'Well, yeah. Maybe.'

By the time he finished telling Drew about his long and well-lubricated conclave with Olsen the previous night, most of the puff had absconded the lawyer's chest, and quite a bit of the color had drained from his cheeks, too.

'I can't believe it . . . they've been on this for weeks?'

Tom put his hands up. 'Well, Olsen, for sure. I can't say about the others. But signs are that Roth's a man who likes to spread his bets. They've had plenty of time to put it together, anyway. I reckon all they're waiting for is Deeley to file the complaint, so they can fire the starting gun. Roth might hold back on the letters, though, until someone pays him for them. He'll want to get something out of this. For himself if not for Deeley.'

Drew was looking like all his plans had slid in the bin, and he hadn't got anything else in the tank. He was staring blankly out the window down at the street below.

'There is one good thing,' Tom continued. 'None of them seem to know about the baby yet. La Marr still has time to get out of here, go somewhere safe until the time comes, and let this other storm blow over.'

Drew turned to him at last, anger mingling with defeat in his eyes. 'You think they won't chase her for this. Try and hunt her down like some rabid dog?'

Tom knew they would.

'Maybe we could play Roth at his own game?'

'What are you suggesting, Tom?'

'Creep like that, he swims in that pool, there's got to be some dirt on him. It's worth a shot, surely?'

Drew looked doubtful. Tom stood up and reached for his hat. 'Could you stall him?'

'I'm not sure I want to risk antagonizing him any further, Tom.'

Tom put his hat on, gave it a tug on the front brim. 'So don't antagonize him, then. Call him now and tell him you're all in. You're going to settle. For the full twenty-five grand. But say La Marr needs twenty-four hours to raise the cash. That'll give us a chance. You know he'll bite at that if you say it right.'

Mae jumped up as he came through the office door, shot a finger to her lips to kill off his greeting, and silently waved him back out into the corridor. Seconds later she was following him out on tiptoe, pulling the door behind her as delicately as she could and flapping him away even further than he already was.

'Your cop pal's inside. Sullivan. I wanted to warn you,' she whispered. Tom couldn't help feeling a pang of mild despondency. He wasn't sure he could handle any more complications.

'Sullivan?' he said. 'So what? Why have you got me out here whispering?'

He went to move past her but she stuck out her arm and blocked him, supplementing the gesture with a glare and a low hiss. 'Shsssush, will you. That's what I'm trying to tell you. The man's in a terrible state. Grey as a block of granite and he looks like he spent the night in a ditch somewhere. I swear to God, I thought I heard him sobbing to himself in there.'

'Sobbing?' It was so out of character he could only assume she had imagined it. But, then, Mae wasn't given to that. 'How long has he been here?'

'Fifteen, twenty minutes, I guess. He already tried to leave once but I convinced him you called and said you were on your way in. He didn't even say anything, just slumped back in the chair. I'm telling you, Tom, be ready for it, he's not in a good way.'

'OK,' he said, his thoughts turning now to the situation with Ramirez. Something must've gone bad with that. He pulled his billfold from his pocket and asked her to go get coffee and donuts, and to take her time so that, whatever the problem was, Sullivan could feel free to unburden himself. She pulled a face, but hurried out nonetheless. Tom could still hear her heels clattering down the stairwell as he opened the inner door and was horrified to see that not only had she not been exaggerating – she'd actually been generous.

'Jesus, Thad. What in the name of God's happened?'

Sullivan looked up slowly, his eyes red-rimmed. He shifted in his seat, automatically preparing to get up. But Tom waved him back down, putting a hand on his shoulder while he took in his bedraggled state – from the hair awry on his hatless head through a hum of baked-on sweat and a general dishevelment of suit and shirt. There were no signs of any violence having been done to him, but that he had experienced some kind of shock was clear, such was the air of lostness and defeat that seemed to emanate from deep within. Tom pulled a chair round and sat down beside him, wondering now whether a dispute with Sullivan's wife could be the cause, given his old friend's capacity to occasionally stray. But he doubted it.

'Stay where you are, man. Don't move. Does Eleanor know where you are? I take it you haven't been home.'

Sullivan shook his head and a pained, guilt-stricken look clouded his features. 'I can't go home,' he said, his voice a hoarse, defeated rasp. 'I wouldn't be able to look her in the eye. That's why I came straight here. I didn't know what else to do.'

'OK, don't worry about that for now. But straight from where? Are you hurt?'

Sullivan moved his head again, more vigorously this time, and winced, putting a hand up to the back of his crown. Tom stood up and, through the gray thinning hair, noticed a vicious-looking bruise and a small, thinly scabbed tear in the skin.

'Christ, how did that happen?' He asked the question automatically but needed no answer. He'd seen enough cosh injuries in his time and this one was a doozie. It must have hit him full force. No wonder the man was in such a state. He was probably experiencing a concussion. He had an image of Sullivan mugged from behind in the dark, spending the night out cold on a sidewalk somewhere.

'Who did this Thad? Did you actually know? I'm thinking you didn't see it coming.'

Sullivan's eyes flicked to the door. 'Is the kid out there?' he asked.

For a second, Tom didn't realize what he meant. 'Mae? Don't worry, I sent her out for coffee. When she comes back, we'll see about getting something stronger. But c'mon, tell me now. What the hell happened to you?'

Sullivan met his eyes for the first time since he'd entered the room. 'They've framed me good and proper, Tom. That's what they've done. And there's nothing I can bloody do about it. Heath suspended me, says I'll be sacked within the week once they've got a board together, that I'll be lucky not to have charges brought against me. Jesus, how am I going to explain it to Eleanor? What're we going to do?'

He put his huge face in his hands and heaved out an enormous sob. Tom, trying to comprehend, pulled the hands away and demanded he pull himself together and explain, but this time to slow down and go back to the very beginning, encouraging him to explain what had happened more clearly and in greater detail. In fits and starts, Sullivan eventually told him how he'd been called up to Heath's office but found Ramirez there instead. After the blow to the head, he'd woken in one of the cells in Central, apparently dragged down there by Ramirez and, as it turned out when they both appeared later in the cell to rough him up a little more, Reynolds. He'd been left there overnight, then manhandled back up to Heath's office first thing in the morning, Ramirez accusing him of breaking in and causing the mess he'd seen them making there. Sullivan, his head still as much of a mess as the rest of him, had tried to deny it but was too befuddled to make his case. The captain, predictably, had never summoned Sullivan to his office and the only proof, the yellow note, had conveniently disappeared from his pocket.

A pretty frame-up, Tom thought, and just enough to get the thorn out of their sides, without the matter having to get too complicated. No matter what happened, there was no way

Sullivan would be permitted to work at Central under Heath again, and the possibility he would be sacked from the force altogether had got to be high, too. And he knew it. Whatever about the injustice of it, Sullivan's fears were already fixed on the impact it would have on his family if he were to be booted off the force. The man was getting distraught again.

'What the hell will happen to my boys, Tom? And Eleanor? We don't have much put away, we spend every dime we have on raising them—'

They heard the outer door open as Mae came in and made some noise to warn them of her presence. Sullivan wiped his face with the flats of his hands and sat up, determined to compose himself, and Tom went out, returning with two steaming coffees and a plate piled with donuts.

'OK, get these down you, Thad. Then we're going straight out to yours, to let Eleanor know you're all right and let her take care of you while you get some rest. After that, I promise you, we will sort this out.'

But the imminent prospect of breakfast hadn't left Sullivan looking any happier. If anything, he was more doubtful and serious than ever.

'I'm sorry, Tom. But I didn't tell you the worst of it.' He swallowed hard. 'Ramirez knows about Los Feliz. He knows about Mikey Ross. I'm sure of it now. That's why he's gunning for me. It won't be long before he's coming after you, too.'

By the time he delivered Sullivan out to his hillside home in Brentwood and got back on the road again, Tom had the full story in his head. Or as much of it as he and Sullivan could piece together between them. As they had feared, Ramirez had somehow got wind of the shootout in Los Feliz five months before. It could only have been one of Cornero's boys who spilled some or all of the story, and how much of it Ramirez really knew they did not and could not know. Sullivan had only heard him refer to it in the most oblique of terms to Reynolds while they stood over him in the cell in Central, thinking he was still out for the count. It wasn't clear either whether Ramirez had said anything about it to Heath, although they had to assume he hadn't, as Sullivan would most likely still be stuck in the caboose if he had. Perhaps Ramirez was saving that for later. The mere thought of that sword being held over him was enough to send a chill down Tom's spine.

Back on Wilshire, heading towards the city at a clip, thoughts turning over fast as the engine now, it wasn't only fear that was coursing through his mind, but fury too. Fury that Ramirez could bring his oldest friend in the world to such a low point. Fury that Ramirez might try to turn his guns on him, too. And fury that the pug-faced runt thought he could use the law as a shield to hide behind while he broke every rule in the book to feather his own nest. Some people are just too goddamn smart for their own good, he thought, as he gunned the roadster on across the blacktop. The streets were no more than a blur now, his foot on the gas, the sparse traffic yielding to his urgency. He had the bones of an idea in his head now. One that might solve all his problems in one go, if only he could be audacious enough to pull it off. If only he could have the luck to make it work.

TWENTY-SEVEN

B y the time he pulled up on Romaine he had it clear in his head. He ran across the road to Metro's colonial entrance and took it as a good omen that the same desk clerk who had been so helpful before was standing there at reception and not only acknowledged him with a friendly nod but also remembered him by name.

'Good to see you back, Mr Collins, what can we do for you today?'

'Is Mr Ingram in?'

'I'm sorry sir, no, he's not.'

That came as no surprise. Tom knew full well that Ingram was already on the train East – no doubt clattering and hooting its way across Arizona by now – with an advance party of publicity folk heading for New York, where he was due to be joined by Alice Terry and a select few cast members later in the week, for the premiere of *The Prisoner of Zenda*. But he needed his next question to sound quite urgent so he could get in on another ticket.

'Is there anyone else in still working on *Black Orchids*? I need a couple of questions answered for that thing I was working on for Mr Ingram. It should only take a couple of minutes.'

The receptionist ummed a little and thumbed through a Rolodex beneath the counter lip, eventually saying, 'Mr Seitz is in, but he's probably over in editing, I guess. Would he be able to help you?'

Tom nodded gratefully and grabbed the pass that was hurriedly written out for him and headed into the building. As soon as he was out of sight, he exited by another door and made his way across the lot, away from the chemical sheds and the editing building, and instead towards the production buildings. The first likely candidate he spotted, a preoccupied young man wearing thick spectacles, a frown and a stub of pencil above his ear, happily pointed out to him what looked like a line of poverty-row tar-paper shacks – the scenarists' and title-writers' compound.

Inside the place felt a lot cozier, if no roomier, than it looked outside; a rabbit warren of interlinked corridors and cubicle offices that appeared to get narrower the further they got from the entrance. Almost immediately, Tom heard the sound of a familiar throaty laugh coming from one of the offices nearest to him and made straight for it. He was just about to knock when the door was flung open and a tall, blond, rugged-looking guy – every inch a mustang wrangler in off the range – barreled out the door and almost collided with him. The man laughed amiably and apologized to Tom, though all his attention was still back in the room, into which he waved a toothsome adieu, excused himself to Tom again, then loped away looking very happy with himself.

Tom popped his head round the doorframe and rapped a hello. O'Hara looked up, beaming dreamily in expectation, and adjusted her smile to one of more ordinary welcome on realizing it was not her recent guest returned.

'Oh, Tom, hello, come in, I'm so sorry, I thought—'

'I can see what you were thinking, Mary, plain as day.'

He laughed out loud to see O'Hara blush and wave away her embarrassment with a hand fluttered across her lips. She was never the type not to look glamorous around the studio – she knew the game too well – but she had a particular glow and energy about her today, her hair newly set and a crisp silk blouse shimmering in the window light. Gone completely the glumness she'd bathed him in at the Oasis just a few nights before.

'So, who's this guy who's put the sun back in your smile?' He gestured towards the corridor.

'Oh, that's Helge. They breed 'em big in Sweden. He's gorgeous, no?'

'I'm not sure I'm one to judge that.'

'Oh yeah? That's not what I've been hearing from Ramon.' She laughed and flapped a hand at him. 'Only kidding – not that I need to apologize. But what can I do for you? You'll have to be quick as I have a rush job and a lot of words to kill by tomorrow morning.' With that she burst into song, her voice a surprisingly pure and melodious soprano.

'*Oh my heart's in a whirl, / Over one little girl*
Oh I love her, I love her, / Yes I do . . .'

Again Tom burst out laughing. 'Whatever that Helge's got, I want some of it. I've not seen you this delirious in months.'

O'Hara stopped, gave him a prim look. 'Now stop it, Tom. He's a friend, that's all. I just thought you of all people would recognize the song.'

'Sure I do. "Peg o' My Heart". Is that where that fake Irish name of yours has landed you now? I remember them shooting it at Lasky a few years back, right?'

She shook her head. 'Right, but it never got released. Which is why we decided to have another go. New scenario, the whole kit and kaboodle. Vidor's directing, and guess what, we signed up Laurette Taylor to play the lead.' She gave him a coy, side-long glance. 'Now see why I'm so happy?'

Tom was impressed. Laurette Taylor was everybody's idea of Peg. She'd been touring that stage play across America for years, to rapturous receptions – then again, she had a fabulous voice. Which wouldn't exactly help in a movie. And he wasn't convinced anyway that it was this and not the Swede that was behind O'Hara's high spirits. What he'd seen in her expression just now had to be down to more than just a job. Either way it spliced in nicely with why he'd come, and wiped away the last lingering anxieties over what he was about to ask her.

'That's great Mary,' he said, keeping it on the up. 'Really, great. Probably a good time to ask a favor from you, then. Yeah?'

'If you're looking for money, you've come to the wrong place.' She was joshing him, but he could tell it was only half in jest.

'No, not money,' he said. 'It's not even for me directly, in a way. But it *is* something only you can give me, Mare, and I need it badly.'

All the humor was gone from her expression now, concern and curiosity mingling in the creases on her brow. 'Gee, Tom, is everything OK? Talk about a mood killer. Is something the matter with Fay? Is that it?'

'No, nothing like that,' he said, more nervous now than he'd expected to be. 'It's just something you might not want to do. It's to do with, uh . . . with Mr Parrot.'

In the circumstances, the mention of her ex-husband's name was like dropping a depth charge into the conversation. Her expression darkened and Tom counted down the seconds, waiting to see if she would explode. But the detonation never came. Instead she just sniffed, blinked a few times, and tried a smile that didn't quite fit.

'So my secret's out,' she said.

'Was it a secret?'

'Well, no, I guess not. I just preferred as few people as possible to know, so I don't have to remember it so often myself. Anyway . . .' again she sniffed and gave him a bitter little smile that fitted the mood better, '. . . what could you possibly want from me to do with that rat?' A pantomime scowl deepened the lines of disapproval around her mouth, but a resigned shrug of her shoulders simultaneously suggested that she did not care all that much. It was encouragement enough.

'I need to see him, and in a hurry. I'm hoping he can help get a pal of mine out of trouble.'

'I don't rate your chances,' she snorted, all sarcasm now. 'I've only ever seen him get people into trouble.'

He pressed on regardless. 'I'm hoping he might make an exception in this case. I mean, if you were maybe to ask him to be nice to me. Or to give me a proper hearing at least.'

Again, she gave him a scornful look. 'I can't think of anything more likely to encourage him not to. You do realize the man hates me, Tom, don't you? Honestly, you would be better off calling that witch of a secretary of his and making an appointment like anyone else.'

'If I did I'd have to say what I wanted to see him about,' Tom said, with a grimace. 'And this has to be completely off the books. No one can know what it's about. Not even you. It's too dangerous.'

Her eyebrows shot up, intrigued, and a mischievous smile danced on her lips. 'Is this something that could get him into trouble? You're not going to blackmail him are you, Tom? I can't think of anyone who would deserve it more.'

Tom could tell the hook had gone in deep and knew now he had a chance at least. 'Not blackmail, no,' he said, looking down at his shoes but feeling her eyes bore into him nonetheless. 'Not as such. But he wouldn't want anybody knowing what I know. I promise you that. And I can promise you twice over that he won't like it. I mean, *really* won't like it.'

At that, O'Hara clapped her hands together and threw herself back in her chair excitedly. 'If you won't tell me what it is, why should I help you?'

Tom looked up at her. 'Like I said, I'm hoping it'll help get a pal of mine out of trouble. A good man, who never hurt anyone who didn't deserve it, and helped a good many through bad times when he could. Might even end up saving me a mess of trouble too. So, I'm desperately hoping this thing I've found out can push that through. It's a long shot, you know, but we're desperate. Which is the only reason I've come to you. Because, as I see it, you're the one who can most likely get me to the place where it might happen.'

She wasn't interested in any of that. 'Sure, Tom, that's all fine. But what I'm interested in is will it hurt *him*? Kent, I mean. Will it?'

'It'll hurt him more than not telling him.' Tom shrugged. He didn't add that it wouldn't hurt as much as handing the information he had to Olsen. Or even to her, right now.

'I got to warn you, Tom. You really don't want to cross him. He has a long, long reach, you know. Longer than anyone else in this damn city. And I should know.'

Tom smiled at her. 'You don't need to worry about me. I'm only the messenger.'

O'Hara grinned broadly. 'I can't guarantee he'll do anything I ask, Tom. But so long as there's a chance it'll hurt him, I'm in.'

She picked up the telephone from her desk, clicked and asked to be put through to a downtown number. 'Kent, it's Mary, yes . . . no, don't hang up . . .'

TWENTY-EIGHT

K ent Kane Parrot couldn't make a space for him until that evening. By the time Tom made it back downtown, darkness was falling, the home-time crowds were thinning, with only a smattering of storefronts still spilling light on the sidewalk. He'd been given directions to a commercial property on a side street near Pershing Square and, as he rode up to the top floor, he had a disquieting sense of being the only person in a vast building that was lightless but for the single flickering bulb in the elevator. The best he could hope for, he reckoned with a shiver, was that he was one of only two.

Parrot's greeting wasn't exactly informal but, then, neither was it unfriendly. He was a big man with a big chin, a strong handshake and a striking physical presence, standing a good two inches over Tom, and broader, too. The muscle and natural athleticism that had made him a star player on the USC football team in his college days was still not entirely subsumed by the fleshy layers of a life lived opulently in the succeeding twenty years. He was a man who bristled with power, exuding the natural authority of one who, born rich, had spent the rest of his life determined only to get richer. In his case, to all intents and purposes, by means of his legal practice and political connections.

Tom was surprised to find himself waved into a room that was laid out more in the manner of a plush parlor than an office. The last place he'd anticipated meeting Parrot was in his private quarters. But that's where this had all the appearance of being. Even the decor, done out in shades of green and brown, seemed chiefly intended to relax, despite bookshelves on one wall laden with legal tomes. Even the small bureau desk butted against the far wall was clear of paperwork or writing implements of any kind.

'I keep this place for private business,' Parrot said, ushering Tom towards a pair of plush green easy chairs, between which was a low table bearing a tray, two glasses and a venerable-looking bottle of bourbon about two thirds full.

'I hear you do a good bit of that.'

The lawyer gave him an assessing look and decided he could afford to ignore that.

Tom accepted the proffered glass, declining the siphon with which Parrot mixed his own drink.

'Well, Mary's got the house and, although they have offered me a private suite in the new Biltmore they're building on the Square, that won't be fully fitted out for a few months yet so this will have to do for now.' He grinned, adding: 'I think I'll probably survive here till then.'

Tom had remained standing while Parrot fixed the drinks but took a seat as the lawyer lowered himself into the chair opposite.

'So, what can I do for you, Collins? Mary says you're a good man and, while she might tell you otherwise now, I have always respected her judgment.' He paused a beat before adding: 'It's a judgment my own sources happen to concur with. You have a rare reputation for a man in your line of business, I'd say.'

'Probably because I haven't been in it long enough.' Tom took a sip of his drink, silently saluting its quality with a lift of his glass. It shouldn't have been any surprise the man had done his homework, and yet he was impressed that he had.

'I also hear they gave you the bum's rush over at Lasky last year. And wrongly, so I'm told.'

'Impressive sources,' Tom said.

'And, of course, I've come across your lady friend, too, the lovely Mrs Parker, out at that delightful club of hers. The Oasis, isn't it? Certainly lives up to its name.'

Tom could see now that he was laying it on thick, that this little power play was Parrot's way of showing him his lowly place in the pecking order, of warning him not to be too tiresome. But, still, it was disconcerting to hear Fay's name brought into the conversation.

'Clearly, you know all there is to know about me, Mr Parrot. So, maybe we should get down to business.'

'Of course.' Parrot smiled. 'But first perhaps you would return the favor by saying what you know of me. Just so we're both sure you know who you're dealing with.' There was an edge to his voice now, a reaction to Tom presuming to take the reins.

'I'd have to be frank,' Tom said with a rueful smile.

The lawyer chuckled and made an inviting gesture with his hand. 'I like the sound of that. Please, be my guest.'

'Well, the truth is I didn't know a whole lot about you, Mr Parrot, until I went asking among people who I thought would know. Not your ex-wife, I should add. I only begged the favor of calling you from her. All she said was to be sure I pronounced your name Parr-*oh* and not Parr-*ot*.'

It was petty to have a dig at the man's vanity so early on, but him coming out with Fay's name like that had done what was intended and got under his skin. Parrot adopted a look of serene unconcern and said something fancy in French, which Tom took to be an invitation to continue.

'To be brief about it, people mostly told me that you are not so much Mayor Cryer's right-hand man, as the man who stands above him pulling his strings.'

The lawyer swallowed that along with another sip of his bourbon. 'Nonsense, of course, but it's hardly the first time I've heard it said. Go on.'

'I was also told that you devote only one hand to Mayor Cryer, because the other is hand in glove with Charlie Crawford, running most of the rackets in this city, or at least creaming off a nice fat cut.'

Parrot's response to that was to curl his upper lip back over his big teeth and emit a barely audible sough of impatience.

'I don't suppose that's anything you haven't heard before either,' Tom continued. 'In any case, it's no concern of mine. The only thing that interests me is what they said about you having a great deal of influence over the running of the police department. And that Chief Oaks is in your pocket. That's the only part of anything that I'm interested in, and why I asked you to see me, Mr Parrot.'

Parrot put his glass down on the table and leaned forward in his chair, reaching out for the bourbon bottle, pouring himself another slug and offering Tom a top-up.

'You're mighty plain spoken,' Parrot said, sitting back again.

'For a man I've never met before, knocking on my door asking favors.'

'You're the one urged me to be frank, Mr Parrot. And it's not a favor I want. It's a trade. That's how most of the big men I've ever met work. Don't like giving something for nothing. I was hoping to make a deal with you. That's all.'

Parrot snorted, his shoulders stiffer now, more aggressive, as if his patience was beginning to wear thin. 'Well, I'm struggling to see any kind of deal I would need to do with you, Mr Collins. But I suppose I'd better let you say your piece, or I'll never hear the end of it from Mary. Go ahead, enlighten me.'

'Well, in a nutshell, a bull from Central is giving a good friend of mine some serious trouble. I thought you might be persuaded to have a word in Chief Oaks's ear for me. Have it stopped.'

Parrot sat forward in his chair with a hearty laugh. 'A word in the chief's ear, is it?' He slapped the top of his thigh like he'd just been told the best gag ever. 'Is that all you want? And no doubt your connections, whoever they are, will have told you that I charge a set fee for such favors, did they? Well, I'm afraid you're on a hiding to nothing there, Mr Collins. Because, contrary to popular opinion, apparently, the chief is not "in my pocket" as you so quaintly put it, and he is not in office simply to do my bidding. Not even something as trivial as this.'

'Don't you want to hear what I've got to trade?'

'There really is no point, Mr Collins. I run a busy law office by day and in my spare time I am honored to assist my political acquaintances with the running of this great city of ours in whatever capacity I may. I hardly need remind you that Mayor Cryer was elected, and Chief Oaks subsequently appointed, on an anti-corruption ticket. If your "friend" is in trouble with the police, let him or her get a lawyer and deal with it through the proper channels, like anyone else. Now if you don't mind, I think we're through here.'

Parrot shifted his heavy frame in the chair and rose to his feet, finishing off his drink with a gulp. Tom remained in his chair, waiting until the lawyer, halfway to the door, turned and saw with some surprise that he had not moved.

'Did I not make myself clear, Mr Collins? I want you to leave.'

'And I will, sir. I have no desire to take up more of your time than necessary, but I do need you to hear me out. It'll be very greatly to your benefit, I promise. And to Mayor Cryer's, too, in fact. Would it help if I told you that my friend is a Central cop, too, and that he's being set up for a murder he didn't commit by one of his fellow detectives. A guy called Gab Ramirez. I think you might know him.'

That last was just a guess, but Tom saw straight away the flicker of recognition in Parrot's eyes, and that he didn't want to betray it.

'Ramirez? No, I don't think so. Should I?' Parrot said cautiously, sitting into his chair again like he didn't want Tom to notice.

'He's one of Captain Heath's boys in the Vice Squad. Just the sort of bad apple Oaks ought to be rooting out on this anti-corruption ticket of yours. Some say Ramirez is running half the dope dens in the city, or at least collecting the dues on 'em. Either way, he has taken a personal beef against my friend – one of the best detectives on the force – and turned it into a vendetta.'

Ramirez's name had only been enough to stall Parrot for a moment. The lawyer raised his hands, palms flat out, in a gesture of exasperation. 'That's all well and good. But I still don't see what any of this has to do with me, Mr Collins. Or why it should be.'

'I was just getting to that, sir. Can I just ask, given your interest in these matters: do you recall the death of Deputy Chief Al Devlin down at the Harbor a few months ago?'

Parrot's brow furrowed deeply but his vanity got the better of him. 'Yes, of course I do. A tragic case. I was on the committee that appointed Devlin.'

'So, you'll know all the bad stuff, too, that came out about him after his suicide.' Tom decided to move on quickly when he saw the lawyer's reaction to that. 'The thing is, Ramirez was a big pal of Devlin's, as it turns out, and he's somehow got it into his head that Sullivan had something to do with his death, although everyone else accepted it was suicide. Now he's trying to get Heath to open an investigation into Sullivan over a body that was found out in Baldwin Hills last week.

He's even gone and set him up for a break-in at the station. Neither of which Sullivan had anything to do with. It is an entirely malicious attempt to stain the character of a man who – up till now – had an unblemished record on the Los Angeles force.'

Ever since Tom mentioned Devlin, Parrot had seemed more and more disquieted by the line of conversation, like a man who wanted to shut it down but needed to hear just a scrap or two more.

'If this Sullivan is as pure as you say, why doesn't he just accept the inquiry and let it play out?' Parrot said, adopting an airy, lawyerly tone. 'Surely, the best way to establish his innocence is to have it proved independently.'

'Because, as you know, sir, these things have a habit of not always working out the way they should. Ramirez has a lot of clout in the department. And he's not above falsifying evidence to get his way. In fact, like I said, he has already done so.'

'That's quite an accusation, Mr Collins.'

'Sure it is. Because it's the truth.'

Parrot let out a long breath and clapped his hands on his thighs like he'd come to a conclusion. 'Well, it all sounds rather troubling, to be sure. And sounds more than ever, I must say, like something into which I could in no way justify sticking my nose.' He gave a little rueful laugh. Affecting an air of amused amiability, he leaned forward confidingly, lowering his voice. 'But I must admit that you did intrigue me, Collins, with what you said earlier about information that might be to the mayor's and my benefit. Now what would that be exactly?'

Long before Tom even got to the punch, Parrot was on his feet again, padding the room like a caged animal, his face flush with a sharply focused fury and a keen sense of outrage at his own inability to see a way round the problem.

'This is an unmitigated outrage! I will make it my personal mission to destroy the infernal woman. Who in the name of God does she think she is?'

'I think we both know she is possessed of an unusually strong sense of who she is, Mr Parrot. Which is probably why she's so beloved by the movie-going public. But I must remind you, sir, as I've said before, Miss La Marr has nothing whatsoever to do with this. She has no idea I'm here, and if she did I have absolutely no doubt that she would be as outraged and as scandalized as you clearly are. Like I said, she is the last person in the world who would want the fact that she's having the child, let alone speculation about its paternity, splashed all over the newspapers. Other than Mayor Cryer, that is.'

Tom allowed himself a pause to absorb the glare of superheated anger directed at him by Parrot.

'No one would dare publish it. We would crush them. It's her word against his.'

'Well, that's just my point, Mr Parrot. You might be able to control the *Times* but the Hearst press has made no secret of its desire to bring Mayor Cryer down, and this reporter I told you about works for the *Herald*. Especially with Hays in town, you know Hearst will direct them to do everything they can to make hay with Miss La Marr's movie connections.'

Parrot was listening but not making a lot of sense himself, repeatedly questioning Tom's own paternity – if only idiomatically – under his breath.

Not that it bothered Tom.

'And it is not really a question of Miss La Marr's word, is it? It's this Deeley who's doing the actual accusing. He says the mayor and her were seen together on a number of occasions, and intimately so – not least by you, I might add. And while you might be able to persuade yourself and the cronies and colleagues who attended these private parties to conveniently forget that fact, there is the matter of an independent witness who has submitted in writing an account in which the mayor retired to another room with Miss La Marr. And that when she retired to an adjoining room – with you, Mr Parrot, I believe – her ears left her in no doubt as to what was going on next door.'

Tom let the flood of imprecation that followed that remark flow like molten lead down around his head and shoulders, grateful now that Parrot resided in a building that was empty this time of night. Had they been anywhere more public, he doubted the lawyer would have given vent so freely to a rage that was, palpably, not that of a man being slandered or unfairly impugned but of one who's been flat-out nailed to the post. Even so, Tom knew he couldn't afford to let it run any further, or risk pushing Parrot beyond the point of cooperation. He had to pull him back and calm him down. Show him the way out and win something back for himself. And for Sullivan. He waited until the lawyer ran out of curses and carpet and, hands flat on the wooden sill, paused to look out the tall, arching window overlooking the lamp-lighted gardens of Pershing Square below.

'You know, none of this needs to happen, Mr Parrot.' Tom's tone was more placating now. 'Even the mayor himself need never know about it. Because Miss La Marr sure as hell doesn't want him to have anything to do with the child. I swear on my life we can make this go away.'

Parrot looked over his shoulder at him, exhausted by his own anger, a look of intense bitterness on his face. 'On your life?' he said skeptically. 'I doubt that that'd be collateral enough. But go on, then, I guess the time's come for it. Hit me with how much you want?'

Tom didn't need to fake the look of disappointment on his face. He shrugged his shoulders. 'I already told you my price. It doesn't seem like such a high one given the trouble I'm offering to save you, but if that's where you're still at in terms of doing a deal, I guess you were right all along, and I should go.'

He turned and took his hat from the side table where he'd dropped it on the way in, and slipped it on his head, smoothing the brim between his thumb and forefinger. 'Before I go, I'll remind you one more time that the meeting with those reporters is set for tomorrow afternoon. If you do decide to change your mind, don't take too long over it.'

He wasn't halfway to the door before the lawyer called him back, indignant resignation the keynote in his voice now.

'What did you say was the name of this detective you're so keen to protect?'

TWENTY-NINE

I t didn't take them long to fix it up between them. It was a good plan that left both sides with enough room for their own way of seeing things, and enough clout to ensure both punishment and silence. Tom's main concern had been to keep Drew out of it as much as possible, to avoid a situation in which Miss La Marr would learn the substance of what he was doing. That was as much to protect her as Sullivan, but still he couldn't fend off a stab of guilt that he had slipped his own deal in alongside it and used her situation to his own advantage. But that was something he would have to live with. Parrot, meanwhile, was a man transformed. Once he swallowed the bitter pill and came to terms with what had to be done, suddenly he was all efficiency, treating the matter as just another business deal. It took no more than a couple of calls to ensure the money would be in place and ready for collection from the chief cashier at the International Savings and Exchange Bank the following day. His call to the district attorney was put straight through. But the matter with Chief Oaks and Ramirez, Parrot said, would have to wait until the morning. Tom had no choice but to take it on trust.

He was back on Sunset and in bed by midnight, waking again only when Fay slipped in beside him in the early hours, the silk of her nightgown cool against his back, her breath hot on his neck, warm arms around him, snuggling in close. What happened after that he remembered only in terms of scent and flesh, a wave of passion built and then released again to sleep. Maybe it was that, or the relaxed balcony breakfast they had together that morning – fresh orange juice, eggs and rolls and strong, strong coffee, the fresh salt air breezing in off the coast and everything they said and did enshrining his belief they were meant to be together – that left his guard down so low, let his stomach lurch with such a sharp stab of anxiety when, as he was about to leave the apartment, the telephone rang.

Fay, with a look of some concern, called him back saying it was Mae.

'Look, I wouldn't want spoil your morning, but I got in early again and just took a call . . .'

The anxiety in Mae's voice seemed to make her stop mid-sentence, and he had to tell her to out with the rest. 'Go on.'

'It was Mr Samaniegos, calling from Venice,' she continued. 'He sounded . . . he sounded upset, y'know. I asked if I could do anything to help and he said no, it was you he wanted, and he kind of gulped that out. So I asked him whatever was the matter and he said, like he was just about to sob, that he . . . he'd done something really stupid last night and got in touch with . . . would it be Gianni, the name? I could barely make him out by then, he was mumbling so low. I don't think he got much sleep last night for the worry of it.'

Tom cursed out loud and looked at his wristwatch. It was only a quarter till nine. Enough time to get out there and be back in time. But he had to call in on Drew first and talk through the set-up with him, and that required a trip downtown. Maybe a telephone call would do it. It would save so much time.

'Was he still at the St Mark?'

'He didn't say he wasn't.'

'Good. I want you to call him back now and give him my number here. Then I want you to call enquiries and get a number for a lawyer working out of offices on Ninth Street – name is Roth, Herman Roth, yeah? But don't call it, whatever you do.'

He broke the connection, thinking hard. He cursed himself for telling Samaniegos that Gianni was still alive. That had been a mistake, he saw now, but the man had a right to know after all. What was the worst that could've happened? Had Samaniegos had a drink too many and tried to get in touch with him? That had to be it. But surely he wouldn't have—

He was interrupted by the telephone ringing again and he snatched the earpiece from the prong, expecting to hear Samaniegos's voice. But it was Mae again. 'Reception desk says he's still there but when they connect me through it just rings and rings. Should I try again in a couple of minutes?'

'Give it five,' he said, nodding. 'Did you get that other number for me?'

He scribbled the number down, hoping he'd never have to use it. Then he clicked again and got through to Drew's office. Joan put him straight through.

'I got what we needed,' Tom said, and prepared to field a spew of pointless questions from the lawyer. 'Look, Frank, I'm not exaggerating when I promise you that the less you know about this the better. I mean, like I never meant anything before. And that goes for Miss La Marr, too. I guess it's what comes of having friends in high places. You'll just have to trust me, OK?'

Predictably that was not OK as far as Drew was concerned, but Tom put some grit in his voice and quieted him eventually. 'It's the only option available to you, Frank. Now, what time did you say you'd settle with Roth today?'

'I went for as late as possible, two o'clock,' Drew said, sounding not unrelieved now that he knew it was out of his hands. 'Roth said that was the deadline for the evening papers.'

Tom cursed to himself, it was still too early.

'OK, that's good. But I need you to push him back until three. That's the earliest we can get this deal in place. Can you do that? Tell him it'll still hit the main editions. And give him some lawyerly excuse why you can't be there to do the deal yourself. Say you've got to be in court or something. And that I will be the man with the twenty-five grand in cash, and I'll meet him inside the window at Al Levy's Café on Sixth, at three on the dot. Be clear on exactly what you want for the money and let my secretary Mae have the details. Got all that?'

THIRTY

As far as Tom had been concerned, getting Samaniegos out to Venice had been simply a matter of getting him out of downtown Los Angeles, full stop. Now, as he gunned the Dodge west along Pico, and onward to the broad, far-reaching vistas of Venice Boulevard, he was cursing himself for sending him quite so far out of town. All the way to the Pacific shore and the plush comforts of the Hotel St Mark, right on the oceanfront. Couldn't get much further west than that. No, sir. Not without getting your feet wet. What a goddamn idiot he'd been. Especially as Venice had been famous since the day it opened for one major pain in the ass – tourists clogging up its fake Italian thoroughfares with endless, slow-moving traffic. No one, not a single goddam one of them, seemed capable of appreciating that even out here in cardboard cut-out paradise, a man could be in a god-awful hurry.

Eventually he made it through the snarl of traffic around the Lagoon and on to Windward, from where it was a marginally less tangled run out to the boardwalk. He found a place to park by one of the carved Corinthian columns supporting the arcade of stores that ran beneath the St Mark's upper floors – only the oversized electric sign for the Owl Drug Store, protruding from the pillar into the street, spoiled the historical effect. But then, that was southern California in a nutshell.

As soon as the heavy plate-glass paneled lobby doors closed behind him, Tom felt a whole lot better. Inside, the hotel's dark, cool interior was as opulent as the exterior promised, and a blissfully quiet contrast to the heat and clamor of the street outside, shaded by half-closed shutters on the internal courtyard windows and dotted here and there with davenports and easy chairs, all of them unoccupied. At the desk, the lone desk clerk, a young man as tall as Tom but skinny enough to be made entirely out of bone, gave him a broad smile and an overly enthusiastic welcome to the hotel.

'I'm looking for Mr Samaniegos. Is he in, do you know?'
Tom followed the receptionist's practiced glance over his
shoulder, towards the tiers of mahogany pigeonholes on the
wall behind, bearing post and room keys. He breathed out
on seeing the key for 403 was hanging there. 'OK, I see that
he is. My name is Collins. Can you let him know I'm on my
way up?'

'Yes, of course, Mr Collins,' the clerk said, picking up the
telephone and clicking the cradle. 'The other gentlemen are
already here. They only just went up ahead of you.'

Tom, already turning towards the stairs, was brought up short
by that and he turned back just in time to reach out a hand and
prevent the young man getting a connection. 'What're you
talking about? What other gentlemen?'

'Why, the two who arrived just before you, sir.' The receptionist carefully lowered the earpiece back on to the apparatus
and returned it to the desk. 'Not ten minutes ago. They said
Mr Samaniegos was expecting them, and not to bother
calling up.'

From the disapproving look on the boy's face, he could tell
something was not right. But then he knew that already, given
that no one but himself, Mae and Alice Terry were supposed
to be aware that Samaniegos was staying out at the St Mark.

'These two guys, eh, what do they look like?'

'Well, I couldn't say for sure—'

The young man was squirming on the twin barbs of decorum
and discretion, so Tom cut him off. 'C'mon, out with it quickly.
Were they Italians? A bit roughhouse, maybe? Is that it?'

The boy quickly looked over his shoulder again towards the
door into the back office, then leaned across the desk, whispering. 'Well, the big one didn't open his mouth but he sure
didn't look like anyone who would be a guest here.'

'Real big, right?' Tom blew out his cheeks a little and bunched
his shoulders like a bear but put a hand up to stop the kid saying
any more, taking his eager nodding as the confirmation he
required. It was not good news.

'The other one smaller, yeah? About so tall . . .?' Tom put
a flat hand up to his shoulder, approximating Gianni's height.
'Good looking?'

A minor eye-roll of consideration and a downward twist of the mouth. 'If you like 'em damaged, I guess.'

Tom considered that for a moment but let it go. 'Now look, this is important. I'm going up to the room and whatever happens don't let them know I'm coming. OK? Meanwhile, have you got a house detective here, or a cop on the books?'

The receptionist nodded. 'Sure, I mean, McNulty does that for us, but he's not due in for another half-hour.'

Tom grimaced. 'OK, so if he comes in early, send him on up. But whatever you do, even if you hear a rumpus, don't call the local cops in unless I tell you or things get real bad. OK? Your boss and me, Mr Standen, we've got an arrangement that Mr Samaniegos isn't to attract any undue attention. You understand? Have you got that?'

Tom left the boy there, nodding in agreement, but with a look of deep uncertainty curtaining his face. He ran for the staircase, taking the steps two at a time, propelling himself up hand after hand by the polished wooden rail. Luckily, no one was coming down so he made it up the four flights to the top floor in under a minute, pausing at the crest to look down the corridor to Samaniegos's room and consider what to do next. There was only one thing for it, he reckoned. Go in mob-handed and take them by surprise.

But before he was forced to act on it, Tom dismissed that idea. Already he could hear the muffled sounds of raised voices emanating from further down the dim-lit corridor on the ocean side of the hotel, a chink of light about halfway along indicating a door left ajar. Approaching as quietly as he could, he thought he recognized Vitale's gruff Italian tones but couldn't make out what he was saying, other than that it was loud, angry and threatening. Then he heard Gianni's voice, shrill, rising in protest, and what sounded like the dull thump of a fist on flesh followed by a crash. He grabbed the door handle and pushed in, stepping into the living room of a suite with an open-door bedroom off to the left. First thing he saw was Samaniegos, startled and terrified, scrambling to right himself on the floor, his shirt and necktie in disarray, a side table tipped over beside him and Gianni uselessly trying to push Vitale back, pleading with him to stop.

Tom's arrival brought everyone to a split-second standstill, all three faces turning towards him, the electric crackle of violence in the air a sharp contrast to the bright sunlight bouncing in through the arched mullion windows overlooking the untroubled blue of sea and sky outside.

'You.' Vitale was the first to open his mouth. 'I remember you. I should ha' known you were in on this when I saw you there. I should ha' dealt with you then.'

Tom said nothing, taking in a scene that wasn't quite how he'd seen it at first. Yes, Samaniegos was on the floor, clutching his chest, looking like a punch had landed him there. But as Tom moved slowly into the room towards him, he saw Gianni was not in fact pushing at Vitale but struggling to get away himself, arched over backwards now by Vitale's lowering grip on the hair at the back of his neck, and desperately trying to retreat from a four-inch blade Vitale was raising in front of his face.

'Don' you move,' the big Italian growled at Tom. He cursed something in Italian and stepped back with a grunt, dragging the goggling Gianni with him, gasping from the pain of the bigger man's grip. Tom could see now why the desk clerk had demurred on the subject of his looks. Gianni's face already bore a number of livid bruises that the careful application of some face powder hadn't entirely managed to mask.

'Wha' the hella you to him, anyhow?' Vitale continued, indicating Samaniegos with a flick of his eyes. 'You his auntie or somethin'?'

In any other circumstances the idea he could be thought of as some kind of sugar daddy might have amused Tom. As it was, the taunt in Vitale's voice showed he didn't even believe it himself. If he had Tom down as that kind, he wouldn't have thought twice about coming at him with the knife. But something was holding the big Italian back. Was it maybe that he took Tom for some kind of cop? The mark of it takes a hell of a time to wear off, Tom knew. Vitale wouldn't be the first.

'I'm here to stop you menacing Mr Samaniegos here,' Tom said, putting as much firmness and formality into his voice as he could. 'And I'm advising you to get out of here right now,

Mr Vitale, while you can. I have already asked reception to call the police. They'll be here any minute.'

He noted how the Italian's brow furrowed briefly at the mention of his name, and for a moment thought it might have been enough. But it was not. The furrowing brow was instantly joined by a jut of furious skepticism in the Sicilian's jaw.

'Cops my ass,' Vitale roared at him. 'If you had help coming, you'd a brought 'em with you. So shut the fuck up and listen – or, better, watch, cos I'm gonna show you and your pansy boyfriend what happens when you do the dirt on me – an' what I'm gonna do to his pretty-boy face if he don't pay up right now.'

With another yelp of pain from Gianni, Vitale wrestled him to his knees and bent over him like he was about to cut his throat, lowering the knife in front of his face. By now, Tom had inched almost halfway across the room towards Samaniegos, who darted a glance back at him. He was back on his feet now, supporting himself on a carved walnut dining chair, pale with fright and the horror of what was about to happen.

A heart-stopping scream from Gianni rooted Tom to the spot. In a flash, Vitale had drawn the blade diagonally up and across the boy's jaw, cheek and forehead, and a flare of blood spilled out across the young man's face. Appalled, Tom saw a smile of carnal satisfaction play across Vitale's features, and knew he had to do something to stop him. This was not a warning. This was a man enjoying his work, who was set on doing worse.

But what happened next took him completely by surprise. Sensing a movement to his left, Tom heard Samaniegos emit an unearthly howl and launch himself across the room, swinging the walnut dining chair above his head and hurling it at Vitale. It caught the big Sicilian by surprise, too. Unable to avoid the blow, all he could do was raise a defensive arm, releasing the shrieking Gianni from his grip just as the heavy chair crashed down, followed by Samaniegos, who he swatted away instinctively and sent crashing into a table on the near side of the room.

Vitale was still standing, still armed and angrier than ever. But he was off balance now and not a little bit confounded.

Tom saw his chance. All he could think of was Joe Martin as he grabbed a heavy seat cushion from the sofa and, thrusting it out, an unconvincing shield against the bloody knife in the big man's hand, ran at him, his right arm tucked all the way back, ready to land the biggest haymaker of his life.

Luck was on his side. As Vitale tried to sidestep him, he caught his foot on Gianni, still cowering beneath him, hands covering his face. The big man dropped his guard for a second and presented an undefended left temple to Tom's flying fist. He felt the bones in his wrist scream in pain as his bunched knuckles connected with Vitale's skull just forward of his left ear and, against the odds, the big man staggered and fell to his knees with a floor-rattling thud, the knife falling from his hand as he went down.

Gasping, cradling his aching hand against his belly now, Tom swung round and planted the heel of his heavy brogue into the side of Vitale's face. Still the ape failed to keel over completely. Alarmed now, Tom glanced around quickly for something solid and heavy to finish him off with. Samaniegos got there before him, rushing in with a large glass ashtray raised ready to strike. But he never got to deliver the blow. Impossibly, Vitale was rising on his haunches, one hand to the side of his head, the other reaching round behind him and pulling a pistol from his waistband.

'Watch out, he's got a—' was all Tom got out of his mouth before lunging for Samaniegos, grabbing him by the waist and rolling him to the floor behind the settee just before the first shot rang out, going wide thanks to the big man's disorientation. Tom looked up, saw there was a clear route from behind the sofa to the door, and gestured at it urgently, telling Samaniegos to get the hell out while he distracted Vitale.

'Go on, go now,' he screamed as he raised his head above the sofa-back, just enough to get a sight on Vitale and hurl the ashtray at him, which struck home with a thud on the forearm raised to deflect it. It was just enough to give him time to run for the door himself, grabbing the scrambling Samaniegos by the shirt-collar as he went and propelling them both out into the corridor. The last thing Tom saw as he glanced back, toppling through the door, was Gianni, his face cascading blood

THIRTY-ONE

Above the deafening thump of his heart and the thunder of shoe-leather as he and Samaniegos raced along the corridor towards the stairs, Tom thought he heard a piercing animal shriek followed by a rumbling howl and, then, the unmistakable crack of a gunshot. And another. Then nothing more. Still they ran.

The noise had brought one or two concerned residents into the corridor and Tom roared at them to get back in their rooms and bolt their doors until such help as might be coming arrived. As they reached the head of the stairs Tom looked over the stair rail and saw that help was, indeed, coming imminently. A couple of cops led by a portly guy in a trench and hat – presumably the house dick McNulty – all with their irons out, were running up the steps at the double. Which forced him to do a quick rethink.

'C'mon, this way,' he said, grabbing Samaniegos's elbow and pulling him towards a service door on the far side of the landing. 'We're better off leaving them to deal with it on their own. There'll be a hell of a lot fewer questions to answer, if we do.'

Tom pushed the actor through the swing door and they found themselves at the top of a plain concrete set of service stairs. He started down them, but now Samaniegos wouldn't budge, refusing to follow him.

'What about Gianni?' He shook himself free of Tom's grip and turned back towards the door. 'We can't just leave him there. He needs help.'

'Are you kidding me?' Tom only just caught him from pushing through the door, yanking him back unceremoniously and shoving him hard up against the wall. 'You can't go back out there.'

'What're you doing? Let me go!' Samaniegos wriggled in his grasp, trying to extricate himself. But even if he hadn't been quaking from head to foot, his efforts would have been in vain. 'We have to help him.'

It was only then that Tom saw the blood on Samaniegos's white shirt, a blossoming bloom of red spreading by the second above his waistline. 'Jesus, Ramon, have you been hit? Are you all right?'

Samaniegos lowered his eyes in panic, a hand pressed to his side as, in sudden realization, he gasped in pain.

'Oh, *dios* . . .' he gasped, pulling the hand away and blanching visibly as he saw it was covered in blood.

He looked as if he was about to collapse but all Tom could think of more than ever now were the precious seconds of time ticking away.

'Does it hurt? Ramon?' Tom whispered at him fiercely. 'I mean really hurt. Can you walk with me?'

Samaniegos took a deep breath, winced, but shook his head. 'It's OK,' he gasped again. 'I'm OK. But . . . what about Gianni?'

'Look, Ramon, I see why you want to help him. I swear I do. But the hotel guys will sort out Gianni. Either way, in a few minutes the cops will be swarming all over this hotel. That's a serious incident we were just involved in, and they're going to want to ask questions. Hard questions about what you were doing there. About how it is you know those guys in your room. Do you want to have to answer that? To a bunch of meat-head cops? If we go now you can always say they broke in. That you were never there when it happened.'

'But, Gianni, I have to . . .' He gasped, hopelessly, like he was on the verge of desperation, even words failing him now.

'C'mon Ramon, please,' Tom broke in again. He looked down, saw blood begin to seep over Samaniegos's belt and drip on to the staircase. He swallowed hard. If they didn't go now, this minute, they might soon not have the choice.

He relaxed his grip on Samaniegos's lapels, patted them down and, putting his hands gently on his shoulders instead, looked the young man directly in the eyes.

'You must know, Ramon, there's not a cop in the county who would stay quiet about this. They'll go straight to the papers. "Handsome young movie star about to break big, Ramon, involved in hotel incident with blackmailer and his Romeo."

Can you imagine the field day the papers would have? How mean and vicious they will be? I promised the Ingrams I would do everything I could to keep your name out of this. That's because they care about you, Ramon. And you've got to think it's not just you that would be finished by this. You'd probably take down Mr Ingram and Miss Terry and Miss La Marr with you too. Especially with Hays in town – can you imagine the fuss? You'd go straight to the top of that Doom List of his. You don't want that, do you? After all they've done for you? And your whole career ahead of you, too?'

'But what will happen if we . . .?' An unfinished question; already the pallor was ebbing from Samaniegos's face, his eyebrows clenching tight as the pain began to break through the shock of what had happened. Then a sudden scuffle of activity outside, voices bellowing – McNulty and the cops again – returned the look of panic to his eyes. In an urgent whisper Tom pleaded with him again.

'We've got to go, Ramon,' Tom repeated in an urgent whisper. 'You more than me. You have to get that seen to, and fast. Whatever happens now, Gianni's going to be in trouble. And the worst thing you could do – as much for him as for you – is drag yourself into it publicly. We can always find another, more private way to help, if it comes to it. Get him a good lawyer, on the quiet, yeah? Now c'mon, they'll be in here after us any second.'

It was enough. Enough to get a distraught and wounded man who barely knew what he was doing any more to nod reluctantly and, trying to staunch the blood with his hands, turn and follow Tom, stumbling down the stairs and out into the dazzling sunlight at the rear of the hotel just as, unknown to them, a truck pulled up on the other side of the building, spilling out an entire company of cops. Tom took his jacket off and wrapped it round Samaniegos's shoulders, leading him away. Three minutes later, they were in the Dodge, making their way out of Venice on the coast road north towards Ocean Park to avoid the traffic and the stares of one or two passing drivers who, not content with the glories of coast and sea and sky laid out around them, wondered instead at the sight of a handsome young man doubled over on the bench seat, weeping uncontrollably.

THIRTY-TWO

F ay was out on the street, waiting, when they pulled up at the Oasis. The door leading up to her apartment above the club was already open, a squat bottle of Napoleon brandy opened and ready on the plate-glass coffee table in her living room, a box of cotton swabs beside it. Tom had risked stopping at a place he knew out near the Hillcrest to call ahead and warn her they were coming in. He couldn't chance taking Samaniegos to a hospital and wasn't convinced he needed it anyway. And it wasn't practical to take him anywhere else. Not in the time he had to work with. He still had to get back downtown ahead of his meeting at three o'clock.

Within minutes a reliably discreet medic of Tom's acquaintance arrived at the apartment to assess the anonymous victim's needs. The patient, Dr Kreutzer concluded upon examination, had been fortunate to sustain a minor and – in the accepted measure of such things – uncomplicated flesh wound. The slug had done little more than rip through a crease of fat and skin an inch or so just below the rib cage. The insertion of a stitch or three, an absorbent dressing, and the regular application of an unguent to prohibit infection, should be all that would be required. Other than rest, of course. It was imperative that the patient should rest as much as possible for the next twenty-four hours, he said, counting out four sachets of a powdered sleeping draught and placing them in Fay's hand – before leaving as unobtrusively as he had arrived.

'It's fine,' Fay said, waving away Tom's repeated apologies, and at the same time cleaning a nick to his forehead that he had somehow, and entirely unknowingly, acquired during the tussle. They had left Ramon to try and get some rest in the guest bedroom, although even behind the closed door they suspected he was wide-eyed and weeping still. 'Poor boy,' she said, 'what a mess to be in, and just as his star was about to shine.'

She sat down, thoughtful, on the low white sofa, and gestured towards the drinks cabinet. Tom mixed her one, thankful to have something to do, even briefly, to cover his anxiety. He was pretty sure Vitale could not have got out of that room before the cops got there; or, even if he had, that there was no way a volcanically angry, vengeance-seeking Vitale could trace them back to Fay's. But he might find his way to the office, and Mae, and that was worrying Tom. He needed to be certain.

'Are you not having one?' Fay asked, surprised, taking her glass from him.

He picked up his half-drunk cognac from the other table and raised it. 'I'll stick to this for now. I've got to get back downtown and I've still got a couple of calls to make. See if I can throw some light on what happened back there. Speaking of which, did you get through to anyone just now?'

Fay nodded. 'Alice Terry was in. She said she would come right over, soon as she could get a cab.'

He looked at his wristwatch for the umpteenth time. 'That'll be any minute now, I guess.'

Fay nodded in affirmation, calm as ever in a crisis. Even when a man who'd been shot in the stomach turned up at her door and trailed blood in across her snowy-white carpet. She smiled at Tom, and he felt a little better about the situation. Just then the doorbell rang.

'That'll be her now,' Fay said, and went to let her in.

'I'll go make those calls then.'

He went into the kitchen to use the wall telephone. He got a connection to the office number in Gower and told Mae to close up quickly, go home, stay away for the rest of the day – and to not ask any more questions. That done, he could think clearly again. He clicked through to the operator, asking to be connected to the offices of the *Argos* newspaper out in Venice, and to put him through to the newsroom. He checked his wristwatch again. Ninety minutes had passed since they skipped out of the hotel. It took the girl a while to make the connection, all lines in and out of Venice were busy for some reason, but eventually she put him through.

'Hello, hello, is that the *Argos*?' The line was so bad he should have been yelling into the mouthpiece, but he couldn't risk being heard in the other room. A distant 'Yeah' crackled down from the other end. 'OK, this is Olsen, chief reporter with the *Herald* downtown,' he lied. 'Someone here tells me there was a rumpus at the Hotel St Mark this morning. Something about shots being fired. Can you put me on to somebody who knows what ha—'

But he could not be put through, because both of the *Argos*'s reporters and its editor were all down at the hotel, and he was speaking with the copy boy who was only there manning the telephones, holding the fort.

'All of 'em out?' Tom guessed anything much would be big news out in Venice. 'OK, son, so can *you* tell me what happened . . .?'

He sat down with a thump on the straight-back chair by the wall phone, his legs quaking oddly beneath him. Outside he heard Fay and Alice Terry's whispered chatter recede as they went down the hall to Samaniegos's room and, with a knock, entered trailing reassuring noises behind them. The muffled murmur of conversation that ensued suggested an element of calm had been restored.

Hunched over, elbows on his knees, Tom held his head in his hands and wondered what the hell would be best to do. Samaniegos was in such a state already, he didn't want to push him over the edge. *If* what the copy boy said could be trusted. He needed to be certain before he said anything. But how to find out? He couldn't risk contacting the cops directly, not even Thad Sullivan. He couldn't risk anyone putting his name to this. Not if he was to have any hope of keeping himself, let alone Samaniegos out of it. Whatever he'd said earlier to get the young actor out of the hotel, it was way past the point of exaggeration now. If the cops or the press – or, God forbid, Hays – were to hear even a whisper of this thing, it would be not only catastrophic but too complicated even for him to find a way of extricating himself. He'd be lucky to avoid the slammer, and his business would be finished. It simply wouldn't be survivable.

There was only one small chance that he could see of containing it now. Someone who had as much to lose as him, if this blew up big. He looked at his wristwatch again. He had just enough time for one more throw of the dice. He clicked the cradle and asked to be put through to a private number in Venice. The likelihood that Howard Standen, friend and owner of the St Mark, would be home in the middle of the day – on this day of all days – was slim. But he couldn't risk the cops tracing a call to the hotel via the operator later. If only he could get a message to him . . . Standen, he knew, had no love for the police, and every reason for not wanting his hotel to become forever associated with a scandal that could easily blow up coast to coast.

Only later, in the dark of the night, unable to sleep, did it come to him. His mother's face, his mother's tears so many years and years back in that cold, dank Dublin tenement, his mother's seizure by some ancient animal madness when she heard his father had been killed and the other kindly, knowing women in the building pulling her back, away into another room where she could scream and cry and claw the walls without terrifying her own children.

So long ago and hard forgotten. Not since he was seven years old had he seen blood drain so quickly from a face, such blindly flailing arms, heard such a howl of anguish as that which emerged from Samaniegos's lungs. Fay and Alice Terry had gasped and reached out as instinctively as mothers to comfort the stricken boy, whose grief filled the room in an instant, when he told him.

He hadn't meant to do it. He only went into the bedroom to tell them he was leaving, and to assure them that Standen was on board and had only given the police the name he'd registered him under. Tom was too shaken by the news himself to want to broach the subject so soon with Samaniegos. As soon as he opened the bedroom door, though, he could tell Fay knew from his expression that he was shaken. Alice Terry did a double take, too, as they were exchanging greetings, enough to make him try and fake a smile of reassurance, which only made it worse.

'You got through?' Fay asked. He could tell she instantly regretted doing so, her gaze flicking anxiously towards Samaniegos, who was by now pushing himself up off the pillows, eyes alert, fearful and questioning. Tom explained about Standen and, looking at Samaniegos and Terry in particular, said, 'So, we have to keep this quiet. If this gets outside of the room, we're all finished.'

'I've got to go now,' he said to Fay. 'You'll be OK till I get back?'

Before she could answer, Samaniegos was pushing out from under the bedclothes, scrambling to avoid the two women's automatic attempts to calm him.

'No, no, wait. You can't just go like that. What about Gianni? Is he all right? Did you hear something?' His face creased up in pain and he clasped his side where the wound was. But his eyes were still fixed on Tom, and his gasp was not a gasp of pain, but a plea of deep needfulness.

'Please, you've got to tell me. I need to know he's OK? Was he arrested? What happened?'

Tom glanced at Fay again. How could she help him, not knowing the weight of what he had to say? But she seemed to see it in him and made a small gesture of inevitability with her hands. He knew then that, whatever he did, it was going to hurt. And better to hear it from him with friends around than on the front page of a newspaper. Still he couldn't help seeking to soften the blow.

'Vitale's dead.' Tom paused to gauge the reaction.

'Dead?' In Samaniegos, a mix of hope and confusion. Fay and Terry were shocked but silent.

'Gianni stabbed him in the neck with that knife you knocked out of his hand. Must've been just after we got out the door.'

'Oh, the poor boy.' Samaniegos's sigh was one of relief. 'He'll need a lawyer. We have to get a lawyer for him. Can we arrange that discreetly? He can plead self-defense, can't he? Where are they holding him? I mean, what about his injuries? Is he in hospital?'

Tom shook his head, wanting to look anywhere but into Samaniegos's hopeful eyes. But he did, in the end. 'I'm sorry Ramon, but Gianni is . . . I mean, after he stabbed Vitale, seems he picked up the gun to finish him off. Then, according to what the cops are saying at least, he turned the gun on himself. They say they tried but couldn't stop him. There's no other way of saying it – Gianni is dead, too.'

THIRTY-THREE

The two men escorting him fell instantly into step and, despite the low devotional murmur of people all around arranging their affairs at tables with clerks and waiting in line for tellers, the urgent slap of their shoe leather seemed to echo up from the polished marble floor and fill the enormous banking hall right up to the lofty, spectacularly gilded ceiling.

He had been picked out as soon as he passed through the imposing doors, and invited to accompany the pair to a more discreet location where his business would be conducted. You couldn't have got a bank closer to City Hall. The thin back end of the wedge-shaped International Savings and Exchange Bank building looked like it was trying to nudge its way stealthily across Temple Square and into the corridors of power opposite. Even so, what surprised Tom most when he stepped through the carved wooden door at the back of the hall, into a smaller but no less grandiose private banking room, was that Kent Kane Parrot was standing there, waiting for him, along with a number of other men he didn't recognize, though three of them he could tell, by their build and sullen demeanor, were cops.

'About time, too, Collins,' Parrot said briskly, but he still came out front of the desk and shook Tom's hand.

'Gentlemen, this is Mr Collins who will be conducting our business for us today. Collins, this is Deputy District Attorney Doran, and Captain Heath from the Detective Bureau.' The others were not deemed worthy of introduction.

Tom did a double take on hearing Heath's name. Could this really be who was causing Sullivan so much grief, Ramirez's boss, this burly but sourly studious-looking man in a lightweight grey suit that looked way too expensive for a cop? And if so, what really was his relationship with Parrot, who had barely acknowledged knowing him the night before? This moment was not the time to bring the other half of their deal up, but when

Tom shot a questioning glance back at Parrot, he was certain he got a barely perceptible nod in reply, as if to say 'it's done'.

Tom shook hands formally with the slightly mournful-looking deputy DA and Heath, who betrayed no sign whatsoever that he had ever heard of Tom before, let alone been forced to do a shady backroom deal to get an innocent man off the hook at his behest. His nods to the other two cops in the room went equally ignored.

'We want this done to the letter, so there are one or two formalities to get through,' Parrot said to the assembly. He nodded to the anonymous bank manager standing silently behind the desk, who rapped on the door behind him, and a clerk came in carrying a large leather wallet which he placed on the desk. All except Tom moved closer as the manager opened it and counted out twenty-five $1,000 bills on to the desk, and with great gravitas wrote each serial number into a ledger, which he signed and asked Doran to witness.

He then placed the bills in a buff manila envelope and slid it across the gleaming mahogany desk towards Tom, together with a pen and a pre-prepared bank receipt.

'You sign that, and we're ready to go,' Parrot said.

'I don't think so,' Tom said. 'That money is never going to be mine and I sure as hell won't be taking responsibility for it. Sign for it yourself. You're the one knows where it comes from.'

Parrot flushed and looked like he was about to say something but, for the sake of either expediency or propriety, he crooked a finger at Heath instead and indicated he should sign the receipt.

'Very well, Collins. If that's how you feel. Heath can sign for it now to maintain the chain of evidence. You'll be travelling in his vehicle anyway. Just don't think you'll get away without giving us a witness statement when this is done.'

'I'm looking forward to that already. It being done, that is.' Tom took the envelope from the desk and slipped it inside his coat pocket. It felt too insubstantial between his fingers for all the trouble it was causing. But he was sure that every second it was in there would drag on his soul like a dead weight.

THIRTY-FOUR

They could have just walked straight down Spring, but Heath insisted on being chauffeured in his big Chandler six. With three big, overheated men in the back, it was not a comfortable option. Slow too, inching through the tangle of crosstown traffic at every intersection. Eventually, they made it past Sixth and pulled into the curb. Tom climbed out and walked the remaining twenty yards to Al Levy's Café, knowing he would be followed shortly by two detectives while Heath remained on watch outside in the automobile.

He pushed through the door and looked around the large, bright, semi-deserted café. Only three tables were occupied. One near the counter by a quartet of office workers jawing over coffee and the remains of a cake, one by the door with two brawlers arguing loudly about the boxing out at the Legion the night before, plus a pair of young lovers cooing at each other in a booth in the dim-lit section at the back.

As agreed, Tom selected a table beside the big plate-glass window that looked out on the people and traffic crowding along Spring. He laid out the early edition of that day's *Herald*, front page up, on the polished ply table, and ordered a coffee and a glass of water from the bored waiter who came to serve him. A moment later the door opened, but it was only the two cops who'd come over in the auto. Without acknowledging him they walked towards the back of the café and sat at a table near the stairs, from where they could witness everything that went on in the room. Tom glanced at his wristwatch; it was still five minutes before Roth was due to arrive. He pulled out the sports pages, leaving the rest of the newspaper on the tabletop, and began to read.

The bell over the door clanged at three o'clock precisely and a tall, angular, balding man in his early sixties, with a shock of white hair above his ears, entered. There was an air of wary alertness in the eyes behind the thin, gold-rimmed spectacles perched on his nose. His smart summer suit was expensive, skillfully tailored to flatter his stick-thin frame, and he had a large flat envelope tucked beneath his left elbow. His gaze ping-ponged around the room before he let the door shut behind him, landing momentarily on the two cops at the back but disregarding them as soon as his glance fell upon Tom and the newspaper on the table. He walked over quickly, nothing whatsoever in his gait betraying any further suspicion or lack of confidence.

'Mr Collins, I presume?'

'Mr Roth.' Tom waved him into the seat opposite and Roth slid in, at the same time waving away the waiter who, alert to the tipping potential of a well-heeled customer, had hurried over.

'I trust we can conclude this business without further ado,' Roth said, scanning Tom's face, noticing the cut on his brow for the first time and wrinkling his nose.

'Sure,' Tom replied. 'Just as soon as I see those letters and the agreement to desist signed by you and Deeley.'

'You'll find everything I agreed with Drew in here.' Roth pushed his envelope to the middle of the table, but kept his left hand spidered over it, tapping it with his middle finger. 'Assuming you brought the cash.'

'Twenty-five big ones as agreed.' Tom pulled the envelope from his pocket, opened the flap and discreetly fanned through the stack of bills, smiling grimly to himself as Roth licked his lips unconsciously. 'But I need to examine what's in there before I give them to you.'

He drew Roth's envelope over and opened it, spreading the documents out on the table and sifting the pages.

'There's only one letter here, I was told there would be two,' Tom said, putting a snarl in his voice to underline his serious-ness. Roth feigned surprise and began leafing through the papers on the table. Tom cursed under his breath, put the envelope with the cash back in his pocket, and reached for his hat. 'Mr Roth, as you'll have gathered from my face a moment ago, I've been having a long and very disagreeable day today. I don't need you adding to that. So, if the letter you showed Mr Drew purporting to be from a girl called Rose is not on the table within the next ten seconds, the deal is off.'

Roth tutted loudly, attracting the curiosity only of the four office workers, and repeated the word 'purporting' under his breath, as if irked by it. He patted down his suit pockets exaggeratedly, eventually extracting from a vest pocket a couple of sheets of folded notepaper and handing them to Tom. 'I'm so sorry,' he lied, his smile insincere. 'I must have forgot to put it in with the rest.'

Tom said nothing and took the pages from him, checking the signature. It was Rose Arthur's all right, and every bit as damning as Olsen had suggested. Only then did he examine the second letter, which to his undisguised surprise contained far worse, describing an evening the previous winter of such Dionysian debauchery that Tom could barely credit anyone of Mayor Cryer's prominence would have risked attending. But apparently he did, though the emphasis in this document was not so much on La Marr's attentions to Cryer but to . . . the name caused Tom's stomach to lurch so hard he looked up, and caught Roth grinning malevolently across at him.

'Yes, I thought you would find that interesting,' Roth said. 'Obviously, I was eager not to publicize that one beforehand, or reveal it to anyone other than Drew unless absolutely necessary – for my own protection as much as that of the young lady, you understand.' The lawyer stopped, palpably restraining himself from saying any more on the subject. Instead he extended a long arm and hand, the bony fingers more suited to a pianist than a blackmailer, and pulled out a document from underneath, turning it towards Tom.

'Come now, you have everything you asked for. You see here, Mr Deeley has signed an undertaking not to file a divorce petition or pursue any bigamy or other proceedings against Miss La Marr at any time in the future, which I have countersigned and witnessed. So could we get on with your half of the bargain, Mr Collins. The money, sir, please?'

Tom cast a quick eye over the paperwork. It seemed to contain everything that Drew and Parrot said it should. He pulled his shoulders back, nodded at Roth and slid the envelope of cash across the table to him. Roth took it eagerly, counted the contents under the table, and folded it into his coat pocket.

'It's been a pleasure doing business with you, sir,' Roth said, rising from the table and holding out a hand to shake.

'I couldn't say the same, Roth,' Tom said, keeping both his hands on the table. 'So I won't.' Instead he gathered up the documents, the contents of which he really did not want to think about, let alone have in his possession for a moment longer than was necessary. He understood perfectly, now, why Drew had not disclosed to him anything about the contents of the second letter.

Roth scowled as he turned away and walked towards the street door, more erect than before, pausing only to look back over his shoulder at the sound of two chairs scraping out from a table towards the back of the restaurant beyond Tom. His expression darkened and he turned around to check his route out, quickening his pace just as Tom felt the two cops sweep past. Roth was reaching for the chromed metal handle when one of the loud brawlers sitting beside the door swiveled in his chair and stood quickly, a police badge extended in the palm of his hand, blocking the exit.

Within seconds the lawyer was surrounded by the four plain-clothes cops, protesting volubly at being manhandled, even as he was informed that he was being taken into custody and should come quietly to the police station or accept the painful physical consequences of resisting. Tom saw one of Heath's two underlings dip a hand inside the lawyer's suit coat and remove the envelope of cash, transferring it to his own coat pocket. Tom rose from his seat, just in time to receive the fierce glare of betrayal that Roth hurled back at him. A moment later the lawyer was bundled out the door into the street, the flow of pedestrians outside parting like the Nile, stopping to stare, hands to mouths. As Tom went to follow, he noticed the cop who had taken the money was lagging behind and, still inside, closing the glass-paneled door with a peaceful thump, all but blocking out the noise of commotion outside. He turned to face Tom and put a hand up, an implacable obstruction.

'Congratulations,' Tom said, grinning. 'That was neatly done.'

The cop ignored the compliment, maintaining the same granite grey flatness of expression he had exhibited all along. 'I think you've got something there, Collins, belongs to us now. Bought and paid for.'

Tom took the comment like a body blow. Somehow, he'd imagined handing the papers over to Drew, that being the pretense of the deal he'd made with Roth. He hadn't actually thought it through enough to take it any further than that.

The bull crooked all four fingers of his right hand, demanding the documents. 'C'mon, hand 'em over. You know Mr Parrot will keep 'em somewhere safe.'

Of course. It wasn't the cops wanted them. It was the price Parrot demanded for putting Roth on ice. And what a bill of goods he was getting for his trouble. Not just a sword to hang over his friend Cryer's head should the time ever come, but a nice bit of leverage over Drew and La Marr, and even Charlie Crawford, into the bargain. All Tom knew was he had no desire to hang on to those papers for a minute longer than necessary, and that he'd be making a hell of a lot of trouble for himself if he didn't hand them over right there and then.

Even as the thought was going through his mind, a blur of sharp, aggressive movement outside in the street caught his eye, accompanied by what sounded like a woman's cry, but distant. He peered out the plate-glass window more intently, so much so that the cop whipped his head round, too, as the crowd of pedestrian onlookers rippled apart again, glancing around in alarm or surprise. A skinny young man in a hat and trench coat had shouldered his way out from among them and was running up to the huddle of detectives surrounding Roth, a raised automatic pistol in his hands. Mesmerized, Tom saw the blue-grey muzzle jerk and spit three times as the compressed 'pop-pop-pop' of its rapid fire struck his ears, saw Roth's tall, thin figure hit twice in the chest and once in the mouth, blood and fleshy fragments spraying out, toppling backwards against the officer behind him, who also collapsed clutching his shoulder. A moment later, the youth was gone already, leaving chaos in his wake as the crowd of panicked pedestrians fanned out in all directions, screaming, diving to the sidewalk, running blind into the street in front of squealing, braking vehicles, even before the dumbfounded officers had time to draw their guns.

'What the fu—' The bull had enough self-preserving presence of mind to snatch the envelope of documents from Tom's grasp even while he was turning on his heel. He wrenched the door open, hurling himself out into the street, going for his gun, and roared at the terrified throng to get out of the way as he ran through them to pursue the gunman, who was out of sight by now, but he ran in any case, the other plain-clothesmen already busy on their knees attending to the fallen.

Empty-handed, Tom stood and stared at the door, seemed to see every scratch and scuff on its pressed steel frame, the spring-loaded automatic closure mechanism above, the slight focal warp of the heavy plate glass and the reversed etched out café name that seemed to block out nothing of any interest in the street beyond, and he did not move. He felt no need to, nor to take any notice of the remaining customers, all now pressed against the windows, gabbling and screaming and pointing and desperate to see what fate might have saved them from outside. Tom felt no need to do anything other than stare and be entirely removed from the twisting, rising nausea in his gut and to notice only details, like the chrome yellow feather from a lady's blue silk hat fallen on the sidewalk and Phil Olsen appearing out of nowhere, running toward the ruck around the dead man and the profusely bleeding cop, mouthing instructions to a colleague with a big Graflex camera in his mitts, taking photographs, exchanging plate cassettes with a calm, professional assurance. That was the image brazed on to his memory. Not Roth broken and bloody in the street but Olsen, notebook in his hand, licking his lips and drinking in the horror before him, wide-eyed and exhilarated as ever he was ringside when a man was up against the ropes taking a real bad beating.

THIRTY-FIVE

'So who do you really believe is the father, Cryer or Crawford?' Fay asked, as she mixed another drink for herself on the marble balcony table.

It was a beautiful evening and the three of them were relaxing outside in the coolness of the day's vanishing light, Sullivan having stopped by on his way home from work. On one of the chairs was a faded late edition of the *Herald*, left out for days now, its front page emblazoned full-width with the headline *LAWYER TO THE STARS SLAIN ON SPRING STREET*, and beneath it: *Assassin strikes in broad daylight on crowded street.* Beneath that again an exclusive eyewitness report by chief reporter Phil Olsen, who had called that very day to profusely thank Tom, whose tip-off regarding the arrest for extortion of a prominent city lawyer had turned out to be one of the bloodiest newspaper scoops of the year so far, syndicated across the nation and beyond.

'I'm not playing that game,' Tom said, with feeling. 'And neither is La Marr. According to Drew she's more determined than ever that nobody should know. And let's hope for the child's sake they never find out. I'm not sure anyone would want to admit to having either one of them for a father.'

'Not unless it has Cryer's nose,' Sullivan threw in, laughing. 'A schnoz like that, there'd be no denying it. The whole world would know whose it is.'

'Whose *he* is, Thad,' Fay corrected him. 'I was telling Tom before you arrived, I took a trip out to the sanatorium this morning to see the proud mother. Talk about cautious to a fault. They refused to let me in at first. I had to call through in order to convince them. The plan is to keep the birth under wraps and have her pretend to oh-so-generously adopt him – from a helpful orphanage in need of a donation – a couple of months down the line. It's such a shame to have to draw a veil of lies around such a happy event.'

'She has no choice,' Tom said. 'They would tear her to pieces, and the child would suffer for it too.'

'I know.' Fay sat down beside him, thoughtful for a moment, then the smile returned to her face. 'And the main thing is that both mother and baby boy are healthy and happy and doing very well indeed. Like everything else in that young woman's life, she breezed through the labor by all accounts. And what a bonny little lad he is. You know, she actually asked me if she might name him after you, Tom.'

'Sure she did.' Tom laughed. 'Just like she asked Drew if she could call him Frank, Ingram if she could call him Rex, and Ed if she should call him Ed. I wouldn't be at all surprised if she told that ape Joe Martin she was going to call the child Joe. Or Martin, come to think of it. That kid's going to have a longer run of monikers than a Mexican prince, the rate she's going.'

Sullivan laughed and handed his glass to Tom for a refill. 'You know, you two, I've had some pretty good news myself.'

'I thought you were looking a degree or two less glum when you came in,' Tom said, darting a knowing glance across to Fay. 'But I hope it's nothing to do with babies, Thad – the last time I was talking to you, you were saying you could barely afford—'

Sullivan wheezed out a horror-struck cough. 'Jesus Christ, don't even say it, lad. No, thank the Good Lord! Just the seven will do me fine, thank you very much.'

Fay burst out laughing. 'Well, that doesn't leave any room for doubt. But do get on and tell us – what's the good news?'

'This fella Ramirez who was causing me trouble, he was transferred out of Central yesterday. Off to the port police in San P., we were told. And Captain Heath said all the charges against me were dropped. Calls me up to his office – I thought it was my turn next to get the boot – and says it was all a big misunderstanding and I should forget it ever happened. I've never been so relieved in all my life. Those prayers I offered up the night before must've done a power of good, that's all I know.'

Sullivan winked at Tom, who had told him over the phone

in only the vaguest terms, the day before, that the threat against them might be about to recede.

'Tom mentioned you'd been having trouble,' Fay said. 'So, did they discover what happened to that poor man? The one in the Baldwin Hills?'

Thad shook his massive head. 'No. The local coroner's come down, all of a sudden, on the side of accidental death. No signs of violence to the body and some enterprising – and thick-skinned – soul from the County Sheriff's office went and climbed back down into that cactus patch and dug out a bottle with a trace of some ferocious moonshine or other in it. They reckon now he must've fell in there when he was blind drunk on the stuff. Lay there for months – drying out, so to speak.'

Sullivan couldn't resist a low laugh at his joke, and Tom joined him, raising his glass in a grim salute. Fay was not so easily put off.

'And nobody missed him? In all that time?' she asked, astonished.

'Seems not. Even if they did, there'd be no way of telling it was the right man. I'm sorry to say it, but there's nothing much left of him but leather. Not a single scrap of evidence on his person to identify him.'

'Nothing?' Fay looked quickly at Tom, then back at Thad. 'But I thought Tom said—'

'The constable in question says he was mistaken about that now.' Sullivan didn't so much as miss a beat. 'So, there's only one thing left to do and that's bury the fella – at the county's expense and under the name he'll have for all eternity now: John Doe.'

This time it was Sullivan who raised his glass. 'As they used to say in the old country: I never knew the fella, but I'm glad to see the back of him all the same.'

'Amen to that,' Tom seconded. He wasn't familiar with the adage, but he liked the sentiment well enough. He turned to Fay now, thinking for the thousandth time how beautiful she looked in profile, and how grateful he was to fate, or whatever it was that awaited him in eternity, that she chose to be with him at all. 'Speaking of new names, I managed to catch Ingram this morning at his hotel in New York. Said he's very satisfied with the outcome and that there's a nice fat check in the post for me.'

'Little does he know.' Fay laughed. Tom had already told her how the director had the day before refused, albeit charmingly, to listen to a word he had to say about La Marr's case other than that Deeley and all his legal threats had disappeared. 'That's Mae's job secure for a few more months, I guess.'

'He sounded genuinely pleased about the baby,' Tom added.

'So long as he stays under wraps, no doubt,' Fay said, drily. 'Whatever she calls the child, I don't fancy her chances of ever working with him again.'

'Unlike Samaniegos,' said Tom. 'That's what I was just about to tell you. Ingram told me – and he sounded happier about this than anything else – that Ramon has finally agreed to change his name. Said he's been trying to persuade him for months and couldn't imagine what had brought on such a sudden change of heart.' Tom paused for a hearty chuckle himself at that. 'So, Ramon Samaniegos is, from now on, to be known to the world as, wait for it . . . Ramon Novarro.'

'What in the name of God difference is that going to make?' Sullivan snorted.

'Oh, no, Novarro is so much more romantic,' Fay insisted. 'It's got a sonorous Spanish ring to it, too. All those Rs and Ns running together.'

She threw her arms up, hands back like a Spanish dancer. '*Rrrr*amon Nov*arrrro*,' she enunciated, clapping out an accompanying burst of hard flamenco rhythm. She glanced at Tom. 'I wonder what could possibly have persuaded him to change it?'

'I can't imagine.' Tom laughed. 'But whatever his reason, I'm guessing his mentor Mr Rex Ingram had a big hand in choosing it. It sounds more like an Irishman's idea of a Spanish name than a Mexican's.'

'Well, I for one have no doubt,' Fay said, persevering, 'that, once the poor boy recovers from his current troubles, the name Ramon Novarro will one day be known all around the world. It has real star quality.'

'I'll drink to that,' Tom said, refilling their glasses and raising his aloft to the moon and to the stars just now emerging from the fading pink of sunset in the sky above. 'To Ramon Novarro. May his name live on for ever.'

'Bloody movies,' Sullivan grumbled. And, laughing, Tom and Fay raised their glasses to him instead, acknowledging the better toast.

AUTHOR'S NOTE

Barbara La Marr did go on to give her baby son Martin to an orphanage for a day and went through the pretense of adopting him back again amid a blaze of ingeniously orchestrated publicity. Her role in Rex Ingram's *The Prisoner of Zenda* propelled her from mere vamp into the realms of real stardom, though her enjoyment of her fame was tragically cut short by her early death from tuberculosis in 1926, aged just twenty-nine.

Ramon Samaniego/s (spellings vary), renamed as Ramon Novarro, went on to become one of the greatest stars of the silent era and, though he continued to act on screen for most of his life, like so many others his career was badly impacted by the advent of the talkies. He retired a wealthy but lonely figure, never forming a lasting romantic relationship in his life. He died in 1968, murdered by two young men he had invited into his Laurel Canyon home.

Rex Ingram continued to make his mark as one of the great directors of the era, but fell out of love with Hollywood and relocated to the south of France where, between making films at his studio outside Nice, he traveled and indulged a lifelong passion for Arabian and Islamic culture until his death in 1950, aged fifty-eight. He and Alice Terry stayed married, though she remained mostly in Hollywood, surviving him by thirty-seven years until her death in 1987.

Black Orchids, renamed *Trifling Women* by the studio against Ingram's wishes, was released late in 1922 to mixed reviews but a healthy box office. The only point on which most critics agreed was that Barbara La Marr and the silver screen's latest young 'Latin lover', Ramon Novarro, were almost as glorious as the outstanding set design. At the time of writing it remains one of the silent era's many 'lost' masterpieces.